PRAISE FOR *SWEET PARADISE*

"Boise Montague, intrepid St. Thomas, V.I. private investigator, returns in SWEET PARADISE. Talented author Gene Desrochers delivers a suspense-filled tale overflowing with duplicitous characters and greed-driven agendas in lushly authentic Caribbean environs. A mature generation is determined to hold tight to the empire that provides them with every luxury, while the next generation attempts to fulfill its dreams ... Others will compromise all that is decent. And Boise Montague will do what he does best as he separates the winners from the losers and the innocent from the guilty. A 5-star read."

--Laura Taylor - 6-Time Romantic Times Award Winner

"Boise is back! Gene Desrochers returns his readers to the island paradise of St. Thomas. You'll feel the warm tropical breeze as Private Investigator Boise Montague must discover [what happened to] the matriarch of a wealthy island rum producer. The deeper he digs, the closer he gets to his own mortality. Wandering and sometimes stumbling through his investigation, Boise learns about family secrets—and they could kill him. Outstanding writing and the vivid setting will keep you transfixed."

--R. D. Kardon, award-winning author of *Flygirl and Angel Flight*

SWEET
PARADISE

GENE DESROCHERS

Sweet Paradise
First Edition

Cover design by Ebook Launch

www.acornpublishingllc.com

ISBN-13: 978-1-952112-38-6 (Hardcover)

ISBN-13: 978-1-952112-37-9 (Paperback)

For The Drunken

CHAPTER 1

Christina's World occupied my attention a lot these days. A replica of the painting, framed to appear more authentic, hung in the passageway outside my room at The West Indian Manner. It depicted a stark, drought-ridden swath of midwestern farm in golden-browns. A distant, unpainted farmhouse appeared ravaged by the dust bowl or some other agricultural tragedy. The odd way the field closer to the house looked neatly sheared contrasted with the unkempt tentacled weeds where Christina sprawled.

Christina was alone.

The painting matched nothing you might expect from Caribbean décor: palm trees, beaches, waves, perhaps a fish. Perhaps a literary something featuring a schooner from the nineteenth century cresting a wave, or a trite sailboat on tranquil waters bathed in light from a glorious setting sun.

Yet here I stood, on the top floor of a Caribbean guest house. The owners, Marge and Lucy, displayed a strange sense of interior design. Antique furniture, scary Indonesian masks, assorted things that instilled a feeling of dread. I was comfortable with dread or I wouldn't have continued living here for the past six months. The Caribbean had welcomed me back from Los Angeles in March 2015 with murder.

To most eight-hour cruise ship visitors, St. Thomas was all positives. The best harbor in the Caribbean. Water so calm and clear you felt like you were floating in weightless space when snorkeling. Tropical breezes and a treasure trove of taverns where you could sample every kind of liquor known to man. Charlotte Amalie was everyone's lover, but no one's wife.

In St. Thomas, you were either a native, a tourist, or someone seeking anonymity. Smugglers avoiding the more chaste and heavily-policed British ports. The buccaneers of yesteryear pirated goods from legitimate British, French, or Spanish ships laden with gold, silver, sugar, coffee, and rum, then came here to hock what they'd stolen. Not nice people who followed the rules. Constant trouble. Titillating excitement.

Once outside, I trotted down the endless brick steps, pausing at the halfway point to inspect my favorite avocado tree. Medium-sized, it was barren of fruit in early fall. The waxy-green leaves glistened in the clear morning. From the crowded street at the bottom of the hill a car horn *bleated* like a dying goat. Everything appeared hunky-dory, except for one thing: the bulbous protrusion in the crook of the two largest branches.

To the untrained eye, the small brunette tumor might appear to be nothing more than a harmless anomaly. Some natural growth that enhanced the bark's defenses. I recognized it for what it was. A killing blow. The harbinger of infestation, devouring from the inside out.

I picked up a stick, stretched up and prodded the nest. Brown clumps tumbled to the ground. Irritated termites swarmed out. It smelled clean, like sand on the beach or sawdust in a mill.

I dragged the stick over some of the enclosed termite highways leading away from the nest and over the branches like veins. Beneath the hardened wood-dust covering, thousands marched in orderly fashion, devouring the beautiful tree molecule by molecule. I poked it again. The nest was hard. Durable. Termites were not easy to kill.

Jabbing the stick deep into the nest, I left it protruding like an appendage and headed for my new office.

Terry Montague often said bad things waited around every corner in life. He was a tough man to have as a father and often wrong about a great many things, but about this he had a point. Nothing had happened for a couple months, which meant I was overdue. Perhaps I'd developed a feeling, or perhaps I was being naturally cautious because of the dangerous business I'd chosen to pursue. Either way, precautions needed to be taken.

On the advice of my reporter pal, Dana Goode, I'd rented office space in the same building occupied by the newspaper she worked for, *The Daily News*. They took up the entire top floor of the building. I had a ground-floor view. Dana was a splendid negotiator, and she'd bargained the landlord down to a rate I could stomach. She had a way of getting her way.

Although I rented space in the building, we were not officially linked. I did advertise in the paper, and had even wound up working with Dana on my last case. She'd been helpful. She'd also nearly gotten me killed--repeatedly. Friends can't be perfect. In the end, I'd hung out my shingle. This was my second week in my new office as a private investigator desperately seeking clients.

I rapped on the thin, fake wood. "You see what I'm talking about, Randy?" I said as my office door rattled like an open shutter in a hurricane. "If I hit it any harder, it'd crack like an egg. Not entirely secure, wouldn't you agree?"

Randy shifted from sole to sole, eyeing the door like it was a cooked chicken and he couldn't decide where to start cutting.

"Yeah, I hear you, Boise." He nodded. "But this here door be new. Like they done replace it before you sign the leases. I done asked them, and they ain't puttin' another door in this frame."

Brand new piece of crap. A lot of new stuff sucked these days. Designed to be replaced in short order. Planned obsolescence had taken over every corner of the world. I'd be dealing with island riff-raff. Some half-assed door wasn't gonna keep them from robbing me or busting in after I'd pissed them off. If I wanted to make a living, I needed a known place of business. Which meant bad guys and good guys would both know where to find me. This door made me nervous.

With my index finger I traced a frame in the air that outlined the door. "Tell you what, if they replace the door, I paint it for free."

Randy chuckled. "Sorry, brodda. They ain't paintin' the door eidda." He turned and waddled up the stairs to the second floor.

"Yeah, sorry I asked," I muttered under my breath.

With the flat of my palm I smacked the door again. It shuddered.

My office faced the parking lot and a weed-infested traffic circle. The lock wasn't even a deadbolt, just a shiny, faux brass knob suitable for the bathroom inside a house.

After shelling out money for the security deposit, some used furniture, and the rent, my savings account wasn't worth much more than Christina's tinder-box house. My accommodations at The Manner and the rent on this new office would be covered for another two, maybe three months, then I'd be out on my *rass*.

The deserted parking lot baked in the hot West Indian sun. My curls swayed in the breeze from my ceiling fan as a drop of perspiration trickled down my sideburn. No clients, no prospects. Story of my life.

The door. Something needed to be done about this door. The sandpaper-brown finish didn't engender confidence, or even a second glance. I hadn't moved back to St. Thomas to live the same boring brown and gray life I'd had as a law firm investigator in Los Angeles. The economy here didn't hum, there were no grand museums displaying works of staggering genius, and the only plays were poorly done local fare. What St. Thomas had was color and natural wonder, and a soothingly warm sea. And a bunch of crazy residents. Like I said, people here craved anonymity and it wasn't because they were nice and normal. Many, many of them were running and hiding. Such people had trouble staying out of trouble.

My ad in *The Daily News* hadn't done squat for business either. Sure, it had only been running for a week, but all I could afford was three weeks. Walter Pickering, the president of the newspaper, claimed that all the publicity the paper had provided me by covering the murder of Roger Black and the kidnapping of Celia Jarl was more than enough. No more free advertising for Boise Montague. Pickering was so cheap his shiny, brown scalp squeaked. It cost me time and money to solve those crimes and the stories had no doubt contributed to increased circulation for the paper.

The other doors on my floor were all the same sandpaper-brown, sporting the same cheap lock. I wasn't being discriminated against. My door was the newest one. My proximity to the three steps that led up to the first-floor landing gave me great visibility. Be grateful. Nah, I'd complain some more the first chance I got.

***

The paint was too damned expensive. Everything in these stores was too damned expensive. Various brands, types, and colors populated the shelves. Much of the selection needed to be mixed to get any colors besides the boring variations on brown, gray, and white. All of that added up to more than I wanted to spend.

Hidden in the back corner of The Paint Depot was a discount shelf of criminally off-beat tones in mostly brilliant pastels that people had tried and returned.

Probably Puerto Ricans.

Maybe I was part Puerto Rican. I could pass. Curly afro and dark skin, check. Attitude, check. Love of brightly colored clothing and houses, check. Rapid-fire Spanish that no one in any other Spanish-speaking country could understand, uncheck. In reality, I was one-quarter black, although it was tough to tell. I had the bushy hair and I was fairly dark, but more in some other native islander of aboriginal descent way.

Rooting through the discount piles, I found three gallons of cantaloupe. Cheap and attention-grabbing. If someone tried to break into my office, everyone within five-hundred yards would notice the shady character standing in front of the blinding melon door. It would also make it easy to explain how to find my office if anyone ever called for an appointment. Maybe I could use it as a gimmick in future ad campaigns, assuming I ever had an advertising budget again.

Would anyone take a detective with a cantaloupe-colored door seriously? I shrugged, picked up two of the cans, and plopped them next to the register with a hollow metal *plonk*.

The clerk snorted and wiped the back of her hand across her nose. She had claws for fingernails, featuring faux jewels encrusted on rainbow-colored backgrounds. She clicked expertly on the register using the tips, as if this was the most natural way in the world to type.

She studied the top of one of the paint cans where a bright orange dot denoted the color.

"You know you can't return these? All sales final."

I nodded. "Hey, how do you type so good with those nails?"

She gave me a sleepy look. "Don't know, just I do it." She squinted at the lid of the can. "You got to buy all three of these cans, da man."

6

"I think three is too much, sista," I said, falling into the lingo. I reverted back. "I'm painting a door."

"Ain't no matta what you painting, you got to buy all three."

Islanders rarely pronounced the "th" in words, so "three" came out as "tree" and "the" came out as "da." You got used to it pretty quickly so that even the state-siders could eventually understand in most cases. There were a bunch of local dialect words you pieced together over the years. From growing up here, I naturally reverted when speaking to other locals, however, I'd also spent half my life living in the continental United States, so standard North American English was no problem either. Since I'd only been back for six months, standard American felt more natural. Speaking in the accent made me feel different. Sometimes it made me feel I belonged. Other times, I felt like a phony; an actor in my own life.

This woman wasn't going to budge on the house rules. If the lid said I had to buy all three, then I had to buy all three. Even at that, the cost was about one-third of one new can. On the bright side, I'd have a surplus to keep my door freshly painted at all times. I was going to need that extra paint to cover up the blood.

***

The first coat was drying. More droplets of sweat rivered between my shoulder blades as I slugged water and Guinness alternately. Two in the afternoon was no time to be painting in the October heat, but I didn't know what else to do and sitting around worrying about my looming penury seemed pointless.

The used old-timey clock radio I'd picked up at Bob's Store babbled on about hurricane warnings as reception fizzled in and out. It was the latter part of hurricane season, and we'd seen minimal storm damage in the region. We might dodge hurricanes for one or two years running, but it was never long enough to truly become complacent about them the way places like New Orleans had.

The overhead fan *whirred*. Outside my door sunlight filtered thinly through a cloud, illuminating the traffic circle a faint ocher. As I considered the faded lines denoting parking spaces and the cracked pavement, a young man bobbed into my line of sight. He was one of those people who walked on his toes at all times, as if the tendons in his calves were so tight his heels couldn't touch the ground for more than an instant before popping up again. He squinted at the building, turning his head back and forth, then perused the sheet of paper clutched in both hands. A green Osprey backpack hung loosely off his shoulders. People in California used them for hiking. He tugged at the built-in sippy straw and sucked. The bubbly slurping of the last drops of water in his pouch filtered up to me. Disappointment clouded his face.

His attention snagged on my door. I grinned and gave myself a mental pat on the back. He shifted one hand to his hip and gave a slight lean. I wasn't sure whether I should let him see me in my ratty painting outfit, but figured that could be explained by the wet door. A spooge of cantaloupe paint dominated the center of my gray t-shirt. I eased the door open a couple more feet.

"Help you?" I asked. "You look lost."

"Nice door." He pointed at his forehead and swirled his finger around. "You got some."

He was college-aged and his face was sunburned, as were his arms. He wore a Hawaiian shirt and khaki pants, a classic tourist outfit.

He continued to stand in the same spot, squinting and considering the sheet of paper. I returned to my inner office, needing another sip of water and the breeze from the fan. Out my open doorway, I could barely make out the top of his Caesar-style haircut.

"You should get a hat!" I hollered out.

His head rose up from the paper and he pushed up on tip-

8

toes so I could see his eyes. "The sun's doing a number on you," I said. "Want a drink of water?"

He stared at me a while with a strange stillness, like he was in no hurry as he weighed every option. This boy was a local, and he would pull me into events that would rock one of the largest industries in the Virgin Islands.

"Do you have Perrier?"

CHAPTER 2

"**D**on't touch the paint," I said, tapping the door farther open to give him room to enter.

While he shook my hand, his wide eyes wandered around my spartan office. "You just move in, Mr. Montague?" I liked the way my name sounded in his mild Southern accent. The "ta" wasn't so harsh.

"Yes."

His eyes stopped on the black and white photo of Evelyn propped on my desk. "Nice lookin' lady. She your babe?"

"She was," I said.

On my desk next to Evelyn's photograph sat a green sheet of paper listing Alcoholics Anonymous meetings. Dana had left it there after my last drunken debacle. I dropped it in the waste basket.

"Some broad left that there," I muttered as nonchalantly as I could.

He nodded, then something dawned on his face. "Oh, hey, man. I'm sorry, my name's Herbie but folks call me Junior, on account of being named after my daddy. I been goin' off to boarding school in Georgia these last years." He slurped down the glass of water in a single gulp.

"Sorry it's not Perrier," I said. "I'm not really a sparkling water kind of guy."

"Thank you kindly, Mr. Montague. Water's good too, but to my mind Perrier improved it. Heat's hot here, even if you're coming from Georgia."

"You can call me Boise," I said. "How old are you, Junior?"

"Eighteen, sir."

"Are you lost?" I asked.

"Sir?"

"Are you lost? Maybe I can help as you don't really look like you know where you are or where you're going."

At this Junior took another drink. "Well, sir…"

"Boise," I repeated.

"Sir Boise, right. I'm lookin' to speak to someone at *The Daily News* I think. I'm sorta from around here and I'm back."

That sounded all too familiar. A stranger in his own land. At least I was a little darker. His milk-white skin made him out to be a classic tourist with greenbacks in his pocket and wide-eyed naivete on his face.

The Daily News was the pride of St. Thomas. The primary source for news in the three U.S. Virgin Islands and the British island of Tortola. The newspaper's editorial and staff offices were housed on the second floor.

I leaned on the corner of my rutted desk. "Are you placing a classified ad or something? You can go online to do that."

"No, sir. Ain't about classified ads. It's concerning my grandma." He kicked at the floor like a kid in a Mark Twain novel. "On account of she hasn't been in touch with me in a while and it isn't like her."

"Maybe her cell phone died or something. Is she over sixty?"

He nodded.

"The elderly can be confused by technology," I said.

"Sir, I appreciate the water, but it's all right, I'm gonna go on up and speak with that reporter. I'm supposed to go talk with him about her...I think."

"You think?"

"It's been a little confusing. I mean, what's happening around lately."

I dragged one of the two chairs I had for clients away from the wall and parked it in front of my desk. I refilled his water glass and held it out.

"You want to sit down, Junior? I've got a few minutes to speak if you'd like to run your concerns by me before you go spilling your guts to a reporter. They're great at what they do, but they tend to do things in a very public manner and you sound like you might not be ready for that quite yet."

That stillness came over him again as he studied me. He took the glass and began running his finger over the condensation. He remained standing like a singer on stage waiting for the music to start. This kid kneaded things before he baked them.

He sat.

"Maybe it'd do to talk with you a spell. What's your line?"

"Do you mean my work?"

"Yessir, your line of business." He made a lazy circle with his glass of water. "In this here office? Whatever it is, it appears you've only begun."

This had somehow started to feel like a job interview. Junior was studying my every move, waiting for me to do something he didn't like, something disingenuous.

"I'm a private investigator. This," I spread my hands grandly, "is my place of business."

He picked a business card out of the brand-new wood holder I'd purchased from a vendor on the Waterfront last week.

"These business cards are a bit flimsy, don't ya think?"

"Uh, no, just economical."

"You mean you printed them at home?"

"No, I printed them at a friend's home. I don't have a printer...yet."

Great, an eighteen-year-old had me scrambling to explain my marketing materials. I debated exaggerating my experience, but something told me he'd sniff it out and leave without another word if I didn't tell the whole thing straight. My wallet was so thin I had to pat my pocket to make sure it was still there.

"I've had two cases with positive resolutions. Right now, I've got nothing going on, so I have time to listen to lost kids tell me about grandmothers. I don't have the extra money for gold wrapped or foil-printed or glossy raised indigo twenty-pound stock business cards."

A stinging sensation shot up my arm and I slapped a savage mosquito dead. Outside, a car crunched over a bit of loose gravel before the engine died, followed by a cruise ship horn's sad blare.

"All right. I'm gonna tell you about my grandma. This is confidential, right?"

"Yes."

"And I don't have to hire you."

I chuckled, but his face remained impassive. Missing grandma, no sense of humor. Check.

"No. I'm offering to hear you out, that's all. If you want my help, we'll talk about that later. Are you going to college?"

This made him sit straighter and his countenance brightened. "I'm fresh-meat at Georgia Tech. Go Yellow Jackets!" He cleared his throat and lowered his raised fist.

"What are you doing here in early October? Don't you have classes?" *Objection, leading the witness,* I thought. This boy must be very concerned about his grandmother to come down here in the middle of the semester from a life he clearly adored.

13

After another sip of water, he muttered, "My Grandma sent me this weird handwritten letter to come see a reporter. It appeared in my actual mailbox. Must have been hand-delivered."

I stared at him. "You mean someone physically in the state of Georgia dropped a letter into your mailbox?"

He nodded. "You believe that? No stamps or nothing. I tried calling her about it, but her phone goes right to voicemail and the mailbox as of yesterday was full, probably from all my calls. Text and email also got me nowhere. I tried locating her phone with that Find-My-iPhone App, but the thing must be dead as roadkill if she even set it up. None of my roommates knows squat. Partying and useless most of the time. No one saw anyone drop off the letter. It looked like her handwriting, but man, I didn't want to just take off from school. Once I heard that full mailbox message, shoot, I had to come, know what I mean?"

"How long since you got the letter?"

"About five days."

"You want to show it to me? Maybe fresh eyes."

"It's been longer. I'm ashamed. More about ten or eleven days." He fiddled with his empty glass some then rubbed the back of his sunburned neck before he went on. "Guess I'm forgetting things. Been away too long. Sun's mighty strong here. Mighty." I waited. "She hasn't been online in over a month. I've called countless times and my texts go unanswered."

The kid was repeating himself. Fear could do that.

"What do your parents say?"

He was eighteen, so it didn't really matter legally. If he hired me, we were good to go, but I doubted he held the purse strings.

"They insist I don't know her like they do. But that's the thing, I know her. Yeah, I know they say she used to be flighty, back when they were first born, but that's long done. She's a reliable lady as they come."

As he spoke these last words, his head drooped. He appeared to be looking through the bottom of his glass at my tattered rug, which was bound to make a man even sadder.

He sniffled some and rubbed his nose making me wish I had a box of Kleenex on my desk. It would pair well with Evelyn's photo.

"So, what makes you think she didn't run off with some hunk of a man or go on an extended vacation. Does she vacation?"

He shook his bowed head. His fine hair was cut extremely short and a one-inch wide bald spot was already forming on the flat part at the back. He seemed young for hair-loss. I wanted to press him about the letter, but he seemed hesitant to discuss the contents.

"Do you like bikes?" he asked.

"Bikes. Sure, bikes are nice. I don't ride much, though. Not for pleasure. If I need to get from here to there and don't have other transport or time for walking, I'd take a bike. Why?"

"I ride. Long distances. In Georgia it's easy. Long, flat roads that meander for miles. Lot of back country. I guess I've become a bit of a Georgia boy. This island feels stiflin'. Too hilly for biking and roads too narrow. But, I'm gonna wind up back here. We all do."

"What's your Grandma's name?"

"Francine Bacon."

The name sounded familiar. Maybe I'd read it somewhere and it was lodged in my long-term memory. Had I known the family in my youth?

"What's your mother's name?"

"Gertrude. But she left long ago. Way long ago. It's me and my dad here, and his brother and sister. I guess aunt and uncle. And my grandma."

"Your mother left?" I asked, stuck on that sad fact.

"Yeah, when I was just born. My dad, Herbie, says she just wasn't meant to be a mom. She couldn't handle it. I've been trying to find her, but no luck. I don't even know her last name."

"It's not Bacon?"

"Don't know. My dad won't talk about it. None of them will. He says she's not worth my breath or thought. He says some women aren't cut out to be mothers. Is that true?"

"Yes," I said. "It's true."

"I guess in my emotions I spilled a bunch on you. Sorry," he said. I filled his water and gave it back. He sucked on the edge of the glass, his eyes far away.

"And who were you going to speak to at *The Daily News*?"

"Me," came the reply from my doorway. "Herbert, Junior?" A slight man with a thick head of hair slipped in like a shadow and extended his hand in one fluid motion. "I'm Adirondack Kendal, the reporter you were coming to see. I started wondering what was keeping you and heard voices coming out of Mr. Montague's office." Kendal turned to face me. "Boise."

Kendal the Jackal was the name Dana had given this one on account of his propensity to steal stories from other reporters. He didn't look happy with me.

"Kendal, don't you knock?" I asked.

He pointed at his nose. "I smelled wet paint and remembered your door wasn't orange when I walked up the stairs this morning. Besides, it was open."

"Indeed it was. You should still check to see if you're welcome before you enter a room."

At this he offered an academic smirk, then shifted his gaze back to Junior.

What was Kendal up to? According to Dana, although he claimed to be a legitimate journalist, his instincts tended more toward scandal and innuendo than fact. Perhaps he recorded every episode of TMZ and watched it longingly in the dark of his pitiable apartment, the television flashing the Kardashians and Pitts in technicolor. Francine Bacon must have some level of notoriety for Kendal to be this interested.

Before he could address Junior, I interjected. "So, Kendal, what do you want with Junior here? Are you solving missing persons cases now?"

Kendal kept his eyes on Junior. "I'm a reporter, I go where my nose takes me." Kendal spun around and faced me. "You know what, I don't have to explain myself to you. Come on Junior, we're going. We need to talk." He took a pause for emphasis. "Alone."

Junior put his water glass on the edge of my desk and started to follow Kendal.

I was working on my reactionary nature, but couldn't resist throwing out one final jab at Kendal's back. "One thing to remember, Junior, everyone wants payment. Just because it isn't cash, well, there's other payments. Aren't there, Kendal?"

Kendal put his hand on the door and leaned into the doorway. He jerked his hand away and cursed. Turning back to me, he held up his cantaloupe palm.

"See what you made me do? Shit Boise, you better..." As I wondered what I'd better do, a faint *whiz* split the air, then a *thunk* as an arrow pierced Kendal through the back. An arrowhead grew from his chest, the tip red as a hibiscus flower.

I hauled Junior down as I dove to the floor. Blood spattered Kendal's smeared handprint on the door. His left hand clawed two long fingermarks into the paint as his arm pinwheeled. A bright red dot oozed down Junior's pale leg.

Junior's lips parted in a soundless gasp. Kendal's knees collapsed. His right eye twitched as his arm slid back down the wet paint, completely ruining the work I'd done. The distant smell of salt air from the harbor was instantly drowned by what smelled like a bag of wet pennies. Kendal's breath wheezed. In-out, in-out.

I dragged him away from the door, then tried to slam it shut. The damned thing was so light, the air caught at the jam, leaving a crack. No time. Back to the wound. My hands hovered around the arrowhead.

No yanking. The head was too large. The tail had plastic feathers. How would that feel coming through the areola of his

17

lungs? Or was it alveoli? Either way, it seemed like a bad idea. I left it. As for life-saving techniques, they had never covered arrow wounds in my C.P.R. course. Compressions were impossible, so I did the other thing they always tell you to do: call 9-1-1 and put it on speaker.

Junior rocked on the floor, legs pulled to his chest. Peeling off my sweaty, paint-stained shirt, I put pressure on Kendal's chest at the base of the shaft while commanding him to stay conscious. I yelled the address at the phone, although it was still ringing. His eyes fluttered. They shut. My hands were slick and sticky all at once as I searched for his pulse. Nothing. The penny-smell overpowered.

I crawled to the door and locked it. Inching my head up, I squinted into the afternoon for the assailant. It was like opening my eyes underwater without a mask. A black blur that must have been a crow cawed from the rotting tree across the street. It soared into the air. Nothing else moved.

The 9-1-1 operator barked through the speaker, "Nine-one-one, what's your emergency?"

I turned back to the phone, but my hand was stuck to the windowsill. Stuck in drying blood and paint. I tugged my hand away, leaving a red-orange handprint on the white trim.

"I have a man with an arrow in his chest. He's just expired," I announced between hitches.

The operator remained calm, as if this happened every day. She asked if I'd confirmed death and was completely sure. I said yes. She said the police and an ambulance were en route after I gave the address I'd been repeating over and over. She told me not to move or touch anything, then asked if anyone else was hurt. I said no, just shocked. I knelt down next to Junior after dropping my phone on the floor.

"Junior?"

Junior mouthed the words: "Is he?" His only sound was a croak.

"Who knew about you coming to meet Kendal?"

His hand jerked at the air. "I don't know. What do you...no one. I didn't tell anyone about coming to the newspaper. The letter from Grandma told me to keep it quiet."

He dabbed at his nose with the crumpled McDonald's napkin clutched in his hand. Would anyone hire me now that a reporter had been...what was the word for being pierced with an arrow? Arrowed? Run through? No, that's a sword term.

"And who the fuck uses an arrow?" I murmured.

A film had formed on the blood puddles as they coagulated. Kendal was lucky not to be a hemophiliac. That seemed a miserable life.

Pounding on the door jamb. Ripping pepper spray from my pocket, I sprang up. My knee protested, but I barely registered the familiar pain. Walter Pickering and Robin Givens stood in the doorway, their hands raised in surrender.

Upon seeing Kendal, Pickering staggered forward and dropped to his knees beside the body. He fingered Kendal's neck as Robin turned away and heaved into my trashcan. The room instantly reeked of urine, shit, vomit, fresh paint, and that coagulated blood iron-fist. I flicked the fan up to high.

The clock radio droned a staticky news story about the upsurge in tourism last quarter. Ten minutes had passed since I'd seen Junior for the first time.

Walter Pickering shut the door, pulling Robin inside with his wiry, ebony fingers. The man was always dressed for a wedding...or a funeral.

He turned and hissed at me, "Did you call the police?"

"Yes." We both had our noses in the crook of our arms like a pair of Draculas. The blood on our hands added to the effect.

He turned to Robin, gazed into the street through my window and vacantly wiped her full lips with a napkin. She opened the door. Robin's tight skirt hugged her full hips.

"What are you doing?" Pickering snapped and shut the door.

"You really think the killer's still out there, Walter?" Robin said through gritted teeth and caked on foundation. She had a pimple on her nose that no amount of make-up could stifle. "Stop being a pussy!"

After a suitably intense reporter-stare-down, Pickering did what he does best, barked some more orders while rubbing his bald head.

"Everyone, start snapping."

He was right. We needed to get our own evidence before the paramedics and cops took control. All three of us snapped photos and video. Junior didn't move. That was fine, keeping track of a statue was easier.

CHAPTER 3

The cops arrived ten minutes after the paramedics pronounced Kendal dead.

They asked us to wait outside. We inhaled the salty air like we'd been held under water for the last hour. My office might never smell normal again. Not to mention Kendal's open, staring eyes. Big, dead eyes.

An unmarked Crown Victoria out of a nineteen-eighties episode of *Simon & Simon* lumbered onto the grass despite three open spaces not ten feet away. Something about cops and especially detectives, no matter what city or state, they loved to park anywhere but in a marked parking space. They behaved like a dog that could piss on a bush, but would rather piss on your mailbox.

Two burly men emerged. The driver wore a long-sleeved white button-down tucked into blue dockers. The other detective dressed like he'd spent the day in a sports bar: t-shirt, White Sox cap, jeans. White Sox had a beard, but the driver looked cooler in a pair of oval sunglasses and a goatee. The skin around his goatee shimmered in the tropical light. I'd seen enough metro-sexuals in Los Angeles to know the look. He liked facials. Had facials really made it this far into the Atlantic?

Walter shook his head while he stared at this phone.

"Was Kendal married?" I asked.

Walter nodded. Junior had parked himself next to the railing on the steps.

"Who's the kid?" Walter asked.

"Junior. Was here to see Kendal, but he wandered into my office first."

"Kendal came looking for this kid and what, an arrow found him?"

"That's about the size of it. You look like you could use some sleep, el presidente," I said, trying to lighten the mood. It was too soon.

"This is no fucking time for your shit, Boise. I gotta tell a man's wife he's been shot with an arrow in our place of business. Hell, I gotta tell all my other reporters that one of them was just killed in our building and I gotta have someone write the story for tomorrow's edition. Do you believe I'm enjoying those things?"

A firm finger tapped my shoulder. Goatee stood there, cool as a block of dry ice. His dark, satiny skin stood out in stark contrast to his dry-cleaned white cotton shirt.

"That your office?" He had a thick voice, honed by years of intimidation practice in the field.

"Yes," I said. I tried to swallow, but my saliva had dried up.

In my experience cops tended to dislike private operators, like we were in competition, although to my mind, I'd always thought the two groups should help each other.

"What's with that door?" he asked.

"I was painting it when all this went down."

"I see." He typed something into his phone.

"Hey, Boise?" It was Junior from his perch on the steps. "How much longer? I'm gettin' a bit hungry." He gestured putting food in his mouth. "Long flight, you know?"

"Who's that?" Goatee asked.

Junior walked over. "Hey, officer."

"Detective," he said, indicating the shield clipped to his belt. "Major crimes."

"Sorry, sir. I got in from Georgia not long ago and I'm gettin' to where I could eat a bushel o' peaches."

Goatee nodded, then sauntered over to his car and came back with two Snickers bars.

"On me. You want a bottle of water?" He raised a James Bond eyebrow.

"Uh, no. Thank you, sir." After accepting the proffered snack, Junior started to move back to his spot.

"Wait. We all gotta talk." He eyed Pickering, then pointed at me and Junior. "How about us three have a discussion in my car."

Through a mouthful of chocolate, caramel, and nuts, Junior said, "You got a-c?"

Once in the backseat, I said, "What about Walter?"

"I know Mr. Pickering. I know where he works and how he thinks. He'll tell me what I need to know, then I'll read all of it in the paper tomorrow. No worries there."

I'd been questioned extensively by cops in my life. Everything from information gleaned while investigating cheating spouses for the firm I worked for when one of them wound up dead later, to the prolonged questioning involved with Evelyn's death. One thing they liked doing was dividing up suspects and witnesses to see if the stories were consistent. His choosing to question Pickering and Givens separately probably had more to do with checking out if our stories lined up than the fact that Pickering was a reporter. Then again, maybe Goatee really was worried Pickering would report everything he heard.

A team of forensic techs trotted up the stairs and entered my office. White Sox leaned in to whisper something to one of them. He ambled over, hitched his jeans again, then plunked into the passenger seat. Removing his hat, he leaned close to the vent, his eyes narrowing as the cool air buffeted his face.

Goatee patted his partner's shoulder. "This is Detective Barnes. I'm Detective Leber. We are in the major crimes division. We've been assigned to investigate the death of," he looked at his phone, "Adirondack Kendal. Is that right?"

Barnes nodded his bulbous head, still leaning into the vent. "At least we got an easy I.D. for once, huh? What's that name all about?"

Leber shrugged, "Mountain range, I think."

"It's in New York state," I added helpfully.

"So, why was Adirondack Kendal in your office, Boise?" Leber asked.

Junior and I hadn't discussed this question, but I'd agreed that our conversation was confidential. I intended to keep that promise.

"I'm not really sure why Kendal came down. A visit, I believe," I said.

Detective Leber stared at me from between the front seats, at least it felt like he was staring at me, his sunglasses were so damn dark. He robotically shifted his attention to Junior, tapping his knee.

"What's your name, son?"

"Herbie, but folks call me Junior on account of my dad having the same name."

He typed into his phone. "Last name? Spell everything."

We told him all the basics. I laid out the specifics of the actual arrow shot, but left out the few details about Junior's family, including his grandmother's unknown status. Junior added a few more specifics, but also left out his concerns. Eventually, they let us go but insisted that they'd be in touch to follow up on our version of events.

As we headed for the Snack Shack a few blocks away, I asked, "So why don't you want help from those detectives on your grandma?"

"I don't know. Just don't feel right, you know?"

"Two burgers," I said. "With fries."

I leaned toward the kitchen and inhaled deeply. The warm aroma of food ushered away the stench of death and decay that had left a foul after-smell in my nose.

When the counter guy didn't give me a total, I realized he was staring at my bare chest. I'd used my shirt to soak up Kendal's blood. He pointed above him at a greasy no shoes, no shirt, no service sign. A large metal fan was the only thing keeping it bearable between the island heat and the smoking kitchen only feet away. Hanging above the register were t-shirts with the restaurant's name for sale. I tugged on a medium and paid the man.

The only beer on the menu was Schlitz and Pabst Blue Ribbon.

"What do you want to drink?"

"I'm vegetarian," Junior declared.

"Fine by me," I said. "I'll eat both burgers. Drink?"

"Perrier."

"Perrier and a Pabst B-R." I shelled out my last twenty. "You eat fish?"

He didn't respond. He was fixated on the spot on his leg. The red spot.

"You want to go wash that off?" I turned to the guy at the counter. "Bathroom?"

He shook his head and pointed to another sign. *NO RESTROOMS*. I remembered California had some law about restaurants being required to have restrooms. This was not California. I asked for a cup of water and grabbed some napkins. Junior wiped his leg. His hand continued wiping the spot so that his skin had begun turning redder and little wet shreds of napkin stuck to his leg. He jerked when I gently gripped his shoulder.

"I think you got it out," I said.

Dropping the napkin on the table, he crossed his leg onto the knee of the other leg and leaned over, examining it more closely. There was nothing there.

He took one sip of his Perrier, then picked up another napkin, dipped it in the water cup and resumed rubbing the spot.

We passed the time in silence until our orders were called--he rubbed, I sipped. Scenarios ran through my mind about why someone would want Kendal dead. The main one for me was that he had an arrogant attitude and cared little about the consequences his stories brought to those involved. As I slathered ketchup over my burgers, I couldn't help thinking this might have turned out for the best as far as Junior's interests were concerned.

"I work up an appetite whenever the authorities come around." I shoved the plate of crinkle-cut fries in front of him and dumped some ketchup on the side of the plate. "Bon appetite."

Did Kendal's demise have anything to do with Junior, or was this a colossal coincidence? Would I ever get my office back? Mostly, I reminded myself that Kendal wasn't paying me and Junior might be. I was determined to keep better focus on this case than I had on Roger's, where I'd gotten distracted repeatedly by a kidnapping Dana and I had stumbled upon during the course of our investigation. The guy whose daughter had been kidnapped had been one of, if not the wealthiest men in the Caribbean, but I hadn't earned a dime for saving the girl.

After ten minutes his eyes had gained some focus. He seemed present again, but smaller somehow. "So, how you doing with what happened?" I asked between bites. Each mouthful of burger deserved its own fry, then I'd dab my mouth for grains of salt or bread. Four napkins minimum for proper dabbing. I had an unnatural fear of food on my face.

Dipping a fry in the ketchup he ate it slowly, bit by oily

potato bit. "I'm still worried about grandma. Somehow feels like this is my fault. The guy comes down to see me and pow, dead. No one else saw the letter or knew about me coming here. The letter didn't even say which reporter was my contact. Must be a coincidence, right? Couldn't be me. Right?"

"That's a very rational attitude, except whenever someone dies in a room with only three people, there's a decent chance it has to do with at least one of the other people. Rule of threes, as my old man used to say."

He slurped some tea and belched into his hand. "'Scuse me. Yeah, I guess you could be right. But you and this reporter are both in a dangerous business, right? I mean solving murders and digging up dirt on folks is bound to make some enemies, right?"

The kid did have a point.

"Then again, you were only two feet away from a guy who got aced with an arrow. That doesn't worry you at all?"

"Two feet might as well be a mile for a pro."

He was starting to shove fries into his mouth with more enthusiasm, a good sign. Focusing on details and solving the problem always provided a welcome distraction from the emotional reality of death, as did hunger.

I looked up from my plate. "What's that mean?"

"The arrow. Did you look at the arrow?"

I dropped my burger on top of the fries and wiped my fingers, but didn't dab, which should tell you something about how much this statement jarred me.

"Nope. It was hard to make out the brand since the damn thing was covered with blood."

"It was pro grade. Not something some rook goes in for, you know?" His eyes grew faraway again for a moment, as if he was perusing the arrowhead in his mind. "Plus, they put that thing into him hard, so almost certainly a serious crossbow."

"How do you know this?" I asked.

He stared down at his leg again and scratched at the spot with his fingernail while wiping off some of the dried napkin bits.

He shrugged his shoulders like this was obvious. "Man, my whole clan's into archery."

I popped off my chair like my four-of-a-kind just got beaten by a straight flush. "When the fuck were you going to tell me this?"

The cashier threw me a dirty look as my chair toppled over. Setting it back on four legs, I leaned close, my words shooting out in a bull snort. "We need to talk! Let's go outside where there's more privacy."

CHAPTER 4

My burger dripped ketchup on the patchy grass outside the restaurant. I ripped another hunk out of my burger then continued my onslaught, bread crumbs flying out of my mouth to emphasize my displeasure.

"What's wrong with you? You get someone killed in my office, and you don't think to mention it!"

He shrugged again.

Swallowing the last of my beer, I flung the can against a rock. I needed another. A piece of bun fell as I lifted my hands to my head, shoving my hat off. The burger followed the beer can into a nearby bush as I spun awkwardly on my good leg.

"It didn't occur to your rational, college-educated mind that there might be a connection between the archery community on this island and Kendal getting one through his chest? Really expect me to believe that?"

"No man, it didn't. Well, not till now. Yeah, it sorta makes some sense," he mumbled.

Three deep breaths. Most times I forgot to do this, but somehow, in the heat of my business floundering, my office posing as a sealed crime scene, and my cantaloupe-colored door needing to be repainted, I managed to shift into a Zen-like state.

When I opened my eyes, Junior sat crossed-legged on the grass, biting his fingernails and scratching that same spot on his leg.

"Tell me more, and I want to see your letter."

"We're archery folk. Hell, my uncle was an alternate on the Olympic team in eighty-four."

That had been the year it was held in L.A. I'd seen the plaques at the Coliseum.

"Does your family have money?"

"Yeah, we do all right," he replied. "My grandma's well-off, anyways."

Then it hit me. The Bacon family had made their money in sugar, molasses, and the most famous export from the Virgin Islands, Bacon Rum. I could picture the Jolly Roger flag waving above the name on the 750-milliliter bottle.

"Who else knew about you meeting with Kendal?" I asked.

"No one. I didn't even tell my dad I was coming down. He wouldn't have let me. He and grandma don't much see eye to eye."

"When'd you get here?"

"Around an hour before I saw you."

"And all you brought is that backpack you're carrying?"

"Yup. I have clothes at my grandma's house."

Unbelievable. First Elias, a college student at The University of the Virgin Islands, who was an intricate part of Roger's murder, then this kid. Young men knew how to find trouble.

"Money?"

"I got my own," he said. "Grandma gives me spending

money. I'm running out, though."

"What's your father going to do when he sees you?"

"I reckon to ask forgiveness instead of permission. Isn't that how it's done?"

Maybe that explained why he was so concerned about grandma's non-responsiveness. Funds running low. Once I'd picked up my hat and dusted it off, I said, "Letter."

He rummaged through his backpack and handed me a handwritten letter on eggshell colored paper.

"Is this your grandmother's signature and handwriting?"

"Yes, as best I can tell."

Dear Herbert Junior,

If you get worried about me and what's happening or if I go off the map...I've got some things going on, noble things...go see a reporter at The Daily News. Just leave a message there in my name and he will set up a meet with you. He is an old friend, a dear man who is helping me sort things out. He will clarify what's happening. For your own safety, I'm not going to tell you about it yet. Do not go to your parents, go see the reporter first.

Love,
Grandma

"How did Kendal know who you were?"

The man-boy shrugged. Blank-lost expression, but not shock anymore. Examining the letter further brought another salient fact to my attention: it was undated. So many questions.

"Okay, here's the deal: I need a job. You are going to hire me to find out what happened to your grandma. You are going to convince your parents to give me a retainer for expenses."

He stopped biting his nails and scratching. Stillness overtook him again. After a brief pause, he nodded. "All right, man. All right. I'll try."

Donning my hat, I offered my hand so he could stand up.

"This is happening," I said. "Let's go see your family."

"They're gonna fight us on this. They don't think she's missing."

"I'm in the mood for a fight."

CHAPTER 5

We arrived at the Bacon house twenty minutes later. The late afternoon sun threw a golden light over the orchard of mango and pomegranate trees.

"No sugarcane?" I said.

"Actually, grandma hates the smell of the stuff. She doesn't allow rum or sugar in the house." He inspected his thumbnail, which he'd already bitten to the quick. "She uses honey in her tea."

"You're really worried about her."

It was rhetorical, but he answered anyway. "I have concerns. You know, it's tiring when no one believes you about something like this."

I did know. All too well.

He rubbed the back of his hand under his nose then wiped whatever it was on his pants. Once inside, Junior excused himself to use the restroom.

Five fans with blades the size and width of a pelican's wing swirled the air, but somehow it still smelled musty.

A Victorian couch littered with buttons beckoned. All the furniture looked antique, like museum pieces from the turn of the nineteenth century. Everything was so busy it made me feel like I should remove my shoes and sit with my legs sideways on the flowered couch. I rapped on the coffee table.

"Yes, it's real marble, straight from England. Nineteen-twenty," said a Caucasian man with slicked back hair and a mustache. He wore natural-colored linen pants, a matching shirt and sandals.

"Herbie, you are such a bore," said a woman.

Feeling naked without Junior to explain my presence, I bolted off the sofa. I waved and grinned like I'd just entered a ballroom clad in boxers and a tank top, which wasn't that far from the truth.

"Hi, I'm Boise." I coughed, then stammered on, "I'm, uh, here with Junior."

The man she'd called Herbie looked at me suspiciously. "I'm gonna call security. I don't know how you got into this house, but…"

Junior returned. "Hey, Papa," he said dourly.

"Junior! What the hell are you doing here?"

The woman smiled and took a sip from her wine glass, "Yes, Junior, your father did not tell me you were coming down today." She threw an icy stare at Herbie, then the ice melted as she turned back to Junior. "Give your auntie a kiss, dear."

Junior obliged, pecking the woman on both cheeks. She did not hug him and her kisses were the air-type.

"Nice to see you, Aunt Hill."

"My, I think you've gotten taller since last I saw you. What is that you're wearing?" She glanced down and put her hand over her mouth. "Is that blood on your leg? Are you hurt, boy? Wilma!"

It was the same spot as the original blood he'd wiped off, but there was now a small cut from his continuous rubbing.

A woman scurried in from the back of the house, wearing a navy smock and rather tight jeans. "Yeah, Miss Hillary. I right here. What you need?"

"Wilma, call Doctor Schneider. Junior's hurt!"

She leaned over, her pink finger shaking above the cut like an angry insect.

"No, Wilma, don't worry, I just scratched it too hard. I'm fine. Don't call the doctor."

Wilma planted her hands on her hips. "Junior, when you get here? Come give me a hug, boy!"

Junior and Wilma hugged warmly, a marked contrast to the greetings offered by his aunt and father.

Herbie piped up. "See, there it is, Hill, overreacting again to nothing. That's what you've taught my son with all your hysterical outbursts. And you wonder why he has trouble letting go of this fanatical concern for mama. Is that why you're here, son?" Herbie's jaw clenched and unclenched, as if he strained to control the need to use the restroom.

My knee ached, so I settled back onto the hard couch. Another man entered from the garden. The smell of marijuana and sage wafted in with him.

"You reek! Get out this instant." Hillary pointed to the back door from whence he'd entered. "You know there's no smoking in the house."

The man choked out a hoarse reply, "I'm not smoking. I already smoked, bitch."

He stalked around her, punched Junior in the shoulder with a cocked grin and a wink, then plodded up the carpeted steps in black and white Chuck Taylors. A door slammed.

"That's Uncle Harold," Junior whispered as he returned to my side and Wilma headed back to the kitchen.

"You see what it's come to," Hillary said, sticking her chin up at the second floor. "He thinks he can do whatever he wants when she's not in residence! I could wring her neck for leaving again with no warning and not taking her lapdog with her. Gurr!"

She pronounced gurr as a word, not as a sound. This woman struck me as one of the most contrived people I'd met in some time. Even in Los Angeles, at the law firm where I worked, she would have kept pace.

"You see why I don't feel confident we'll convince them?"

"Convince us of what, Junior?" said his father.

Hillary gazed at her nephew then danced into the kitchen, returning with a fresh glass of white wine in one hand and a bottle in the other.

"Wine anyone?" No one spoke. "Fine, more for me." She downed the glass and filled it again then parked the bottle on the bench by the grand piano.

"Hillary," said Herbie, "you know that can stain the wood. Mama would not approve."

"Hmmm. Well, no one else around here seems interested in the rules anymore, so why should I care?"

Snooty rich people, yay! Keep cool and get a retainer.

"Mr. and Ms. Bacon?"

They turned in unison as if the family dog had just spoken. Hillary leaned against the piano, striking a key on the end. A deep *bong* filled the room.

"I'm Boise Montague, a private dick Junior has asked to look into the disappearance of your mother."

At this they looked at each other and for the first time seemed to connect as siblings. Hillary erupted with laughter. She clanked her glass down on top of the piano and pounded out three dramatic notes.

Herbie stroked his mustache in a downward motion as he realized I wasn't joking.

"Junior, do you really expect us to continue indulging this

36

paranoid fantasy about mama? Really?" The last word came out as "rally."

A door on the second floor creaked open. Harold descended the curved staircase. Hillary sneered at him over the rim of her glass as she guzzled more wine. He seated himself on the bottom step, leaning back on his elbows and throwing his legs straight out. Lounging. After casually smoothing back his wavy locks, he slid a pack of cigarettes from his shirt pocket and tapped them against his knee. The box made a hollow *pop, pop, pop* on his tattered jeans. He opened it and held the cigs out to each of us in turn. Although I didn't smoke, I took one. This seemed to please him.

He said, "Boise, huh?" as he lit my cigarette. His lighter had little green palm trees on it.

"Oh god, the prince has deigned to grace us with his presence," slurred Hillary as she poured another glass of wine. The liquid in the bottle looked dangerously low. Her forehead matched the yellowish tint of the white wine and had an oily sheen to it. This family descended from colonial landowners, probably a mix of Spanish and Danish ancestry.

"Hey man, let's hear what the little dude has to say. So, Junior, what's the haps? Why'd you bring Private Dick Boise by?"

"I think grandma's missing. Something's not right. You know we talk regularly and she didn't say nothing about a trip or..." He paused, seeming to search for more things she could be doing on the sly. "...I dunno. What do you think Uncle Harold?"

"Well, little man, you're a thinker and a damn observant hombre. You had your ear to the ground on mama. If you say something's amiss, I'm inclined to give it a ride."

"Good God, Harold. You're stoned. What do you know?"

Harold belted out a plume of grayish smoke and declared into the cloud, "And you're drunk."

At this Hillary shot off the bench, knocking the wine bottle to the floor. The bottle didn't break, but white wine seeped out onto the baby blue rug. That rug probably cost more than I made in a year.

"Look what you made me do!" She marched away calling for Wilma. The wine bottle remained on the carpet, the buttery smell of chardonnay melding with the cigarette smoke.

"See, Junior, it's never too late to act like a child," Harold said with mock enthusiasm. "Mr. Montague, welcome to our slappy home!" He lifted his arms and slouched against the stairs, taking another drag. "So, what are we talking about, Junior and Boise? You guys sound like a dream team. The Samoan and the Southerner. Like some kinda movie."

"I wanna hire Boise to find grandma. I miss her and I'm missing school on account of I can't focus with this on my mind."

Herbie sneered and wrung his hands. Hatred dotted his cheeks like acne as he glowered at his younger brother while addressing his son.

"Oh no. Junior, this ends now. Your grandma has been doing shit like this our whole lives. We are not…"

"I dunno, man," interrupted Harold. "She hasn't done this since I was in my twenties." He threw me a sideways look. "That was a while ago. Definitely since before Junior was conceived, which is why he doesn't know about that side of her. Give the kid a break. Let him have some ideals." As he finished this last plea, he mouthed at Junior and me, *fuck 'em*, then stuck out his tongue.

"I saw that," Herbie declared. "F-you too little brother. You always did lack class."

Harold put his hand over his open mouth in mock shock. "My virgin ears are burning! Three business degrees and that's the best you can do, dude?"

Hillary charged back into the room, arms akimbo, the now empty wine glass clutched in her right hand by the stem. As she rounded the corner, the top of the glass struck the wall and shattered.

"Ahhh! That woman's crazy! She means to bash me. Help!

38

Help!"

Behind her, Wilma held a wooden rolling pin still covered with flour aloft, while casually following the hysterical Hillary. Not quite as threatening as Medusa, but I suppose close enough for Hillary.

"I ask her leave me alone. Jus' leave me be. I making food and she want me to drop everyt'ing to come clean she mess." Wilma pointed the rolling pin at the bottle Hillary had left on the carpet. Flour dusted the bottle like a snowfall. "You mean to tell me you can't pick that up by yourself, Miss Hillary?"

Hillary cowered behind Herbie. Harold let out a peal of giggling that matched his stoned demeanor. The only sane ones seemed to be the eighteen-year-old and the housekeeper brandishing the rolling pin.

"What do we pay you for?" asked Herbie with solemn authority. The volume on Harold's giggling turned off abruptly. His torso became rigid as he rose off the steps and moved to his brother. Harold cocked a fist at Herbie's flushed face. Their noses nearly touched. I could almost feel the steamy warmth of Harold's bull-snorts from the sofa. The physical contrast between Harold's muscled and tanned body and Herbie's lithe, pale features belied the stereotypical differences. A man of the earth who on some level detested his wealth and a colonial invader hell-bent on keeping the European family fortune intact. I wondered which son Francine felt closer to.

"You do not pay anyone, Herbie," Harold growled. "All of this. All of it. Is paid for by mama. We are tenants, and poor excuses at that."

A whimpering sound emerged from Hillary as she held the broken glass by the stem out to ward off her enraged younger brother.

"And you, Hill, what are you gonna do with that?" Harold ripped open his shirt, a white button landed on the smooth black surface of the baby-grand, spinning like a top before settling. He stuck out his chest, daring her to stab him with the shattered tip. "Maybe you'll whine and dine me to death." He let out another peal of laughter.

"Crazy people," muttered Wilma. She picked up the wine bottle and headed back into the kitchen, her head shaking as she continued to mutter the word "crazy."

Then, as if things could get any stranger, Hillary fainted. The wine stem bounced across the carpet, rolling to a stop under the piano.

Harold insisted she was faking it to get attention, that she'd done the same sort of thing a thousand times whenever she didn't get her way. Herbie and I carried her upstairs and lay her down in bed. When I returned, Junior and Harold stood outside in the orchard dropping bits of bread into a koi pond as a dozen of the bulbous fish lazily gulped the proffered crumbs. An open field with arrow bullseyes mounted at the far end stretched off to my right. The field was also marked with soccer goals at each end. It appeared to be a regulation sized soccer field. The place reminded me of a cartel boss' estate in Colombia or Mexico I'd once seen photographed for an architectural magazine. In the distance, a section of grass was fenced and marked as a tennis court. Two barren net posts stood guard outside the doubles alleys.

"So, my little man tells me he wants you to find mama. You up for that? I mean…" He nodded toward the French doors behind us. "…we ain't exactly the Swiss Family Robinson. You sure you want in on this fiasco?"

Harold started a second cigarette. Mine smoldered in a ridiculous green ashtray on their marble coffee table. He offered me another. I waved him off.

I nudged Junior. "It doesn't sound like your family is much for your theory. Not your dad and aunt, anyway." I addressed Harold. "What do you think? Could she be missing, or were you just saying that to get a rise out of them?"

He pointed the business end of the cigarette at me. "You

don't smoke, do you?"

"No."

"Cool. Cool. Yeah, well, I don't really believe she's missing, but who cares? I'm happy to help my nephew out with his beliefs. All the better if it pisses them off. So what, you came here to ask for an investigative bankroll?"

"Yeah, Uncle Harold, I was praying you'd indulge me on this seeing as I'm really concerned about her and she's your mother. I mean, what if I'm right?"

"Yeah, kid, or maybe you wanted an excuse to ditch school."

"Man, you know I like school."

"Yeah, I know, that's why I'm inclined to say fuck it and pay this man for his services."

"Really!" Junior's eyes lit up. "You'd do that?"

Harold nodded and his nephew hugged him. I felt like hugging both of them; I had a paying gig.

"I see you have an archery range over there," I said.

"You shoot?" Harold asked.

"No...well, once at a camp." Something small and brown scurried across the open field. "Was that a rabbit?"

"Yeah, when we were kids, we had a pair of rabbits get loose. That saying about multiplying like bunnies is for real." Harold sniggered. "What say, champ? Should we show him the ropes?"

"Sure," said Junior.

We made our way over to the range where a small shed housed the equipment. Harold brought out a complicated device that resembled a bow.

"Funny looking, huh? These things have gotten pretty high-tech. When I competed, they were much more like this."

From the back of the shed, he brought out a bow painted army camouflage and sporting a more traditional look, but made of some high-tech alloy.

"I use this for hunting, not competition."

He let me hold it.

"Wanna try?" He winked at Junior. "What about you? Been practicing?"

Junior shrugged. "More into biking lately, but I go shoot sometimes. I'm gonna get some water."

Once Junior was gone, Harold dropped his cigarette on the ground. He pulled a quiver out of the shed, and we positioned ourselves next to a painted brick marked with a white "20."

"Dude, archery one-oh-one. You put your hand here. Nock the arrow here." He hadn't given me an arrow yet, probably a good idea. You don't give a loaded gun to a child. "No, like this, man." After adjusting my hand, he pointed at the multi-colored target. "This is a pretty rookie distance, but if you don't shoot it'll be tough enough."

"It seems plenty far enough to embarrass me," I muttered.

My left arm had some bend in the elbow. He straightened it. "Extend your bow arm." He tapped under my right elbow. "Elbow up. Level. Good." He handed me an arrow. I nocked it. "Turn more sideways, like this." He demonstrated. "Nice, except, ah never mind. Let 'er rip."

I pulled back, trying to control my breathing as I'd learned to do when shooting. The arrow flew, hit the edge of the target and careened off into the grass.

Harold pursed his lips and rubbed his hands together. "You almost hit the target."

I held the bow out to him. "Let me watch you."

A grin spread across his tanned features. He appeared ruddier and more rugged-looking than his siblings. He gripped the bow with practiced ease, shook his right hand like it was a wet rag, set the arrow, and released. The arrow hit between the first and second gold ring.

"Too much weed today."

"What do you mean? That's amazing."

"It's all right."

"I hear you're an Olympian," I said.

As he picked up the stuff and dropped it back into the shed, he said, "Why would Junior be telling you about my archery exploits?"

"We had an archery-centered discussion at lunch today."

Harold sighed. "I'll bite."

"A reporter Junior was going to speak with got shot with a hunting arrow in front of us through the open door of my office." I patted my chest. "He's dead."

His expression remained passive, almost strangely so.

"The blood on his leg?" Harold said.

"Actually, he wiped off the other guy's blood hours ago, but he won't stop messing with the spot where it was."

"Jesus," he muttered. "Does Herbie know?"

I shook my head.

"Yeah, probably for the best, dude. He won't enjoy hearing that his son was in a room where someone was killed. Might make him more inclined to refuse your assistance. This got anything to do with mama ghosting us?"

"No idea," I said. "I've been a part of this game for an action-packed couple hours. All I know is a man's dead and your nephew's conviction that his grandma's missing. Why don't any of you believe him?"

Junior exited the house with a determined gait and crossed the grass, holding a glass of water.

"What's up, kid?" asked Harold.

He pouted and kicked at a rock. It tumbled toward the target. "Dad's being a dick."

Harold nodded. I could see he wanted to agree, but he held his tongue.

"What'd he say?" I asked.

"He complained about wasting tuition money since we lose fifty-percent of this semester's money if I drop out now. He also bitched about the cost of airline tickets. Like just 'cause he's afraid to leave this rock, I should never do anything?"

"Hey man, your dad's, like, thrifty." Harold said.

"No, he's a cheap-ass." Junior waved at the estate. "Got all this and acts like we're broke. Shoot, if you hadn't agreed, I wouldn't even have Boise here on my case. She's his mother."

Harold rubbed his neck and winced. "Look man, you gotta understand, your grandmother wasn't always Missus Reliable. She had some wanderlust back in the day."

"Where'd she go?" Junior questioned.

"Shoot if I know. Foreign lands? She'd go off with people then come back with 'em and they'd stay a week. She'd call 'em uncle-this or aunt-that, but none stuck around long. They'd go and she'd stay a while, then wander off again. We got raised by the maids and manservants back then mostly. I was the youngest, but those two," he cocked his head at the house, "they got into some terrible mischief. Undocumented carousing. They got me started early. Heck, I'm still doing it." At this last statement he grinned his stoned smile, eyes dull and dreamy. His teeth had a yellow tint, which reminded me that I hadn't brushed since our last meal. "But, I'm willing to spend some bucks to be sure she's still around. She straightened out and has been more reasonable the last twenty years. Also, she's my mama."

"Can I use your bathroom?" I asked.

"Inside to the right," Harold said.

I flossed and brushed, stealing a gob from a tube in the medicine cabinet, sticking my blue fold-up toothbrush back in my pocket after shaking off the excess water. My floss was running low.

Through the French doors, I could see Harold and Junior talking. Harold mussed his nephew's hair and said something that made both of them laugh. Thank God for uncles. I wished my Uncle Jim and my dad had been on speaking terms because I liked the guy a lot. But they weren't, so we weren't.

The sound of running water issued from the kitchen but otherwise, the house had fallen silent without Hillary to incite chaos. The maid was washing dishes when I entered the kitchen.

"Hi, Wilma, is it?"

She started, flinging soap suds into the air. They paused mid-air, then began their slow descent.

"Aye-yay-yay, mi son, you startle me!" Her hand covered her large bosom. It matched her wide hips. She shook her head as she leaned over the sink. A small smile broke on her lips.

"What I can do for you? You want some water?"

"No, nothing like that. I wanted to say I'm sorry about how Hillary acted to you earlier. It didn't seem nice," I said.

She began washing the dishes again. "They pay me, so she think she can tell me anything and I have to do it. Miss Bacon, she say otherwise. I work for she, not dez brats."

"Do you live in this house?"

"Yeah."

"How long since you last saw Miss Bacon?"

"She done gone for da past weeks. Maybe three or four she done gone. She sometime go away. Not my place to say where da missus go."

My eye suddenly felt irritated. "May I?" I indicated the water. She stepped aside and let me put my face under the faucet. "You think she missin'?" I asked from inside the sink while rinsing out my eye.

She turned her ear to me and cupped her hand. "You ask if she missin'?" She leaned back against the wall and looked out into the back yard. In the distance you could see a hazy expanse of endless grayish-blue desert. The ocean. It was quite the estate. "Could be. These children." She shook her head with resignation. "I younger, but I had to work me whole life. Me whole life. Work make you grateful, you know?"

She handed me a brown dish towel.

"Did she used to take off randomly?"

"Not no more. She change in da last ten years. Since Junior get to be seven or eight. Even before that she was more docile.

45

She more like the family. But, I think she have somet'ing else in mind too."

"Something else?" I was confused. Wilma seemed to be in a stream of consciousness state.

"Yeah, somet'ing she read. I see them arguing a lot recently." She returned to the sink, washed a plate and a fork, then drained the brown, soapy water. The gurgling pipes forced me to speak up.

"With each other or with Francine?"

"Both." Sounded like, *boat.*

"What do you mean something she read? What would she read that would create such animosity within the family?"

"Da sugar business. She no want da family to stay in it. Nothing good come from it. Not no more. She want to give back. She talk about something, like she find her god."

She ran the faucet, pulled the sprayer out and killed the suds in the bottom of the sink, then headed into the back of the house, leaving me standing there like a wallflower at the prom.

A powerful shout erupted from the living room. I poked my head out. Herbie had opened the French doors. He was commanding Junior to come inside. They needed to talk about his cavalier attitude toward his studies and money. Junior slinked inside and upstairs, his father on his heels. Herbie walked with the pathetic confidence some men gained from deflating their sons.

I moved into the living room and watched them ascend. At the top of the staircase, Herbie turned and looked down at me. A nobleman gazing down at a serf.

"You are dismissed. Leave my son alone. Your ideas are infecting this family. You're not welcome here."

Exposing secrets. It brought out the worst in people. Harold was in the driveway cleaning the blackened old wax off a surfboard. He offered me a ride home.

"Was your mother a reader," I asked as we jostled down the road in his brick-colored jeep.

"Pardon? A reader. Who doesn't read if they know how? Who's gonna willfully be a fool?"

We jounced over a pothole as we left the long, smooth driveway and hit the badly rutted "main" road outside the Bacon estate. Behind us, a wrought iron fence ambled shut. The gate man waved at Harold, who threw out a mock salute, which made the older fellow grin. From what I could see the private street serviced three houses, of which the Bacons' was the last. We passed another gated driveway bordered by hedgerows. Up a hill I could make out a Mediterranean style roof surrounded by coconut trees.

"You'd be surprised," I muttered. "You taken a good look at humanity lately? Not brimming with intellectual curiosity."

Without slowing, he whipped around a bend, crowding the middle. Another car swerved around us, laying into the horn. The man threw his finger out the window. Harold smiled and waved.

"That's Jerrimy. He's always angry because his parents spelled his name weird. We had classes together up in New England."

"You attended boarding school like Junior?"

At the next intersection, a blue Toyota Rav-4 was parked in a dirt spot on the shoulder. A fat white guy with questionable facial hygiene had a paper open on the steering wheel. He didn't look up as we flew by.

"It's a Bacon family tradition. Man, I was so pissed I told mama I'm never leaving again unless it's to visit another island. No snow. Endless summer. That's my motto." His tan face lit up and it was like I could see waves foaming in his eyes. "You surf?"

"Used to, out Hull Bay. In L.A. it's territorial and you need a wetsuit. I also smelled funny when I got out."

He stuck out his tongue and wrinkled his nose. "Wetsuits suck, but if you gotta. Where you headed?"

"The West Indian Manner."

"In town?"

"Yup. East of downtown near ... "

"I know the place. It's almost as big as our house."

We drove in silence for a few minutes. Dusk overtook us. He eventually flicked on the headlights. Traffic was light.

"You believe this traffic," he said as we halted at a stoplight with four cars in front of us. "What a hassle."

I looked at him out of the corner of my eye as I pictured nine p.m. in L.A. on a capillary having more cars per block than we'd seen in eight minutes of driving. He punched me in the arm.

"I'm messing with you, man. You mentioned L.A. so I figured I'd complain about this piddly shit! The look on your face when you were contemplating how anyone could think this was bad. These are the little moments I live for." He pouted his mouth and broke into a silly British accent. "Now, I know you're dying to ask some more questions about me lost mum, so out with it, dear boy."

"Well, I was asking about her reading habits," I said. "Do you recall her reading anything ground-breaking lately?"

"Ground-breaking. Hmmm. Breaking ground you say? Hmmm." He was still having fun with me.

We swerved around another bend. To keep from leaning into him, I gripped the door handle and someone honked. Nothing much seemed to phase Harold.

"You want we should swing by your office? The cops probably left everything open."

I hadn't even considered that. "Yeah, great idea," I said.

As we passed through Havensight, a small sign you could barely read said "Daily News" with an arrow pointing right. "This is it coming up," I said. Harold flung the wheel and cut off an on-coming auto.

"You have a way with other drivers," I said. My stomach did a somersault.

My office door was indeed wide open. Darkness had settled in and street lights illuminated the parking lot. A few reporter's cars remained, but otherwise the place was deserted.

My door looked like a three-year-old had spent the afternoon finger painting on it. Kendal's blood splatter had dried on the lower right below the doorknob.

"Is that?" Harold pointed at the blood.

I nodded with a shudder.

The bloody arrowhead flashed in my memory. Morbidly, I thought of the bottle of champagne used to christen a ship. Kendal had christened my office.

I limboed under the police tape and surveyed the inside. Nothing missing. Thank God for small favors. For what it was worth, I locked the door.

"Getting back to your mom's reading," I said once we were back on the road. We passed Island Pharmacy, and I remembered my short supply of floss and the need for Kleenex in my office. I asked Harold to stop. He pointed at the "CLOSED" sign. I had gotten used to late-night pharmacies in L.A. In St. Thomas it seemed everything except bars closed by six or whenever they felt like it.

When growing up here, my father had no trouble spending his lunch hour, breakfast hour, and dinner hour sauced, all the while holding down a job. The islands were full of functional drunks like Terry Montague.

"Hey man, I've been thinking, maybe we ought to rummage through her room. She didn't tell me much about that stuff but lately she was on about something, like all these years of shutting us out was for our own good. There were more, I dunno, varieties of people milling about. I mean, there's always someone who she had business with, but these seemed more like social-activist types or something. Younger. I figured it was some charity she was starting and she'd tell me about it when she was ready."

"Varieties of people?" I asked as Harold flashed his high beams at an oncoming car whose lights were blinding us.

He opened his fingers then dropped them back on the wheel as he shifted. "I dunno. More, you know, islanders. Locals."

"People of African descent?" I said.

He looked at me then back at the road. "Good way to put it. I hate the word black. Hate the word white too. Never seen anyone who's white or black, you know?" I waited for him to continue. "Just, I dunno, mama got friendlier with our workers lately. More respectful, you know? Not that she was disrespectful, but like they were more equals than before." He paused, perhaps waiting for me to say something that made it okay. When I said nothing, he went on. "I know, it's fucked up."

The man had a bit of white guilt, as he should. I pointed to Wet Willy's, a bar with brick facing and slatted shutters that hadn't been painted since prohibition. "I'm gonna have a beer before heading up. You want one?"

"Guess I'm buying," he said.

We bantered about insignificant stuff as I swilled down the last drop of Guinness from my pint.

With a belch of satisfaction, I *clanked* the glass on the wooden table and bookended it with my hands. My eyelids were going to need toothpicks to keep them from falling shut like garage doors, but I had two last acts of business to conduct with Mr. Bacon and my buzzed demeanor would help.

"About the retainer," I said.

At this he waved his hand for me to shut up. Pulling a bulky Velcro wallet featuring a beige surfer riding a white wave on the flap, he counted out twenty hundreds.

"What else?" he asked. "Are you going to tell me not to drive?"

"When can we rummage through your mama's things?" I asked.

"Soon, maybe even tomorrow if I can get those home bodies out. Just be ready when I call."

I shared my cell info. As I rounded up the hill toward the guesthouse, I turned back.

"Two more things," I said.

He lingered next to his car, peering at me through his own heavy garage doors. "I'm not Samoan."

"Did I say you were Samoan?"

"Yes."

He lifted an eyebrow. "What's the second thing?"

"You shouldn't drive."

I didn't wait to see if he followed my advice.

CHAPTER 6

Junior's father was in no mood for games. Herbie popped some Dexedrine, an amphetamine prescribed for ADHD, but in his case used for alertness. He'd started the drug because of the focus and self-esteem boost, years of constant use evolving into dependence.

Herbie's hand raked across Junior's face, raising an angry red knot on his cheek and sending him to the floor. He had come out of the bathroom after taking a shower to find his father sitting on the edge of his bed. Junior knew it was coming. He knew what the situation demanded. He'd gone outside the chain of command. Aired laundry.

Junior's face ached, but this was nothing. He had pride, but in this room, pride got you hurt. His father had never said "I love you." Well, more precisely, he'd never said it in a loving way.

"I show you love. I raise you. This is how you repay that kindness? Bringing this country stranger into my house. How dare you?"

The boarding school language. The highbrow berating. The street-level beating. All of it happened so fast.

"And now my dumb ass brother is going to involve other people. He agreed to pay this, this fool detective, didn't he?"

Junior nodded from his position on the floor. Something dripped out of his nose. Junior watched it splatter on the hardwood. Not blood. Clear.

"You are going to repay me for both the cost of the ticket, and…"

Junior's temper slipped silently from his grasp and shattered like a glass ornament. Still staring at the wetness on the floor, through clenched teeth he said, "I'm not going away. I'm here to find grandma."

His father bent down, his hot breath pasting his son's ear with each word. "You will do as I say, boy. You will go complete your schooling. You will make this family proud, or you will get nothing."

I don't want nothing from the likes of you, Junior thought. Although he felt rebellious, he dared not stick his hand into the shark's mouth again. He kept his mouth shut. He let thoughts run free, but voiced nothing. Not now. Not in the dragon's lair. He would wait for the right time, then he'd make his father proud by taking the initiative. Finally, he'd see Junior for the leader he would someday be.

The small act of rebellion had taken every bit of courage Junior could muster. Confronting Herbie terrified him. He really wasn't ready for this. He was a man, but not that man, not yet. Wasn't sure he ever would be. Today, he felt like a gambler who had edged his one-thousand dollar chip toward double-zero, then pulled it back right before the roulette dealer waved his hand over the table. He didn't know what had happened to his mother.

Herbie gave the same evasive answers every time he brought up Gertrude. In August, right before leaving for college, Herbie's anger over the questions had intensified to fury.

"You ask me again, boy. I dare you to ask again! Your so-called mother, Gertrude, abandoned us. Forget about her, or I'll beat your skull till you cannot remember that cursed name. Do you hear? Gertrude put her heart in a cage and threw away the key when she abandoned us."

Junior had then scurried off to Georgia Tech, but he kept searching for his mother. Whenever he wasn't doing school work, archery, or biking, he ran through databases, social media, had even tried background check companies. His father had threatened to cut off his credit card if he saw another related charge, so Junior had filled out one of the dozens of credit cards offered at the student union. He was eighteen. He was a man, even if he didn't feel like one right now.

He thought if only he could find his mother, answers about himself and his discontent with life would come. Little did he know, finding her would lead to darker paths and no real release from the painful realities of being human. It didn't really matter who your mother was.

"Now, you will go to sleep, then you are heading back to Georgia on Sunday. I'm pleased to see you and so is Aunt Hill. I'll let you stay a few days, but we are not wasting your tuition over this mission to find your grandmother. First it was your mother, now it's your grandmother. Leave it alone. They're both hopeless causes. You understand me, boy?"

"Yessir." Junior snatched a change of clothes out of his dresser and shut himself inside the bathroom. Thirty seconds later, he heard his father leave the bedroom. Using the clothes, he constructed a pillow and crunched into the fetal position on the bathroom floor.

Thoughts of the women in his family he actually knew swirled in his head. Aunt Hill had always been distant, formal. She was family and greeted him with her own brand of enthusiasm, but underneath she was cold as white marble. She avoided the sun, but her skin remained a hue or two darker than Herbie's. He possessed the true colonial European look. Who lived on a tropical island their entire life only to shun the sun? But he had some warmth for his Aunt Hill. She was never cruel to him like papa. She never defended his father's abuse, but he sensed her loyalty was to papa.

Grandma, on the other hand, had helped Junior. She had sent him off to boarding school and college in a place where he'd fit in. He didn't function in New England schools. Too formal. He needed the relaxed atmosphere of the South. Grandma Francine knew and respected that. For all practical and emotional purposes, she was his mother. He was damned if he was going to let her disappear without digging up every grave on this island if he needed to. At least that's what he used to think.

Now, his respect for her had begun to slip. He had learned things about all of them. Heroes were people, too, it turned out. When you looked closer, your so-called protector was often the same person who set you up to need protecting. Besides, she'd also avoided telling him about his mother. She'd claimed not to know her last name or where she was from. Junior wondered if Gertrude was even her real first name.

As he tried to imagine what his mother looked like, he fell into an exhausted sleep on the cold tile.

CHAPTER 7

Walter Pickering, a man who never seemed to sleep, woke me at nine. I trudged down the hallway to the bathroom and showered next to a stateside tourist who wouldn't stop yapping about how authentic The West Indian Manner was.

"The place is so real. I feel like I'm in the mess with the locals, you know?" He kept on about how this trip was on his bucket list and he was running out of time. "So's Charlize Theron, but I think that ship has sailed."

As I left my room, I paused to admire *Christina's World* once again. A dark underpinning beneath the midday glare of a relentless sun.

Why was Christina on the ground? Was she hurt? Was she tired? And the streaks of gray. You couldn't accurately judge the woman's age. She had a slender figure and a dress that could be worn by a woman anywhere from fifteen to fifty. Even more intriguing, an open-minded person might ask if Christina was even a woman.

Then there's the house. Is it deserted? What's that ladder on the side? Are they painting or patching the roof? The place looked like a tinderbox ready to explode into flames if a stray ember grazed it.

Christina's longing seeped through the back of her head, like a second face. No need to see her eyes, her mouth, or her curled lip. The crush of her shape and the way she stretched toward the distant farm told you everything. It also told you that whatever she longed for would always be just out of reach.

I fingered the top edge of the frame and leaned in, searching for someone in the window of the farmhouse. Only shadows greeted me. Empty shadows. Such darkness on a golden canvas. No one there. Christina was alone.

After an egg sandwich prepared by "Silent" Marge, a name I'd secretly given the nearly mute co-owner of the guesthouse, I hoofed it over to my office. I figured I'd put a clean coat of paint on the door, but a police officer was there. He said they had a few more forensic matters to take care of before I could have it back. The island shrug was his response when I asked exactly when he expected my office to be released. Loosely translated, this meant he didn't know and didn't care.

"You know you are not supposed to hold the crime scene for any length of time after the crime scene guys are finished. Back where I used to live…"

He waved me off. "I don't know nothing about that, but I was told to keep it clear. Check?"

Admittedly, I was cynical about police specifically and the government's use of our money in general. We needed the police and my office had to be properly vetted before I could return, but it was my office and my rent money going down the drain. I clenched my jaw as I turned to leave.

Watching all those years when my father, Terry, drank too much and made a fool of himself taught me something about discretion, especially around cops. Terry had wound up very close to a felony conviction. It should have been a felony, after all, since he clobbered a fellow bar patron over the head with a beer bottle. The guy needed twenty-six stitches and nearly lost sight in his right eye from a stray shard. A damned talented and expensive attorney my maternal grandfather paid for had negotiated a misdemeanor. My parents had promised to pay him back, but never managed to.

I never heard from or spoke to my grandfather again after moving to St. Croix in 1994. None of us did, including my mother. Patrice Montague's father had principles to replace family. Mom never forgave her dad for that.

The tension in my household, which had always been high, permanently ratcheted up to a ten out of ten that year. For some reason Patrice loved Terry and willingly gave up her family to stay with him. To her, "Till death do us part," was literal.

The stack of hundreds Harold had handed me the day before bulged contentedly in my front pocket. A real retainer. Legitimate private-detecting. Dana Goode, the reporter who'd helped me on my first case on St. Thomas and the closest thing I had to a partner, would be proud. My mother, on the other hand, would continue to be disappointed that I hadn't become a pulmonologist.

A text came in from Harold: "Meet me at the house at four. They have some fundraiser to attend. We'll have a couple hours to rummage."

I replied, "I'll be there."

I didn't relish discussing Kendal with Pickering, but why worry? I knew nothing. I'd say Junior's presence must have been a coincidence. Pickering probably didn't even know Kendal was working the kid or Francine.

Robin Givens threw me the twittering-finger wave as I edged

past her desk and tapped on Pickering's doorframe. He held up a finger, then dismissed a young reporter with a clap on the shoulder. Pickering's scalp had a spattering of growth, something I'd never seen. He was really letting himself go.

"Hey, Boise." He pumped my hand once and gave me a tired nod. "Mind closing the door?"

It would be one of those conversations.

I shut the door and sat. "What's up?"

"If Dana weren't on assignment, I'd have her in here with us. As it is, she's swamped over in Tortola."

"What's she doing?" I asked.

He shot me a don't-change-the-subject stare.

"Do you see my people out there?" His open palm extended to the cracked horizontal blinds behind me. Bags under his eyes and the deeper grooves across his cheeks had aged him noticeably in less than twenty-four hours.

My back cracked as I swiveled. Seven reporters milled about. They all had forlorn faces, except one guy talking on the phone whose hands moved wildly as he spoke. I turned back to Pickering.

"They're my family. You understand?"

When I didn't say anything, he repeated the question, an edge in his voice and a menacing lean over his desk. "Do you understand?"

"Yes, Walter. I understand."

He leaned back. "Good. I want you to write out a statement about what happened."

"The cops have my statement, and I don't work for you. Writing is not what I do, otherwise I'd be a reporter."

"I have a copy of that. I want another one. More details. More about that kid who was with you."

"Sorry, he's a client. I'm not telling you about him."

"I'm not asking, just being polite," Pickering said, plopping a yellow legal pad in front of me. "In fact, it's not formal at all, I want you to stream of consciousness anything you know onto this pad."

"Look, I'm happy to…"

Pickering stood. His chair rolled backwards and thudded against the wall. "Get a fucking waiver from your client! I want to know everything about everyone in that room."

"What's in it for me?" I asked.

"You do realize a man was murdered in your office. A man who worked for me. We are reporters, not cops. Dying is not part of this job."

"Yes, but again, just because your man came into my office and died, does not make me beholden to you or your newspaper. I'm an independent operator who rents space in the same building."

"Free advertising for one month. Eighth section." He sounded like he was giving up his first born. "That's the best I can do."

I'd been working on my codependency. I wanted to appease Pickering. The guy had some father-figure thing going on with me, but I resisted the urge. Instead, I did what Henry "Batey" Bateup, the guy who'd trained me in Los Angeles, had told me worked better than anything in the world both when negotiating and questioning people: I waited in silence.

Pickering rummaged through a file drawer in his desk. He placed a legal waiver on top of the pad. "Fine, a quarter-page. You happy? You know the newspaper business is suffering. I need that ad space for paying clients."

I picked up a blue pen he'd placed on top of the legal pad and clicked it a couple times.

"That's the form, but I'm happy to shoot an email version over to your client. You know his address?"

I texted Junior, who responded immediately. He agreed to sign the waiver and for me to detail our investigation, so long as I left out the identity of the missing person.

Pickering grudgingly nodded. "I'll get it out of him myself. Give me your version of events. Call the missing person Ramona."

"Ramona? Why not John Doe like everyone else?"

"Call them Ramona."

"Fine, I'll call them Ramona," I said.

I started writing, then paused. "Hey, when's the funeral?"

"Not for a while. Autopsy. They have to send him to Puerto Rico for some reason. Probably not for a month. But, we'll have a memorial service at Kendal's favorite watering hole on Saturday. Informal, but we'll all be there as will his family."

"Can I come?"

"Why? You two didn't exactly hit it off."

"Still, he was someone I knew. I mean, we worked together in a sense. Same building and all."

Pickering lifted his jacket off a hook and draped it over his arm. "Fine, it's informal, I doubt anyone will care. But you have to dress decently." He looked me up and down like I was a rodent with rabies. I wore my usual t-shirt and shorts ensemble with a straw fedora.

"What? This is a new t-shirt," I said, tugging at the thin material.

He picked something out of his teeth, flicking it into the wastebasket beside his desk, and tightened his tie knot in a fold-up mirror propped on his desk. After replacing the mirror in a drawer, he huffed on his sunglasses and rubbed them with a cloth.

"Okay, okay, I have something nice," I conceded.

When I'd first returned to St. Thomas, Aunt Glor, my deceased friend's grandmother, had made me get something presentable to attend a mass at the local cathedral. She was a religious firecracker of a woman, who liked to ply me with peanut butter and jelly sandwiches and a glass of milk.

"I'm going to let you stay in my office for one hour. Stay and write whatever comes to mind. I'll be back."

It felt good to spill the events onto a sheet of paper. Like I was releasing some stored trauma or throwing up a rancid bratwurst. My breathing flowed as if I was a car with a new air filter. When next I looked up, Pickering stood in the doorway.

"So?"

"Why are you back so soon?"

He held up his gold watch. "Been an hour and fifteen." He read my face. "Got more to say? I'll work at Dana's desk. You keep at it."

He shut the door, but the spell was broken. A few more details, then I wrapped it up. One new observation had occurred to me as I re-examined the events surrounding Kendal's death. Something struck me about the angle of the arrow's entry. I thought it had come straight through the door, but in fact, Kendal had been facing to the left of the doorway slightly, so the arrow had come in from that side of the parking lot. After I finished, I made a copy of the pages and handed the copy to Pickering.

"I want the original," he said, squinting at the pages.

"Sorry, but I'm keeping the originals."

After a tense moment, he shrugged, stapled the copied pages together, returned to his office and shut the door.

CHAPTER 8

"That Pickering guy called me," Junior said when I walked into the Bacon house. "The guy's relentless. I spilled that it's my grandma who's missing, but said that stuff I always hear about being off the record. He didn't like it but I stood my ground. Whaddya think?"

I sighed. "Well, as I said, newspaper guys want to print things. They aren't in the business of keeping secrets, but if Pickering says it's off the record, I think you're all right. Don't tell him too much more."

"Why'd you?"

"Guilt, I guess," I muttered. "I have a load of guilt about things like this. Even Kendal the Jackal has a family. In the end, we all want the same thing."

We walked into the expansive backyard. Harold was taking

aim at a target. He hit a bullseye. Junior picked up the joint Harold had balanced on the edge of a portable table and took a hit.

"How does your dad feel about that?" I asked.

"He doesn't know," he said pointedly.

I wiped sweat off my upper lip. "He won't hear it from me, but hard to miss the smell on clothes."

"I'll blame him," he nodded at Harold. "Second-hand smell, right?"

He cracked a smile at his uncle who gave him a knowing look. "Those two been blaming me for all the negative habits of this one for years. Why ruin a good pattern?"

Junior pinched the edge of his shirt and sniffed. "He's a dick. Uncle Harold's the only good one besides grandma around here."

Junior offered me the joint. I waved him off.

"Ready to do some recon, amigo?"

After Harold and Junior each tugged on the joint one more time, Harold killed the spark. He dropped the roach in a dime bag, and pocketed the bag. The three of us headed upstairs. Wilma was in the kitchen, banging pots around as usual. The smell of fried food occupied this section of the house.

"Shouldn't you guys have a bunch of servants running all over the place?" I asked.

"Not grandma's style. Right, Uncle Harold?"

"We used to have more, but mama's been simplifying over the years. She's more and more uncomfortable with servitude."

"How long will they be gone?" I asked.

"Who knows. Hill's afraid of her own shadow at social gatherings. She acts tough, but they might have to break off anytime. Then again, if she drinks enough wine..."

Harold took out a key and unlocked a room at the back of the house. We ascended a mahogany staircase that ended at a single door. Outside the door on the right was a Haitian-style landscape painting vibrant with yellows, reds and blues. Once inside, the far wall was dominated by a set of African masks, some

64

smooth and simple with red and gold lines, others more elaborate, with strips resembling hair, eyebrows and beards. You felt watched. The walls were painted an earthy color. A window overlooked the ocean. Shadows from drifting clouds played across the shimmering sea.

There was one photo on her nightstand of the entire Bacon clan at what looked like a luau, complete with tiki torches and a boar on a spit in the background. I had met everyone in the photo except Francine, who stood in the center wearing a hula skirt. A petite woman with short, silver hair. She resembled Betty White. Using my phone I snapped a photo of the photo.

Next to the picture, facing the spot where Francine presumably slept, was a small painting of reeds. Above the reeds, looking almost like it was rising out of the water, were the bold words, "If not me, who?"

There was more to that quote, but I couldn't remember it at the moment.

"So, what are we looking for Inspector Gadget?" Harold asked. The pungent scent of weed hit me as he edged toward the dresser. "And what's with the limp?"

"War wound." I turned in a circle, taking in the rest of the room. "What happened in here?"

Harold and Junior gave me blank stares, so I clarified. "The furniture." I indicated the bed and side tables. "Not Victorian. Appears to be African and some Caribe style. Simple. Much more suited to the island than the rest of the house. Either this room was changed or the common areas downstairs were. From the looks of things, I'd say it was this room that underwent the most recent transformation. Am I right?"

Junior put his hand to his chin and got very still again. "Yeah, it is different here. What used to hang on that wall with the masks?"

Harold puffed his cheeks and made a farting sound with his lips, then said, "Oh yeah. Man, it used to have a really big painting of our rum plantation done by this semi-famous artist in the eighteen-hundreds. A landscape of the production facilities in St. Croix. Barrels of rum being hauled away for shipment by workers. I'm guessing, but maybe Mama got tired of it."

"So, is the rest of the house the same?"

Harold opened the mosquito net covering the bed and plopped down. "Who cares, man?"

Junior examined a wooden chest at the foot of the bed. A quilt lay neatly folded on top. Junior put the quilt on the edge of the bed, revealing a scene of men being hauled away in chains on the lid.

"I never saw this before either. Seems kinda dark for Grandma to have in her bedroom, don't you think, Uncle Har?"

Harold didn't respond. He stared up at a ceiling fan, which sported large palm-frond shaped blades.

"I'm hot." He got up on his knees and pulled the cord. The fan began a lazy arc, and the room cooled. I cracked the window to the right of the ample balcony.

A table with four chairs around it filled the balcony. "Did you guys ever eat meals out here?" I asked.

"Once in a while," Junior said as he examined the inside of the trunk. "Usually, we'd sit and drink iced tea or tamarind water and play cards. I remember that. Hey, I found something."

He handed me a photo-copied article. It was entitled, "The Price We Pay." Below the title, written in black ink and underlined, it said, *who does she think she is?* As I submerged myself in the words, I heard the distant sound of Harold speaking to Junior. Then, Harold wiggled my shoulder.

"Come on, man, let's go. I hear them in the driveway. We gotta go." The mosquito net was already back in perfect position, waiting for Francine to return to her clean bedroom. We scrambled out the door and down the stairs. We hit the living room. I bumped into Junior, who bumped Harold just as Herbie strutted through the front door followed by Hillary.

66

"What was that?" Herbie said, throwing up his hands. "Why did we go there again?"

"Hon…" Hillary stopped and looked at us all as we gaped at them.

I caught a glimpse of the bow leaning against the wall outside. The others seemed tongue-tied, so I jumped in.

"Hi," I said, waving like an idiot. "I'm, uh, back. Harold invited me over to show me some archery skills. Right, Harry?"

"What's he doing back here?" Herbie directed the question at Harold.

"I invited him."

The two siblings stared at me like I was a roach they hadn't yet decided to squash or spray with Raid.

Junior leapt into the chasm of silence. "Hey, why are y'all back so early?"

Herbie dropped a leather two-toned man-purse on an immaculate ottoman then emitted a huff of disgust. Hillary strutted by in high heels like a flapper on the runway, and shouted into the kitchen.

"Wilma! Wilma! I need something to eat, pronto! Wilma!"

Wilma yelled back, "Thirty minutes! I still be cookin'. You and Mr. Bacon eatin'?"

"No, I need something now!" Hillary said. "I feel faint."

She melted onto the nearest chaise lounge. It felt like a photographic moment, so I pretended to send a text, and instead snapped a photo of Hillary's reverie. She had her arm across her forehead, her other arm hanging over the lip of the aqua-colored lounge chair. Even her hair looked eerily similar to a photo of Rita Hayworth I'd once seen in a book. Other than Francine's bedroom upstairs, this house had me feeling more and more like I had entered the roaring world of Jay Gatsby.

"God, what a fiasco. Honestly, Herbie, why do we indulge these pedantic politicians? They can't even provide a decent meal at these luncheons."

"Hmmm. Yes darling, I believe that's because we need them for our financial interests. If this guy continues to push up wages, we'll have to raise prices and our sales took…" Herbie stopped abruptly. "Let's talk about this some other time. We have people."

"I'm not a person," Junior said with disgust. "I'm your son. I want to find my grandmother. While we're at it, I want to know more about the business."

Herbie threw up his hands. "Always with you and the business. Don't worry, when the time is right, we'll teach you the business."

"Why? I'm going to school as you asked. I'm studying engineering so I can make our processes better. Shouldn't I have some idea if those processes are going to even exist when I graduate?"

Hillary took her hand from her forehead, leaving a red blotch on her lily-white skin. "Must you boys always bicker about this? Can't we just teach the boy about the business already? What's the harm, Herbie?"

Herbie glared at me then pursed his lips. "Once again, we should discuss when we are not," he paused, "entertaining."

I was desperate to read the article we'd swiped. Maybe it was the reading Wilma had mentioned. Junior and I would need to have our own private conversation. I motioned to Harold that I'd like to go outside and shoot some more.

"Where do you think you're going?" Herbie spat as we headed to the French doors.

I started to speak, but Harold held up his hand. "Please, allow me. Herbert." He cleared his throat. "Once again, this is not *your* house. You do not decide who I can bring or not bring onto the archery range, into this living room, or anywhere else, although I promise to keep my guests out of your boudoir and our chaste sister's quarters as well. We wouldn't want anyone stumbling on any bones in the closet, would we?"

"Boys! I'm famished. Herbie, be a dear and bug Wilma to

hurry something along. Herbie!" Hillary's shouting broke the spell of hatred flowing between the brothers. Junior merely stared at the ground, kicking at the corner of the piano. "Junior! Stop kicking at my piano this instant."

Once on the archery field, Harold made a show of demonstrating proper technique, but instead of talking about archery, he and I discussed the close call and my burning questions. Through the French doors, Junior gesticulated as he presumably renewed his onslaught about his lack of involvement in the family business or his grandmother's whereabouts.

Throwing a faint nod toward the house, I asked, "So, what's he on about?"

"Who, Junior? Every few months since he turned fifteen he goes on a kick about learning the business, but what he doesn't realize is that none of us really know the business. Mama saw to that. Herbie's at the rum distillery a lot, but from what I understand he's more of a figurehead. Throws social events, runs the charitable arm." He aimed quickly, pulled the string back till his hand touched the corner of his mouth and released. The arrow whizzed and plunked in the gold area next to two others he'd shot earlier. He held the bow out. "You try again, but keep talking. We need to make it look good, since old Herbie is eyeing us right now." I started to turn, but Harold stopped me. "Don't look, man!"

While I studied the smooth surface of the composite bow, I asked, "So none of you know anything?"

"Nope. Well, Herbie's been snooping. Digging up financial info I think. It's a privately held corporation, so there's no official filings, but online there's always speculation. Mama doesn't bring much home, she keeps her important documents at her office. The way I understand it, we make rum and have some small interests in molasses and cane sugar, but not much at this point. Mostly, the fields have been bought by larger guys. I think cane is making some kind of comeback lately because it's healthier than corn syrup."

I nocked the arrow and aimed. I was scared to touch my face with the string, but pulled it so close the little hairs from the string tickled my lip. "Which is where?"

"Nisky Center is one place, and she has an office at the distillery, as well."

Nisky Center had cropped up in my last investigation involving the daughter of the billionaire owner of major real estate developers, Payne and Wedgefield. Their offices were also there.

"Can we get in?" I asked.

He pressed my hand against my face. "You need to actually touch skin. Also, relax your grip on the string. Two fingers below and one on top, like this." He moved my fingers then tapped the back of my hand. "See, too tense. Relax."

I slid the arrow forward and shook my hand out, then gripped the string again.

Harold pushed up on my arm. "Elbow up."

He stepped back and nodded. I aimed low as he'd told me. The arrow flew, a faint hissing sound and a satisfying *plunk*. Blue.

Harold clapped me on the back. "Not bad."

"You need to find a way into her office," I said.

"Not sure that's possible. She's got security, and it's completely stand alone."

"What's that mean?"

"It's not officially the company office. It's really her own private office in a separate part of the building. The company has a whole floor…hey, man, it doesn't matter. What I'm saying is the woman had some kind of paranoia. She didn't tell anyone much of the gory details about the rum and sugar cane business. Herbie wants in, more to see how much money we have coming than that he gives a shit about the actual day-to-day business. Me, I like liming although if I got to, I'll go to work. Hillary, well, she's definitely not the laboring kind."

"Isn't Francine getting pretty old? Doesn't she need someone who knows the business to take over?"

"I think that's what has them worried," he said, pointing at the now deserted French doors.

Patting my pocket, I said, "What about this article?"

"Doesn't ring a bell. Hey, man, read the thing. I'm more into doing than reading. You research and let me know what we oughta do next. Cool? Aren't you the detective guy in this organization?"

I couldn't argue with that. I needed to start acting like I knew what the hell I was doing. The only problem was, what little I knew about the sugar business suggested you could be dead before you made it.

"All right, I'm heading home to do some light reading. I'll also run some searches on the company and your mother."

"That'll be a blast. I'm gonna keep shooting. Later, dude." He picked up the bow and shot another bullseye.

When I got by the koi pond, I looked down at the fish, all swimming in close proximity I imagined Harold standing over the clear water, his arrow aimed at one of those beautiful, clueless creatures. How easy it would be for him, from any distance.

CHAPTER 9

Back at the guesthouse, on the veranda I munched on carry-out pizza and sipped lemonade. A vague need to guzzle Guinness in the late afternoon had dominated my end-of-the-day thoughts over the last week. Budgetary constraints in the country of Boise demanded the villagers accept lemonade or water as the new national beverage. The sugar would keep me from falling asleep, but it did not fill my belly like a stout.

The article from Francine's room was about slavery. Anti-slavery. Not a subject I expected to find in the trunk of an octogenarian leader of a sugar cane empire going back generations. I was no historian, but it was a safe bet that a white family in the Caribbean making rum and sugar for more than two-hundred years had made much of their fortune on the backs of West Africans.

The article detailed the damage done to Africans forcibly taken from their homelands in Ghana, Angola, and Nigeria, then brought to colonial islands like St. Thomas, St. Croix, and Jamaica. Far more slaves had been transported to the Caribbean and other outlying colonies than to the United States. Jamaica alone accounted for over 1.2 million captured slaves, according to the stats cited in the article.

Islands were brutal, isolated places, which was why England and other wealthy countries had a hard time getting anyone to move here. Among slaves brought to the Caribbean, mortality was high and human reproduction low. In the United States, slaves had better working conditions, lived longer, and reproduced, so fewer needed to be imported. Thus, more slaves were brought to the Caribbean to replenish the voracious appetite of sugar mills, which devoured the workers when the foreman wasn't fast enough to chop off a slave's arm before his entire body was sucked into the mill.

Some of the information shocked me, as I had never really studied my African maternal grandmother's roots or considered that the famed slavery in the southern United States was only a minor part of a much larger system. Francine had highlighted a passage.

Slavery was about economics. Slaves were chattel, as much property as the conveyor belt on an assembly line or the cotton gin. In ending slavery, property was annexed from people who had paid good money for what they owned and, in many cases for slave-owners who did not own the means of production, their sole source of income was in leasing out their slaves to perform tasks for others in the community. Abolition was a taking without compensation, as surely as taking someone's home or land. In some instances, a small compensation was given to the slave owners, but not nearly enough in most owners' opinions. Abolition bankrupted many slave-holders.

In the next paragraph, a single sentence was not only highlighted, but underlined in black ink and an asterisk had been penned in the margin beside it: *If the slave owners felt cheated, imagine how the slaves felt.*

After finishing the eleven-page article, I gazed at downtown Charlotte Amalie. A smattering of old, wooden homes dotted the flats at the bottom of the hill. They stretched away. Above it all, slightly to my right, sat Government House. A white, colonial structure that housed the sitting governor, Abioseh "Abbey" James. The intricate balconies and majestic placement jumped out from the rabble of galvanized roofs and utilitarian architecture.

I flipped the stapled pages to a photograph of a plantation home in Cuba in all its aristocratic glory. Holding up the photo, I compared the real colonial structure on the hill in front of me to the picture. Although I didn't know the history of Government House, I suspected it was a plantation owner's dream: top of the hill, looking down on all the peons.

An article on slavery. I kept coming back to one question: why? Why would Francine Bacon give a rat's ass about slavery at this point? Junior and Harold never mentioned her interest. Either they were holding out or she didn't share her hobby with them. Did she share it with Kendal? And what about the asterisked sentence?

Marge was into computers. When you considered it, computers and a nearly mute person fit together nicely. She could communicate with her fingers, like sign language. In an effort to capture the millennial market, three months earlier, I had suggested Lucy go ahead and install wi-fi in the building. In true Virgin Islands fashion, the install had sputtered at the starting line, needing a replacement router twice before the service finally worked. After a mere nine weeks, they printed new flyers saying they had "free wi-fi." Marge updated the website, and I witnessed two couples under twenty-five roaming around the grounds a week later. One of them even had hacker-hair: purple tips on green roots.

I ran a quick search on my iPad for Bacon Sugar and Rum.

Sure enough, in both St. Thomas and more extensively in St. Croix and Puerto Rico, they had employed slave labor before it was outlawed in the mid-1800s.

Did anyone still grow sugar cane? I thought sugar cane had been done in by beet sugar in the nineteenth century. What were they producing rum and sugar from now in the Bacon business? Again, the internet answered quickly and easily. Cane sugar was all the rage and the finest rum still fermented from Caribbean cane, at least that's the notion pushed by the marketing.

Corn syrup and other sweeteners were on the decline as once again, good old cane sugar weathering the economic hurricanes and roaring back in the last twenty years. Out in California places advertised Mexican Coca-Cola because it was made with cane sugar instead of corn syrup.

My phone rang.

***

"I told them. I told 'em," Junior said dejectedly. "If we'd started looking sooner."

"We don't know that it's her. Not yet," I said.

Junior let his head loll to the right until he gazed drunkenly at Harold from the waiting room chair. Despite his dejection, his speech came in clear, certain tones.

"It's her."

"Will you two shut up!" Herbie growled. "How would our mother have washed up on Hassel Island? It's just some half-eaten body."

A technician came out of the hospital morgue, cleared her throat, then said, "This way, please. Are all of you family?"

"No," said Herbie pointing at me. "He's not coming in. He's not a member of this family."

Junior started to protest. I waved him off, settling into the waiting room chair. The white walls and chilly air made me shudder. When no one returned for over ten minutes I knew they had located Francine Bacon.

Farther down the sterile hallway a fat white guy sprawled in a chair, thumbing through a newspaper. He had a beard, but then again so did every hipster who could grow facial hair in the last five years. I trotted out to the parking lot, locating a blue Toyota Rav-4 five minutes later. After jotting down the license plate number, I returned to the waiting room. Fat guy gone.

My knee throbbed, but I couldn't stop pacing. Who was that guy? I was itching for a beer, but I didn't want to leave before they came out.

Twenty-five minutes later, Junior and Harold lumbered out, eyes red, cheeks flushed. Junior's pale face had blotches matching his sunburned arms. Neither man seemed much in the mood for talking. Harold, Junior and I drove straight to a boat slip. A man in khaki shorts and a baby blue tee stood next to a white fishing boat with the moniker "High Hopes, St. Thomas, USVI" stenciled across the rear end above two large motors.

"Where are we going?" I asked.

They hopped into the boat. My stomach was already doing cartwheels in anticipation of the ocean voyage.

"Guys, I get seasick. I need something."

Harold lifted the cushions of a seat and fished out a Canada Dry Ginger Ale. I sipped the lukewarm soda as we motored out of the marina toward Hassel Island.

An alpha-male in blue steered. Harold had seated himself on the bow, arms hugging his knees. The wind whipped through his stringy locks. Junior paced around in front of me, wringing his hands and muttering, "I knew it, I knew it, I knew it."

I wanted to say something to alleviate his guilt. "Junior, it wasn't your fault."

He spun, planting both hands on the cushion next to me. "Not my fault! I'm the one she talked to most."

"But you weren't here."

"Yeah, that's true. I've wanted to be gone for a long time. But I should have stayed. She needed me."

"Why'd you want to be gone?"

"It's complicated. My dad put me up in boarding school, so I figured I'd prove that I was okay with it. Like, hey man, I got this handled. I'm a man. Plus…"

He pushed up and started pacing again. Although he was moving he had that same frozen look in his eyes I'd seen when Kendal was shot.

The boat jounced over a wave. Ginger ale sloshed on my hand. I sucked it off and took another sip. My stomach started to churn. Behind us, the clutch of houses and low buildings that made up Charlotte Amalie shrank. A white cruise ship dominated the right side of the harbor. I tried to make out my office building, but the docks and other buildings concealed it from view. Bluebeard's Castle stood above to the east and below it, The West Indian Manner nestled behind two tall coconut trees and the avocado tree. I knew the termites were devouring it, but from here, the tree looked whole, at peace.

"I know what you mean," I said without turning around. "I went off with the same intention. Fathers seem to do that, but maybe that's how it works. Fathers shove their offspring out of the nest. You fly or fall."

"Falling. Done a fair amount of that," he said.

I didn't know what else to say to Junior. It all seemed so stupid. Harold in the bow, his dirty-blond locks whipping in the wind, looking too cool in his Oakleys. The kid had more family than I did, as well as more opportunities. Boarding school sounded pretty good to me. I envied Junior. It's why I'd left New Orleans where we'd started living with my mom's cousin after my father went on disability. To disappear. To stop being seen. To stop being a part of the dysfunction. All Junior wanted was to be included. To be let in on the business. In the end, we both had different solutions for the same problem.

Harold groaned as he stepped down from the edge back into the cockpit area.

"Yo, man, this is fucked up. Can't believe we're going to see where mama bought it." He looked at me. One of his eyes was black.

"Creepy, right? I sometimes burst a blood vessel under extreme stress. I think this qualifies, dude."

"Who's showing us what here?"

"We know people, like this guy." He nodded at the blue-shirt wearing pilot. "Former cop. Eddie, say 'hey' to Boise."

Eddie grunted acknowledgement without turning around.

"Eddie," I said to the back of his head. "Okay, what's Eddie's story," I asked.

"Friend of mama's. He heard and called his buddies on the force to get us some photos and an unobstructed look at the crime scene. Eddie's the man, right, Eddie?" Harold slapped the thick man on the shoulder. Eddie gave a slightly more cordial grunt. "Detective named…what's it again, Eddie?"

This time, Eddie spoke with a thick West Indian accent. "Leber."

CHAPTER 10

Leber. Did this guy ever take off his sunglasses? The Bacon family had pull. Detective Leber wore another billiard-ball colored button-down. Eddie and he nodded at each other in some cop greeting. Leber must have made the journey over in the police boat moored at the dock.

We stood on the beach in front of some stone and brick ruins I'd hiked through once on a cub scout trip. Hassel Island was home to a few hundred folks who were mostly hippie types that liked to be more isolated than the bustling tourist trap of St. Thomas allowed. A ferry serviced the island. In elementary school one of the girls, who cut her hair short and smelled like sage, lived over here. I'd had a crush on her for a minute in fourth grade.

"Eddie, this better be good. I already spent the morning doing my rowing workout in this harbor, now you got me out here again. I don't like motorized vessels. Too noisy." Leber shifted his attention to Junior and me. "We really should stop meeting at murder scenes."

"Wait, you're saying my grandma was murdered?"

"That's what I'm saying. Someone killed her."

"How do you know that?" Junior demanded.

"You certainly are more rambunctious today than when last we met," Leber said scratching his arm. "Look, I'm doing a favor for Eddie. That's it. I'm not here to be interrogated. We'll save that for the suspects when I locate them. All of you, including you." He pointed at me. "Have a date at the station for questioning tomorrow."

Harold nodded plaintively. "Yeah, yeah, we'll be there."

"Don't gimme no sass, boy. Y'all done gone and involved yourselves with two people who're dead, and we are gonna want answers."

"Two?" Harold asked.

Junior stepped forward. "Can we stick with this outing. We'll be there tomorrow, Detective Leber. Promise." Leber glanced at Eddie, who again gave a nod. This seemed to relax the detective.

A patch of sand on the beach. The waves surged in and out. A hint of chop on a fairly calm day. My stomach settled more and more the longer we stood on solid ground. I bent, getting closer to the sand, then looked sideways at Leber.

"Evidence?" I asked as I stood and made a mental note of our proximity to the main island.

Leber shrugged. "She drowned. She had some signs of small fish nibbling at her extremities." He looked at Harold and continued speaking. "She was in fairly recognizable shape. Drowning, if that's all it is, leaves the body in fairly good condition." He squinted at his phone. "The report says something about bruising on the backs of her thighs, like a board hit her there, but not too hard. She'd bruise easily at her advanced age."

"Do the police have any idea where she'd have drifted into here from?" I asked. "She died somewhere out there, right?"

Leber nodded. "They think she must have been in the water at least two days before washing up here."

"Hey man, if you offed someone, wouldn't you weigh the body down or something?" Harold asked.

"Let's get back on the boat," I said.

"What for?" Junior asked.

"There's no evidence here, is there, Detective?"

This time Leber shook his head, a gleam in his eye. "You're a little brighter than most of the P.I.'s around here, I'll give you that." He turned to Eddie. "What's his name again?"

Eddie spoke in a tone so low, even I wanted to date him. "Mr. Montague."

We returned to High Hopes. Leber stood off to the side, his arms crossed over his bulging chest. Junior fell into his soft stillness. He'd witnessed a murder in my office and now we had confirmation that his grandmother was also a murder victim. My thoughts returned to one of my father's tried-and-true remarks that things, usually bad things, happened in threes. If you included Roger's death almost three years ago, this was my third, but I had a feeling that didn't qualify.

"What are you doing?" Harold asked once we were back on the boat still moored to the small concrete pier.

Leber's skepticism oozed over me as I hunched over, examining the inside edges of the area around the steering wheel, fisherman's chair, and the entrance to the below-deck cabin. Nothing appeared out of the ordinary except for a little nick in the otherwise immaculate white fiberglass over wood finish. After snapping a photo of the small gouge, I straightened up.

"Where's your partner?" I asked. "What's his name? Bales?"

"Barnes, but you already knew that," Leber said. He still hadn't taken off those oval sunglasses. Mr. Cool.

"Are your eyes sensitive to light?"

"You want to look deep into my baby blues?" he asked.

"Nope, but I do like to see the eyes, otherwise how do I know who I'm dealing with?" I shot back.

Leber waved his hand in a let's-get-on-with-it circle, so I did.

"How tall was your mother?" I asked Harold.

He looked at Junior and shrugged. "I dunno, what you say, Junior, five-two."

Junior assented to the estimate.

"And how tall are you, Harold?"

"Five-eight and one-quarter."

"Would you stand over here?"

He moved against the railing of the boat. Taking hold of both his shoulders I positioned him directly in front of the mark I'd found.

"Please lean back so the backs of your legs are touching the edge of the railing."

"Hey man, you're not gonna push me in, are you?" When he said this, everyone's eyes lit except Harold's. "What? Wha'd I say, man?"

"Where's it touching the back of your legs?"

"Hmmm. I dunno. Maybe just below the knee here."

"What kind of shoes was she wearing when you examined her?" I asked Leber.

"I don't know."

"Do you have reception?"

He checked his phone, then climbed out onto the dock and strolled to the shore. I pointed at the nick in the rim of the boat, then laid back and put my sneakered foot on the edge and banged my heel against it.

"This could have been made by a shoe kicking down with the heel as she was shoved over the side." I stood and leaned over to look at the starboard hull. There were no marks there. It was very, very speculative on my part. A mark. Not much.

My stomach had begun to churn again, so I got out of the boat and sat on the dock, giving myself a good view of the spot where Francine was found. Junior settled next to me, squinting up at the sun, his forehead redder than ever.

Junior said, "She wasn't wearing shoes, but she had on stockings when they found her. Sounds like she would have worn some kind dressy shoes with heels."

Picking up a pebble, I chucked it into the green water. "Women in their eighties, they like shoes like that. Let's go look at her closet and find out who had access to this boat."

Leber returned, clicking off his phone. "You sound like you think you're in charge of this investigation. This is a police matter."

"You find out anything about her shoes?" I asked.

"No."

"No, you didn't find out anything or no, you're not sharing?"

He turned his face toward the sun. "Beautiful sunset tonight. It's best ya'll go grieve your loss and be ready to answer some questions tomorrow."

I put my arm on Junior's shoulder like a friendly neighbor. "If I didn't know better, I'd think these po-lice were more interested in snagging a collar than in figuring out who killed your grandma. Would you like to take a piss on the deck?"

He peered around at Eddie, who had positioned himself back in front of the steering wheel in a possessory manner. Eddie tilted his head. He had brown skin and a football-thick neck. His blue shirt flapped in the breeze.

Leber said, "It isn't like that. We want to figure this out and all help is appreciated. Much appreciated. But, we need to be kept in the loop. You share everything with us."

At that Eddie turned and fired up the engines. Leber disembarked.

"How do I get in touch with you, partner?" I asked. "I only have your office number. What about your cell?"

He wrote his cell on the back of a business card and handed it over. I noted its thickness. Even the government had better business cards than me. We motored into the channel and around the point. Leber remained on the pier, watching us cruise away.

Harold and Junior surrounded me, after looking at each other with a blend of fear and exhaustion.

Junior said, "So you think grandma was killed on this boat?"

"I don't know. It's a theory, but a shaky one at best."

A wave of nausea swept over me. The rest of the trip I hung over the water, puking my guts out.

"It says in here she was killed on or about October first. Could be off by as much as thirty hours in either direction, but based on the feeding around her nostrils and ears, it looks like it happened in the late afternoon. Where were you on that day?"

He tapped his pocket. "As you can see, I'm not big on preserving brain cells. Probably right here smoking weed or cigarettes and shooting arrows, or just smoking weed. What day'd you say?"

"October first."

"Naw man, what day, like day of the week?"

"Thursday," I said.

"Thursday, that's tough. Not a day I typically have a set routine for, but usually around late afternoon I'd be relaxing out here smoking. Don't think I even left the house again that day after surfing till about eleven."

"Were Hillary and Herbie here?"

"Prob-ly, but Hill stays indoors a lot, and I'm outside on my balcony or out here." He raised his arms to the sky. "I mean, what's the sense of living here and staying inside, right? Anyways, the place is so big, how am I supposed to know if they were here. I likes to get over in my wing."

"So that afternoon, you don't remember seeing them or them seeing you?"

"No. You know, Boise-boy, if I didn't know better I'd think you thought I did in my mama."

"All the bases, Harold. All the bases. How long had she been gone before October first?"

"Junior freaks out too much. She's a grown woman. She was out of touch for a few weeks or a month. I dunno, maybe more. Man, I ain't got time to track my mama's whereabouts. You track your mama around?"

Where was Francine during the weeks Junior hadn't heard from her? She wasn't dead until about a week ago. That left up to fifty days unaccounted for. All of September and maybe a chunk

CHAPTER 11

The next day, I solicited a copy of the coroner's report from Leber via Eddie via Harold.

"How do you know Eddie?" I asked Harold from a chair on the archery range. Using his old bow, Harold was taking shots from the one-hundred-yard block.

"Eddie and I went to Antilles together. We had classes all through middle school and high school after he transferred over from Charlotte Amalie."

"Not too many kids from Charlotte Amalie High School get to Antilles. I mean public school kids usually can't afford a place like that, right?"

"Man, his mama went and won the V.I. Lottery. And wouldn't you know it, that woman was smart with those winnings. She didn't act like those usual lottery winners and splurge on cars and televisions and a big house with fat payments. She stuck to the program and fixed up the same ratty house she lived in that her parents owned and then focused on her kid. Oh yeah, and she bought a rental property. Eddie went on and studied criminology and became a detective, too. Good dude that Eddie. Doesn't talk much though, except when he gets in an emotional mood and knows you real well."

His phone dinged. "All right, the report's in my inbox."

"Can he get the report on Kendal, too?"

"Kendal?"

"Yeah, the guy who was arrowed in my office."

"You know, man, I'm not about using up favors on dudes I don't even consort with. Why do I care about Kendal again?"

"Cause your mother told Junior to go speak to Kendal. I think his murder's connected."

He gave me a sideways stare, shot another arrow then typed something into his phone. He kept mowing down targets while I waited patiently and considered the difference between darts and archery. On one target was a photo of the governor's grinning face at some pep rally or other. Harold put one right between the man's smiling eyes.

After a time, I sighed. "So, can we print out the report?"

"Yeah, yeah. Lemme finish this set. Hold your horses."

He took ten more shots, then we returned to the house. Shortly, he retraced his steps clutching a printed copy of Francine's autopsy report.

I held the pages aloft. "That's fast, even in more advanced jurisdictions."

"It's no accident. Eddie and the coroner have history. He got us pushed up. He says Kendal got sent to Puerto Rico, so no way to expedite there." He shrugged.

No surprises in the coroner's report. She drowned. Salt water into the lungs and all that technical jargon about asphyxiation and doses. "Homicide" was checked under "Manner of Death."

"What's it say about the cut on her forearm? I noticed it when we ID'ed the body."

I leafed through the report. "Nothing much, som superficial wound."

"Superficial? It was pretty deep."

I shook my head. "It doesn't mean the wound was means it wasn't why she died. Who uses your boat? besides you and your siblings?"

He snickered. "Hillary? Man, Hillary wouldn't go ou tub. A cruise ship or a yacht's her game. Occasionally, take a run with me. He's not much for taking it out on but he's capable."

"What about you?"

"Me?"

"You use the boat?"

"'Course. I go to some remote surf spots. You sound cops. They were here for hours, questioning all of us and through our shit. Then we had to go down to the station fo questioning and fingerprinting. You believe that shit?"

"Harold, your mother is dead and an associate of hers The family are always strong suspects. They are gonna be you and this house for weeks."

"Come on. Hillary and my brother are jerkoffs, but mama? No way."

I gave him a blank stare, then said, "Family. They lo the most, and they hate you the most."

He stared at me a moment before lining up another tar suppose. Whatevers." He shifted back to answering my que about the boat. "Eddie and I do some fishing. Couple n ago, we caught us a nice king fish and some pompano. eating."

"Sounds like you use it a lot. When was the last time today?"

His eyes squinted down to slits. "I'm guessing little c month ago. I've just been out Karat Bay and Hull surfing Waves been nice, so no need to go excursing about."

of August. No one seemed to know, and Junior was the only one who really cared.

My phone rang. Walter Pickering.

"Yeah, what's up?"

"I need you here."

"Mr. Pickering, I'm not an employee of *The Daily News*." Heavy breathing into the phone. "Gimme an hour."

Leaving Harold to his archery, I returned inside where Hillary whisked by in a kimono. She ignored me as she glided back up the stairs, the red silk tail flowing after her. She held a flute glass with orange liquid. I suspected a mimosa. Along with a bloody mary, an alcoholic's go-to morning drink.

"Be bold," I whispered into my fist before calling up the stairs. "Hillary?"

She stopped so abruptly, some of the mimosa sloshed on the back of her hand. "Damnit!" She turned to me with clenched teeth. "Must you make a habit of causing me to spill everything? What is it?"

"On October first, it was a Thursday, were you here?"

"Yes, we were all here all day."

"Wilma wasn't."

"Wilma doesn't count. I mean Herbie, me, and Harold. We were together here all day."

"Harold's not sure."

"Harold's always confused, but that's from all the smoking. He loses track of the days. I do not. He was out there and we were in here most of the day. No one went anywhere."

Herbie came to the top of the stairs. "Will you stop pestering my sister? We were all here on October first, as we told the police."

With that, she stormed into her bedroom, Herbie went into his study. The doors slammed simultaneously. My affirmation to be bold only went so far. I didn't have the guts to knock on their doors and further incur their displeasure. Dana would have done

89

it. She would have pushed to make sure neither of them were lying. I wasn't so persistent. I would accept them at their word.

In the kitchen Wilma was once again washing dishes. The islands had never been much for automatic dishwashers, but I figured rich folks like the Bacons bucked convention. However, I saw no dishwasher.

"Hi, Wilma."

She didn't turn around. She rubbed her eyes with a soapy hand and sniffled.

"Wilma. Are you okay?"

"Yeah, I good. What I could do for you?"

"No, it's okay. Never mind. Sorry for your loss."

She grabbed a dish towel and dried her hands. "What? You trying find out what happen, right?"

I nodded.

"I wish to help." Her mouth curled into a frown as she fought off tears. "I love Miss Francine. She was good to me da last few years. She in a betta place now. I should not be sad."

"I'm sorry for your loss, really." I paused.

She stared at me, then spread her hands and inclined her head.

"Were you here all day on October First?"

"Last week? No, that was Thursday, right? No, I was at the doctor that day. I have tests done." She held up her cell phone calendar for me to see. "Den I had to go rest at me son's house. I didn't work that day." She put her hand over her mouth as she realized the significance of my question. "That was the day?"

I nodded solemnly, then said, "When you don't come, is there someone else?"

"No, because the odda woman who come also be sick. They on their own that day." She opened the screen door and went out into the yard. She sat on a stone bench and put her face into her hands.

Everyone was dealing with the revelation in their own way.

Hillary drank and isolated. Harold shot arrows. Wilma cried and worked. None of them were currently available for further questioning, so I took my leave.

***

As my taxi motored down the road, I spotted movement behind a tree.

"Stop," I said. The driver halted in the middle of the hot pavement.

I held my breath. Nothing moved except a plump ground lizard that skittered across the road, its tail flinging pebbles as it went. A breeze kicked up and the flap of a shirt billowed from behind the tree then vanished again.

"Hey!" I hollered as I got out of the taxi. "Hey, man, I see you."

The fat guy from the hospital and the Rav-4 darted out from his hiding spot and took off down the road, a newspaper flapping in one hand. I gave chase and after only about one-hundred yards, he was wheezing so heavily I started reviewing my CPR training. He pulled up as I was about to catch him and held his hands high, then leaned over, holding his knees.

My pepper spray was out as I limped up. Despite my aching knee, I was considerably faster.

"Hey, hey, hey," he said, seeing the pepper spray. "I'm unarmed. Be cool."

Sweat poured off his forehead. He wiped his beard with his left hand. He still held the newspaper in his right. He smelled like cheap cologne and dried sweat.

"What gives? Why are you snooping around this place?"

"Nothing. Nothing. I've done nothing."

The taxi eased up next to me. The driver dead-panned. "Hey, da man. Da meter runnin'. You want me still."

"I'm a little busy. Uh, yeah, keep it running. Just wait."

91

"Irie." He pulled to the shoulder and killed the engine.

"Unless you want your eyes to burn badly, tell me who you are." I tried to sound threatening, but a spray bottle lacked the same cachet as a gun. Luckily, this dude would soon crack.

"I'm here checkin' on Junior. Francine asked me to keep tabs on him."

"Francine Bacon?"

"How many other Francines you know?"

"Keep talking," I said. "What else do you know about Francine and Junior?"

"Nothing." I started to depress the trigger. He held his hands over his eyes. "Don't man, that shit stings like a mother."

"So what, you're some guardian angel."

He smiled at this. "Yeah, buddy, a guardian angel, that's me. Sent from Georgia to keep the boy safe and sound. I'm the king of hearts."

"Did you send him that letter?"

"Yeah, buddy, Francine said if she didn't stay in touch I was supposed to get that letter to Junior and get him the hell down here, then come on down too. Well, hell, you know things kinda went bad."

"Bad how?"

"My kid, well, not so much a kid as a man now, at least he looks like one, he got hisself arrested same day I was hoppin' on a plane to follow Junior. I had to go bail out the little bastard. You believe that? Me a former law-man and my kid in the pokey?"

"You work for Francine?"

"Yup. That's correct. Francine Bacon. She pays me, but not so much I want pepper in my eyes. I'm too old for this shit." He finally straightened up and half-leaned, half-sat on the edge of the cab.

"You're the one in the Rav-4?"

"Yeah, I knew you were on to me. Couldn't sit in that car no more in plain sight. Got out here 'cause I'm worried. Besides, it's hot as a mother in a car around here. Hey, buddy, is Junior okay? Haven't seen him for a while."

"I think he's in his room grieving," I said.

The guy nodded. "Makes sense. Yup. My granny died, I did that. We was close. She taught me craps. Well, my granny on my daddy's side, not my mama's granny. She wasn't nice."

"Name?"

"Daryl. Daryl Evans. I hail from Decatur."

"Okay, Daryl. I'm Boise. You know anything else?"

The cabbie piped up again. "Hey da man, your meter up to fifteen. You still goin'?"

I looked at Daryl. "Where's your car?" He pointed down the road. I paid the cabbie and he drove away after sucking his teeth at me.

When we got to *The Daily News* building, I sent Daryl to the Snack Shack. He said his blood sugar was low and kept apologizing for scaring me.

"See that door?" I pointed.

"Hard to miss."

"That's my office. I'll meet you there in thirty."

"You got it, buddy."

Daryl waddled off toward the Snack Shack.

"Bring me a burger," I yelled after him.

My office was cleared and the door still looked like a dead guy had smeared blood all over it. After a quick once over to make sure nothing was missing, I trudged up to the top floor. Walter waved me into his office. He patted a laptop with his hand.

"Is that Kendal's?" I asked.

"His wife got it over to me. Look at his notes on Francine Bacon."

He tapped a button and the screen glowed. It's hard to overstate the thrill of entering another's private world, whether in their computer or in their home. I'd always had a bit of a voyeuristic bent. To be a fly on the wall in the most private moments of someone's life when they're at their most vulnerable, their most real. Computers could give you such a glimpse. Searching Francine's bedroom gave me a similar thrill. Nothing was better. Nothing except finally seeing all the clues click together like magnets.

The notes detailed basic things about Francine. On page four things changed. A charge bolted up my spine. Two words: slavery and reparations. Reparations. Reparations for slavery. Other than once hearing mention of forty acres and a mule, I knew nothing about this, but it jibed with the article I'd found in her bedroom.

"What is this saying?" I asked. My skin felt hot. Without waiting for his answer, I left his office and headed for the cooler in the corner. Three tiny cups of water later the heat in my gut started to subside.

When I returned, Walter said, "Just keep reading."

Walter went out, I heard a refrigerator open and close, then he returned munching on a sandwich and opening a bag of chips. The notes were copious. They detailed a plan, as well as how Francine had come to have such a plan.

When I was too tired to read anymore, I raised my head. I expected Walter to be looking over my shoulder. He wasn't even in the office. Out in the bullpen, he was leaning over a reporter and pointing at the man's monitor. Above him, printed on the wall, was the mantra that *The Daily News* beat into the minds of young reporters before they left for more prestigious papers: "The News Never Sleeps."

As he walked back in and shut the door, he said, "It's big right? Provides clear motive."

"Are these numbers right?"

Walter settled back into his throne. He waved off an approaching reporter. The man scampered away.

"I know you're not a Kendal lover, per se…" he said. I started to protest, but he held his long fingers aloft. "It doesn't matter. The man was thorough. He was also ruthless and his loyalty left something to be desired, but he was thorough. Besides," he tapped the computer again, "Francine Bacon's a primary source. If she said it about her fortune, what's not to believe?"

"Maybe she had dementia," I said.

"Nope. Kendal insisted on her having two tests done by a psychiatrist and a neurologist. She also had her own done by a doctor in Florida. None of them had ever met her before the test to ensure objectivity. One even witnessed the creation of the Bacon Trust Fund."

I took off my hat and rubbed my thick, oily curls. My eyes dropped to my sneakers, then shot back up to Walter's face. "Do any of them know?"

"How the hell would I know?" Walter muttered. "Even not knowing, it had to be one of them, right?"

Greed. For a fortune worth over one-hundred million to parcel out this way would drive any heir to at least consider homicide. It's funny how fast one-hundred million shrinks once you divide it up amongst four or five people and pay the taxes, outstanding debts, etc.

It didn't seem like Francine accepted counsel from her children. What had Herbie said? She was paranoid. Hillary needed the money since she had no discernable desire or ability to earn a living. Harold was fun, but eccentric. Who knew what was going on in that surf-obsessed, reefer-driven mind. Besides, he certainly knew how to wield an arrow.

I wanted it to be Herbie. The guy was an arrogant weasel who stunk of entitlement. He would never pass the smell test. In the parking lot below a mangy dog took a leak on one of Pickering's Armor-All'ed tires, then trotted jauntily away. The yellow liquid beaded and rolled off the shiny, black rubber, making a steaming puddle on the pavement. They were all archers in the Bacon family, although Junior insisted his dad was not that great, I suspected "not that great" in their world only meant he wasn't Olympic quality.

Walter shot an arrow into my musings. "How well do you know your client?"

"Junior? I've known him since, well, since about eight minutes before Kendal bought it," I said in a shaky voice.

CHAPTER 12

Junior and Leber sat across from each other at the large dining room table at the Bacon residence. A light breeze carried the scent of hibiscus from the estate's expansive garden beyond the soccer field and tennis court.

"Impressive place you got here," Leber said as Wilma placed a glass of water in front of him. "This glass of water looks more expensive than my car." Wilma shuffled back to the kitchen. He sipped the water. On his extended pinky finger, he wore a thick gold ring encrusted with red jewels. "What's the story?"

"It's my grandma's house," Junior muttered.

"Mmmm. Even the water tastes better up here."

Junior shifted. The wooden seat felt harder than usual this morning. He was supposed to hold his tongue, waiting for his dad to get back. Leber had arrived, fifteen minutes early for their appointment, so Junior had texted his dad, who replied in all caps: "REMAIN SILENT UNTIL I GET THERE."

Junior hadn't replied. Although only eighteen, Junior had studied the human animal. He'd read a lot of books. He liked to watch people's behavior. It reminded him of going to the zoo, except the animals were all around in their natural habitat, every day of his life. Some of them needed cages, but most left you alone if you faded into the background. He was pretty sure his father qualified as a narcissist. His aunt's condition was less clear. He guessed all the categories were like breeds of dog, some people were pure, but most were mutts.

This cop had some kind of hero complex, or he enjoyed power. You could apply that analysis to almost every cop.

"What's your story?" Junior asked.

Leber was surprised by the question. People didn't ask cops questions like this. They were too uncomfortable. Afraid to do anything wrong lest they incur his closer inspection. Junior had gone there. Willingly. Leber could use that.

"I started out as a beat cop, then worked my way up to detective. Took some criminology courses at the local university. My mother enjoys calling me Poe after Edgar Allen, who she says wrote the first and best detective story. Maybe it was her influence."

Junior fell into his stillness, examining Leber to the point where the seasoned cop felt slightly uncomfortable. The kid had wells for eyes. A little creepy.

"You have solid alibis," said Leber.

"I do."

"So why not talk to me?"

Junior slid his phone across and showed Leber his father's message.

"I see," Leber muttered. "But don't you want to help Boise and me solve this thing?"

Leber met Junior's gaze. The kid didn't look away, but didn't speak either. Wow, another very rare occurrence. Only crazy people stared right back when he was there to question them about a murder. Sometimes mothers made eye contact when pleading for their guilty sons. Junior Bacon wasn't a mother. Was this kid just plain crazy?

The front door banged open. Herbie Bacon stormed in, Aunt Hillary on his heels. That left Uncle Harold as the only missing piece for the business of data gathering today. This case would be a marathon. He didn't have any substantial evidence implicating any of them. He needed cooperation from Francine's family, otherwise this investigation would devolve into legal posturing for every bit of information. He didn't need that complication. Keep it friendly.

"You came here early on purpose, you weasel, looking to take advantage of an impressionable young man who is distraught over the loss of his grandmother."

Leber felt like a garter snake being attacked by a mongoose. He remained seated, his hands resting lightly on the table in front of him. This man wanted to be the alpha in this family, but he wasn't. He was a sniveling bully who lived in this little world because outside of it, his weakness would be exposed. Men like this did cowardly things. Killing an old woman and a reporter from long-distance qualified.

"Dad."

"Not now, the grown-ups are talking," Herbie barked.

"Dad."

"Now, this conversation and interview are over. Wilma!" The housekeeper did not respond or appear. "Hillary, go find her!" His voice squeaked as he said the last word.

Hillary stared at her brother, then plopped into the sofa in her favorite pose and yelled. Her voice projected much more than Herbie's, but it also grated more, like one of the women from a 1930's gangster film who all sounded like uneducated New Yorkers. Her speaking voice was more refined, more proper.

"Wilma! Come now, Wilma! Herbie needs you for something. Be a dear and bring a bottle when you come."

Wilma appeared moments later, a Chardonnay bottle in one hand and an empty wine glass in the other. She handed both to Hillary.

"This isn't cold enough."

"Then chill it yourself. You know where the chill machine be," Wilma shot back. "Now, what you want, Mr. Bacon?"

"Wilma, I tire of your tone. Please escort this policeman to the drive."

"I'm afraid I need you all to answer some questions."

Herbie swung around on Leber, like Dracula in a bad vampire film.

"We do not have to speak to you. Is anyone under arrest?"

Leber remained seated, his body and face stoic. Junior piped up again, with more determination. "Dad!"

"I told you…"

"Dad, I'm eighteen. You cannot stop me from discussing this matter with Detective Leber. He's been a pro since he showed up at Boise's office that first day."

Herbie sent a chair skittering across the rug that stood between him and Junior. "How dare you … "

"Stop, right there, Mr. Bacon." Herbie froze. Leber had silently risen to his feet, his hand across his torso, resting on his still-holstered gun. "There is no need to escalate this situation. I'm merely here to get some answers that only those closest to the deceased can provide. Can we all please sit down and discuss this in a calm fashion?"

Hillary stared at Junior, her lips wet with wine. "What did you say, Junior? Why was Leber at Boise's office?"

"I was there when Adirondack Kendal was murdered."

"What?" Hillary screeched, bolting to her feet. She moved to the young man and put his head against her bosom. "Please stop this. Please don't keep after this." She lifted his face to hers with

100

both hands. "Promise me you'll stop pursuing this, this inquiry."

"I can't, Aunt Hill."

She wiped a tear from the corner of her eye and turned to Herbie. "This is all your fault. If we'd done things differently back then."

"Shut up!" he yelled, his hand raised. He stopped mid-slap, realizing the cop was still there.

CHAPTER 13

When I got back down to my office, I heard snoring. Daryl was sprawled across my desk, his beige safari hat had slid down over his spongy features. He snorted awake when I tapped his shoulder.

"My man, Boise. What's up?" He held up his hand like he wanted a high five. His breath smelled like chewed lettuce and dried ketchup.

"Sorry, took longer than expected with Walter." I gave him a half-hearted pat on the hand.

"No problem. Jet lag's a sombitch."

"Is there even a time change right now?"

"Don't matter. Still messes me up. Seats are so damn small these days."

"Tell me about Junior," I said, pulling my burger out of the white bag next to his elbow.

"You owe me eight fifty-seven," he said rummaging in his pocket and pulling out a crumpled receipt. My business card tumbled to the floor. He snatched it up.

"You need a professional business card. Wha'd you do, print this at home?"

I handed him a ten and told him to keep it.

"So, tell me about Junior and Francine."

"I'm not in the habit of telling guys I just met about my clients."

"What if I buy you a beer?" I said.

By the time I'd returned with a six-pack of Red Stripe, he'd dozed off again. I plonked a bottle next to him. He groaned, toasted to my health and chugged half the bottle in one pull. I followed suit. He tilted the bottle again and finished it, setting it hard on my desk with a glassy *clang*.

He held a second cold bottle of beer against his neck before popping it and chugging. This time he nearly emptied it. Warming up.

"Ahh! Damn, boy, what kind of beer's this?"

"Jamaician."

"Well, them Jams know how to make beer."

"Can we get back to Junior and Francine?"

"Francine, that woman, she's a piece." He belched loud and long out the corner of his mouth, then winked at me. "A bit paranoid or something. Tightly wound broad."

"Oh, yeah? Why do you say that?"

"She acts like a man, you know. Don't know about you, but women like that, they aren't really my thing. I like me nice southern girls. Make-up, nice, long hair." He belched again.

He reached for his third beer as I finished my first. Although I wasn't ready to drink it yet, I snagged one of the two remaining bottles and parked it next to my elbow.

"Did you meet with her in person?"

"Nope. She contacted me through my website. Said she had a little basic job for me as long as I kept it to myself."

"So why are you telling me?"

"Professional courtesy. I looked you up. You did some investigating out in L.A. and then headed here after your wife passed. Sorry, by the way. Is that her?"

I stared at him a while, then said, "Yeah, that's her."

"Nice lookin' lady."

"How'd you know all that?"

"I'm good at what I do, friend. I know I don't look like much, but I been in this game a while. One piece of advice: that door might be a bit loud for a private deuce, you know?" When I didn't respond, he continued. "Now, hows about you tell me what you got?"

The words came out of his mouth slowly from a distance, then picked up weight and speed as they approached shore and crashed. It seemed strange how sharing this guy was after a couple beers. Was I plying him, or was he plying me?

"Francine Bacon is dead."

He took another long swig then shook his head sadly. "I didn't mean to speak ill of the dead. Guess my job's done here. I delivered the letter and made sure Junior arrived safely. You know any good watering holes around town? Better yet, you know any with scantily clad women and a card game?"

I knew about Lucy's card game at The Manner on Wednesdays, but I didn't want this man that deep in my world.

"What triggered you delivering the letter if it wasn't Francine?"

"I didn't say that. It was her. She emailed me last week and instructed me to hand deliver the letter to his mailbox and watch that he got it. I was all ready to come on down to make sure he got here safely when, as I told you..."

"Right, you had that emergency."

"Don't say it like that. You hurt my feelings. People have

emergencies. Things happen to family from time to time." He scratched his beard and finished another beer. "You mind?" He pointed at the last unopened bottle in the cardboard six pack holder.

"You know anything else?"

"What about? Francine died. Suppose she was sick or something and wanted him to come on down."

"You were a law man? You think she had you hand deliver a letter because she was sick?"

"The lady was skittish as hell. I suspect she worried about the unreliability of the mail, but by the way you're speaking, should I suspect foul play's at play?"

I nodded.

"That's a damn shame." He swallowed another half a beer in a gulp, making me wonder where it all went so damn quickly.

"Anything else you want to share to help me figure out what happened to her? She was your employer after all."

"How'd she perish?"

"Drowned," I said, looking out toward the harbor. You could see Hassel Island in the distance. Everything was slathered in green trees and brush. One ruin stuck out and one white house. All that life. All that death.

"Out there? Double damn. I hear drowning ain't no way to die. You know all those years in Decatur, I only investigated two killings and both were pretty poorly conceived. We caught the bitch and bastard in one day both times. They didn't even run. Nothing like what you see in the movies. But shit, the guy, he got off on a tech. Too bad. Guy had to kill again before we got it right. That one's always itched me, you know?"

"She washed up on a beach right out there on that small island." For some reason I too felt like sharing.

"Not much drowning goes on where I'm from, but I remember hearing at a law-enforcement seminar that those water deaths are a lot harder to nail down, what with critters eating and evidence washing away and all."

"There's not much to go on, you're right. What do you think about reparations for slavery."

He bellowed and slammed his hand on my desk. "I'm not sure a Georgia boy and, well shit, whatever you are, should be having that conversation. You got some, can I say black, in ya?"

He finished the beer and gave a satisfied belch. "Burping helps digestion. I try to do it as much as possible." He held out his hand. "My work's done here. If you ever come up Decatur way, look me up, Boise. I'm in the one-story brick house on Sycamore Street and Sycamore Place."

"That's it, you're leaving?"

On his way out the door, he eyed the wrecked paint job and leaned into to study a glob of red. "She didn't pay me enough to get involved with murder. I leave that to young bucks. One piece of advice: don't be shy about using that pepper spray, and get some new tennis shoes. You never know when you gotta be light on your feet and those soles look slicker than deer guts on a doorknob."

With that, he got into his Toyota and headed out, swerving around a car before remembering to drive on the left.

I spent the rest of the afternoon repainting the door and cleaning up what remained with a mop and bucket borrowed from the super. Back at The Manner, I paused at the bar. Four bottles of Guinness later, I staggered upstairs and passed out.

CHAPTER 14

One thing was good, when you had a bunch of suspects with skin in the game, time was on your side. Where would the killer go? He...or she...needed to stick around, or it was all for naught.

Reparations for slavery. I was still having trouble wrapping my head around that idea, because virtually no one believed in it except former slaves and their descendants. There were a handful of examples where former slave owners freed their chattel and awarded them generous offerings as payment for years of unpaid labor.

In the U.S. there had been numerous suits over the years by individuals and organizations, but none had been granted anything by the judiciary system or the legislature at the federal or state level.

Even with a black president, no meaningful discussions on a major political stage had taken place. However, according to the notes from discussions Kendal had with Francine Bacon, she planned to give the vast majority of her estate to the descendants of the slaves her family had owned before slavery was abolished in the Virgin Islands.

"Forty acres and a mule, my ass," I whispered.

How would that make Francine's kids feel? Betrayed. Slighted. Worthless. In general people were not fond of being disinherited. I doubted Harold, Hillary, Herbie, and Junior were exceptions.

I needed a list of the people involved on all fronts. In other words, I needed a list of those who would benefit from reparations to go along with my list of those aggrieved by Francine's generosity.

Walter was in his office. He seemed to be expecting me.

"I got something you might like to peruse," he said, handing me a sheet of paper.

I glanced at the heading. "You must be a mind-reader."

The details of the trust fund appeared to leave the bulk of the estate worth approximately one-hundred-fifty million dollars to forty-four descendants of the original slaves who worked for the Bacon's when they procured sugar plantations in St. Croix, Puerto Rico, and St. Kitts, as well as those who lived in St. Thomas and worked at the docks and in the warehouses that shipped out the goods produced by the plantations for sale around the world.

The slaves in Puerto Rico were hardest to track since the Spaniards set them free long before the other colonies, provided they agreed to convert to Catholicism. Who the hell was going to quibble about being Catholic or keeping their name when the alternative was slavery? Morals always lose to freedom, unless you're Nelson Mandela. With their names changed and everyone intermarrying, coupled with poor record-keeping, those people got left behind when reparations were being handed out. Francine was a stickler for details and her paranoia made getting in on this huge windfall nearly impossible. She would rather leave someone out than give money to someone who was not part of the group.

Attached to the trust was what Kendal and Francine termed the final list of beneficiaries, including the Bacon kids who would receive small amounts for basic living and remain the owners of the family home. They were actually going for something akin to a modern version of forty acres and a mule. Each of the forty-four descendants would receive an acre of land on any of the current sugar plantations owned by the Bacons in St. Croix, St. Kitts, or Puerto Rico, or they could sell the land back to the trust for the tidy sum of five-hundred thousand dollars. In addition, they were entitled to a full, four-year scholarship to any university in the world, and everyone, no matter what they choose to do with the land, also would receive five-hundred thousand in cash in two payments of two-hundred-fifty thousand over a two-year period.

An email from Francine's estate attorney recommended that she keep the rest in trust to run some non-profit. That was a hell of an endowment: around one-hundred million dollars.

Part of this trust fund was clearly meant to punish or at least force her children to take responsibility for their own destinies and stop living off the "sugar tit" as she termed it. My own thoughts ventured the same way. As a man who never got much help from his family, I had trouble feeling sorry for them.

Harold needed to grow up. He spent his time smoking doobies, shooting targets with a stick, and surfing. All admirable pursuits after a full day's work, not instead.

Hillary was a diva. She liked being treated like a lady, but she lacked any real class or substance. Had she watched a bunch of films from the 1920s and decided she was Veronica Lake? A femme fatale she might indeed be, for her mother.

Herbie was the most obvious choice for father-of-the-year. The guy liked to lord over his subjects, especially his son. Weak men made sport of berating their offspring if they were boys, and molesting them if they were girls. Sometimes, it was the other way around.

Junior genuinely loved his grandmother. He brought me into this mess. Elias, the boy whose father had been the victim in my last case, was the same age as Junior, or close enough. A small island. Maybe Elias knew Junior and could fill me in on Junior's high school proclivities.

I texted him, offering lunch. He accepted.

***

Fans blew hot air around The University of the Virgin Islands cafeteria. A fly buzzed in my ear. I swatted at it to no avail. The lunch lady slopped some mashed potatoes next to some slices of turkey and watery peas. Elias selected an apple, a bottle of orange juice, and a slice of pie. We dined outside at a white plastic table as coeds meandered around and lounged on the grass in shaded spots. A few sun-bathed. Cell phones and books were scattered around like toys on Christmas morning.

Elias propped his backpack against his chair and waved to one smiling girl, who scurried by, likely late for class. Her tight top and tighter yoga pants stirred a longing I hadn't had in some time.

"You dating?" I asked.

He made the you-cannot-be-serious face, dropping his chin into his slender chest. He'd filled out some since our last visit months ago, but still had the sinewy look of his drug-dealing father. He gave off the tone of a man very interested in walking the straight and narrow. Tightly cut hair and preppy clothes.

He dropped the apple into his backpack and dug into the pie. I shuffled my food around the plate, taking the occasional bite and watched the scene some more before trying again. I attempted to recall if I was as stoic with adults at that age, then realized I had been worse.

"How's school?"

"Fine."

"What about Roberts?"

Roberts was the lawyer Elias worked for, answering phones and scheduling clients between classes. The office wasn't far from campus.

"Yeah, it's fine, you know, it's a job. Pays better than most. He gave me a guilt raise."

"You pick a major?"

"Criminal justice with a concentration in, you ready for this?" He drummed his fingers on the table.

"What?"

"Cyber security."

I nodded, a grin breaking across my face. "Nice. Why don't you major in that? Talk about job cyber-security! Get it?"

I playfully punched him in the shoulder.

"Man, that is bad. Real bad. Besides, they don't have a cyber-security major or minor. It's called a concentration, which really amounts to, well, I'm not sure, but I can put it on a resume."

The silence dropped on us again like an anvil. Another girl waved and I could see him getting antsy as he scarfed the last bite of pie, then chugged his juice.

He started to push up from his chair. "Well, it's been real, amigo."

"Wait, I gotta talk about something with you."

He eased back into the chair.

The girl had stopped. Elias turned and made the thumb and pinky, I'll-call-you sign. She shrugged and continued on her way, head held high like she was trying too hard to come off as confident while her heart wilted.

"Always something with you, huh Boise."

"No. Not true, Elias. Last time…"

"Last time you were doing your duty to my dad. But, now that I'm okay, I don't hear shit from you for weeks. It's cool."

He tried to act nonchalant, but I could see under his coolness was a simmering cauldron. I was pissed too, with myself. His father was dead. I was the closest thing he had.

"I'm...I'm sorry, Elias. It's not cool. Not at all. I was just, I don't know, trying to give you space."

"No, yeah. Space. Yup, I need space, you right."

Running my fingers over my two-day stubble, I winced at him. "Let's set a meet before we part, all right?"

Another nonchalant single-shoulder shrug. "Whatever, man." He looked at his phone. "I gotta go."

"Did you know a kid in school named Junior Bacon?"

"Herbert? Rich kid from up the way? Why? He do something? That kid weird. Always standing still and staring at people. Weird. He was friends with one kid who was mean. M.S.D."

"M.S.D.?"

"Marjory Stoneman Douglas."

Who's Marjory Stoneman Douglas?

Elias read the lost look on my face and sucked his teeth. "You grown-ups, always think you know so much, but you don't know M.S.D. What about Columbine? You heard of that?"

I nodded, realizing Marjory Stoneman Douglas was a more recent school shooting. The shootings flooded off the news feeds so rapidly these days, I'd stopped paying attention to the names and numbers a while ago.

"We used to worry about some of the kids, you know, like that. Herbert was one of them types. Why? What's this about? Come on, Boise, you gotta spill."

Confidentiality. I wasn't always good at it, but in this case, I didn't have to be since Elias was like an assistant, or so I reasoned with myself.

"He came by to see me about a missing family member a few days ago. The person turned up dead and when he came to see me a guy got shot with an arrow in my office."

"What the fuck, man? When were you gonna tell me this? You mean that reporter? Your office?"

The Daily News article Walter had run the day after the murder. He must have left out that it was my office. Probably just said it was in *The Daily News* building or something equally vague.

"You know, we agreed that we'd let each other know about anything big happening," he reminded me.

"I didn't want to distract you," I replied hollowly. "Besides, my line of work ... "

"Fuck your line of work! Are we friends?"

"Of course!"

"Then act like it." He stormed off then had to come back awkwardly. "Forgot this. Asshole." He jerked his backpack off the ground and slung it over his shoulder.

My phone buzzed. It was Dana, texting me that I was an asshole. She wanted to know why I hadn't called yet to explain about this shit that went down in my office. Her gruff attitude shined through even when texting. She wasn't much help lately; too many bad politicians to chase down and expose in *The Daily News*.

"Winning friends and influencing people," I muttered to myself. "The Montague way."

CHAPTER 15

My brains primal-oozed out of my ears. A pizza box lay on the floor next to my bed. Six Guinness empties crowded my bedside table. The smell of rum made me gag. I capped the half-empty flatty of Bacon rum that I'd somehow managed not to knock over. I'd bought it to punish myself and do research. One headache with two alcohols, so to speak.

As I reached for my phone to check the time, two empty bottles tumbled to the carpet. The stale smell of warm beer wafted up as some trickled out of one bottle.

"Shoot!"

I scurried down the hall, washcloth in hand, wet it and dabbed at the carpet. My phone buzzed.

"What the hell's going on over there?" Dana asked.

I croaked out, "Morning."

"It's almost noon, Jabuti."

"Shit, Dana, I gotta go."

"I'm picking you up. You think I wouldn't come back for my colleague's memorial? Thirty minutes."

Advil. I popped two and my colitis meds. Five minutes, just need five minutes to gather.

More pounding. My eyes fluttered open. Crushing the pizza box with my foot, I stumbled to the door. Woman with black hair. I stared a long moment, then realized it was Dana. The whole time I'd known her, she'd had red hair. I decided it was probably a bad time to ask her what her natural color was.

She held her hand over her eyes like she was staring into the sun. "Jesus, Boise, must we repeat this all the time. Put some clothes on. Do you drink alone in the nude? Have you been to a meeting yet?"

"What happened to your hair?" I asked. Behind her the giant print of *Christina's World* in its cherry frame whisked me away to a vast mid-western expanse.

"The best hair colorist in the Caribbean works out of her house in Tortola. Got tired of the faded red."

"Weird," I muttered as I turned back toward my bed. "Why're you here already?"

Dana shook her head. "You're like a goddamned teen. Get dressed and brush your teeth. It's been forty minutes. I got caught up talking to Lucy downstairs. She's worried about you."

I shrugged into a t-shirt, boxers, and jeans.

"No," Dana said, wagging her finger like a schoolmarm. "You ever been to a memorial?"

Instead of her usual ensemble of casual clothes and her red Carnegie Mellon cap, she looked, well, elegant and put-together.

"Yeah, but it's in a bar."

Then I remembered promising Walter to wear something nice if he invited me. While Dana jabbed at her phone, I changed. The Advil was slowly unscrewing the vise.

115

"What's up in Tortola?" The inside of my dressy shirt collar had a ring of dirt. The armpit smelled. It needed a trip to the dry cleaners, but I kept forgetting because months would pass between wearings.

One good thing about murder: my wardrobe would get more use and, of course, people with dead relatives were potential clients. Highly motivated, money-is-no-issue kind of people. The lawyers in Los Angeles had clients like that as well. Like those on trial for murder. When your eternal freedom is on the line, saving money becomes a distant secondary objective. Murder puts things into perspective. And from that perspective, money don't mean shit.

Finally, Dana looked up from her phone. She tilted her head, assessing my duds. I started to pull on socks. "Jabuti! What the hell, m-f? My granny takes less time to curl her hair than you do to pull on a decent outfit. Let's go, put the shoes on in the car."

We headed out the door, then she seemed to recall my Tortola inquiry as she pulled her keys out of her cavernous straw purse. "Same shit, different rock. Pick one, the U.S., Korea, St. Thomas, or Tortola. Corrupt politicians. They've got some British thing called a Deputy Premier, who does something, I'm not sure what. The ass has been taking bribes and gave himself some crazy salary."

It was one of those oppressive, tropical days with no breeze. The sun cooked me like a roasted chicken in a bad suit. At some point, a nice linen outfit in beige would do better than the stifling charcoal grey bag I currently wore.

At a no-name bar, evidently a favorite amongst reporters, we jostled through the front door. Pickering ignored us as he patted shoulders and exchanged somber nods. Soft calypso music hummed over the festivities. The smell of rum and sweet syrup permeated the bar area as we sidled up.

"What it be?" asked the bartender.

We got drinks, I with the usual Guinness, and Dana had

vodka on the rocks. Two other reporters came over and hugged Dana, then acknowledged me politely.

I'd never officially met either, but they had the look: eager and haggard. Reporters always needed another story or were cursing the deadline for the current one. A world of pressure that in recent years had become more convoluted by the proliferation of free news. Pickering made it over to us.

"So, Boise, what do you have?"

I filled him in on my notions about the family and my reparations findings. In short, I suspected everyone and trusted no one, except Junior. He didn't set off my radar.

"Reparations." He gave Dana and me a sideways glance. "The two of you know anything about that? It was a pet project of Kendal's."

Walter Pickering was calling into question whether two people, who did not appear to be of African heritage, living in a nation full of citizens of African descent, should be the ones on a case about reparations for slavery. Dana was white and my quadroon heritage not obvious enough for the optics. If your blackness wasn't self-evident, then you might as well not be black. He had a point, but optics weren't everything.

"Boise, Dana's back because I want her on this. She's my most relentless and you're not moving fast enough for my tastes. Dana, you need to kick this into high gear. Whatever it takes. I want every goddamn detail about Kendal, and I want a clean copy in a week."

"Walter…" I started to protest, but he cut me off.

"I'm not done. The Tortola matter can wait, right?"

Dana gave a non-committal nod. "Whatever you want, Walter." Even the feisty Dana could see her boss was in no mood for push-back on finding Kendal's killer.

I understood, I really did. I'd already been down this road on our last Marvel Team-Up, and I didn't intend to be split like a coconut again.

"No, not whatever you want, Walter."

Walter's face rotated toward me as he did a slow burn. "What? How dare you!"

"No, Walter, you know I usually do what you all want, even though I don't work for the *News*. In fact, I pay for advertising in your paper, so far from being on your payroll, I'm a bonafide customer. I have a client who hired me to solve Francine Bacon's murder."

My big mouth. I'd never excelled at keeping things under wraps. I took a deep breath and jabbed a finger at each reporter. "That's not for print. Shit."

For a moment we all stood like points on a triangle, the sounds of steel drums from the overhead stereo system intensifying the tension. Suddenly, Dana burst into laughter. Walter and I tried to contain it, but we couldn't. Laughter burst from each of us in spits and starts. Some of the others stared.

As we gripped our knees and caught our breath, Walter excused himself. Clinked glasses sounded. He gave his usual politically correct speech about the great career and even greater integrity of Kendal. He thanked Kendal's wife, Savannah, for being there. She graciously accepted his words through a veil of grief.

When he finished, Walter walked the widow to the exit. She apparently had had enough for one night. I turned to Dana, who looked puzzled as she watched Walter hug, then usher Savannah Kendal into a cab.

"What is it?" I asked.

She kept watching them. "I'm not sure," she said haltingly. Her squinty gaze followed Walter back to his staked-out spot at the bar, where he went back to conversing with the associate editor whose name always escaped me.

Dana swallowed her vodka and doubled back for more. Three drinks later, she called her belle, an aging debutante from an island family who owned a thriving crystal shop called Little

Switzerland, as well as tracts of commercial real estate throughout the Caribbean. Annie was a stretched-out Dane with perfect, chrome-white skin. Sometimes, I wondered how people like her and Hillary Bacon didn't liquify south of the Tropic of Cancer.

Annie and Dana were alternately fondling each other and kissing while Walter continued down the same road to intoxication Dana was travelling today. I acted the prude, suckling my second pint fearfully.

The afternoon eased into night. Dana kept on with Annie and Walter's eyes turned a shade of devil red. A steel-drum band was setting up on the tiny stage.

Walter wandered over, sloshing a bit of his drink en route.

"Do you know what they call a steel drum musician?" Walter asked. He had a habit of quizzing you on inane facts when he drank.

Dana and I looked at each other, then at Annie. No one had a clue.

"Pianists," Walter said triumphantly.

"They call them the same as piano players? That doesn't seem right," Dana said, raising her eyebrows.

"You sure they aren't percussionists?" I asked.

Walter threw an annoyed, tired stare at each of us in turn, then said, "Not pianists. That's not what I said, Dana. You got to pay better attention to details, Dana. And you," He pointed at me with a slightly bent finger. "'Percussionist' is a general term, Boise. I'm being spec-sif-ic. Pannists. They're called, pannists, Dana and Boise and nice Danish lady."

"Her name's Annie," Dana said with flaring annoyance.

Walter plowed on. "Maybe 'cause the, the thing looks like a frying pan." He gestured at one of the silvery drums on stage. "Heat that boy up and fry some johnny cakes right up."

"Sure, Walter, that sounds about right," I remarked.

"Hey, Boise, I was pondering about what you said earlier."

"What was that, Walter?" I asked, going along with his constant use of everyone's name.

"I'm going to hire you for Kendal. I'll hire you. The paper," he pointed out the front door. "They won't pay for shit. But, I can do it. I can hire you. Tell you what, I'll pay you eight-five per hour plus up to five-hundred a week in expenses. But here's the kicker. If you get this bad boy solved in a week, I'll throw in a nice bonus."

I held up my hand. "Hold on, Walter, where'd you get eight-five?"

"It's what my golf coach charges. I figured it was the going rate for private lessons of the investigative type, also."

"You figured you'd pay me the same as a golf pro? Is your golf pro dealing with murder?"

He laughed. "You haven't seen me hook a seven."

"I work for one-fifty." Really, I didn't, but it seemed insulting that I was making the same as a golf pro who spent his days on manicured grass yelling "Fore!"

"One-hundred. Final offer. Oh, and I'm dropping the weekly expenses max to three-fifty. Besides, let me finish." Walter paused

I waited.

He tilted his glass, and the ice cascaded into his face, crackling on the floor. "I'm em'py. Hang on."

I grabbed his shoulder. "No, Walter, finish your offer. I want to know."

He pulled away. Dana and Annie were caught up in their own little world. The live music had started, hypnotic drumming and a soft crooning by a woman with a gravelly voice. Walter returned.

"So, if I figure out what happened in the next week, yes?"

"I'll throw in a thousand-dollar bonus. Cash bucks." He pulled out his wallet and opened the flap showing four twenties and a five.

I stuck out my hand. He shook, a more watery shake than his usual manly pump. I tugged him close enough to smell his stale breath. "Are you going to remember this deal tomorrow?"

His eyes were sleepy as he muttered, "I'm drunk, but mind's-till sharp."

I held up my phone and hit record, holding it close to his mouth. "Repeat the deal."

He did.

Walter left right after that. So did Annie and Dana.

CHAPTER 16

I'd done it again. Somehow, despite swearing up and down I would not split my attention onto another case, Walter suckered me into it. The difference this time, I had a deadline to get that extra cash, which I needed. Despite two paying clients, I'd be back to zero before long. I was certain of it.

Dana called. She wanted to meet at my office.

"What's with the door?" she asked.

After letting her in, I shut the door and joined her at my desk.

I started to sit but paused half-way down when she said, "Walter's sleeping with the widow."

"What?"

"You heard me."

"You followed him last night?"

"Yup," she said, a shit-eating grin breaking on her face. She loved digging dirt. Not gossip, but real, case-altering dirt.

"Were you even drinking?"

"I stopped after my third. That's the beauty of vodka, no one can tell if it's water and the smell is light, so if I really am plastered, the cops can't tell when they pull me over." She winked at me. "Show some leg or boob," she shifted her blouse slightly to the side, "and they give up fast. Too many sexual harassment lawsuits in the last ten years."

"Back to Walter," I said.

"Riiiiight. He's banging the Widow Kendal. How very boss-like of him."

"Does that feel like motive?"

"Motive? Hells, no! Walter? Come on, Jabuti. You think our Walter … I was just … well, shit, who knows. I didn't think he slept with the employee's wives, so what do I know?"

Dana rubbed her nose a few times. The tip was as red as her Carnegie Mellon cap, which was back in its proper place.

"Allergies?"

She blinked and curled her lips. "I guess. Anyways, old Walter must think he's hiding things well, 'cause he went straight to Kendal's house after the memorial. For a newspaper man, he's not keen on keeping his affairs secret."

"Or maybe he doesn't care if we know. Isn't he single now?"

"Yup, but I doubt last night was their first time. He's been banging her for a while. Did you see them at the bar?"

"I saw, but didn't seem that obvious to me."

She shook her head. "You men. What's obvious, him rubbing his cock on her hip?"

"Sure, that'd do it," I said grinning. "Really, though, you're probably right. What's this prove? Walter makes questionable life decisions and he got unlucky, probably. In that case, lock us all up.

Really, this is just gossip for Robin to hash out in the 'Island Waves' column."

"Right."

The word hung there in the air between us. We were both thinking it. Sleeping with someone's spouse was always, always, always a strong motive for murder. Did I stress always?

The motives were starting to pile up like cardboard recycling at the Bovoni landfill. Walter had motive for the Kendal murder. For that matter, so did I. Kendal was in my office, and it was no secret I didn't much like him. He was helping Francine with her reparations, meaning anyone with motive to kill Francine had motive to kill Kendal through association.

"So, that's how we got a hold of Kendal's laptop so easily," I said. "I mean, it did seem easy, but I wrote it off to her wanting to help figure out what happened. Speaking of motive, what do we know about the wife?"

Dana pulled a metal water bottle out of her bag, took a swig and rubbed her nose again. "I know she does something online. Some kind of sales."

I pointed out the window, where Walter was picking his way over the gravel toward the building. Dana went to the door and called out. Walter entered my office for the first time without a body on the floor.

"We need to talk," Dana said as she motioned for him to sit. He looked dried out, dusty. I set a glass of water on my desk in front of him.

"You got something for me?" Walter said.

Dana fidgeted with her phone and adjusted her hat before she said, "You could say that."

Walter threw her his thousand-yard stare. His dark brown eyes caught the diffuse light from the window. Dana didn't meet his eyes for a moment, then she brought her head up, let her shoulders relax and set her jaw.

"I know. I just told Boise, so he knows too. Please don't

waste our time denying."

He kept staring at Dana. Two people on stage, me in the audience. Behind him, a roach inched along the edge of the wall. It found a crack and scurried into it.

"What is it I should be denying?" Walter intoned. "Did I kill someone?"

"Walter, no one's suggesting that," I said, trying to sound as neutral as possible. My heart thumped. Cornered animals were dangerous. If Walter had actually done something, there was no telling what he'd do next, no matter how confident Dana was in a peaceful resolution. This confrontation could escalate rapidly. I squeezed the pepper spray in the pocket of my shorts.

"No one's talking to you," he said, his eyes still fixated on Dana. "Tell me exactly what you know about whatever it is I'm accused of."

"You're gonna make me say it?"

He gave a solemn nod.

"I saw you go home with Kendal's widow last night. I saw you put your arm around her waist and when she opened the door to that dead man's house." She paused, giving him a chance to interject a defense. When no parry came, she continued. "I waited three hours. You never left that house."

Walter's nostrils flared. His chest rose and fell like a buoy in the ocean before a storm. I wanted to throw him a life preserver, but I owed it to Kendal and perhaps Francine to get some answers or at least come up with more questions.

Two minutes felt like an hour as we all let the room settle. He could have denied it. He could have said he slept on the couch as a kindness to a woman who just lost her husband. He could have said nothing happened, and how dare Dana and I insinuate impure motives to a man and woman of such high moral character as Walter Pickering and Savannah Kendal. It occurred to me as a non-sequitur that both Kendals had location-based first names: Savannah and Adirondack. A town and a mountain range.

North and South. High and low. Walter's name didn't fit in that geographic montage. His was merely a name. He had disrupted the perfect symmetry with his blatant non-geography.

My father had cheated on my mother and Evelyn had done the same to me shortly before her death. A silent, yet poetic expression of guilt and denial radiated out of Walter, absent verbal confirmation. A visceral urge to tackle and beat him buzzed in my ears. Stars swam into my vision, the rage whip-sawing against my civilized conformity. My clenched jaw ached as my crumpled fist thumped my hip. No sinking into this abyss. Not today. Keep a clear head. He still wasn't answering Dana's question.

"That superior look of smug indignation isn't fooling anyone," I said in a deep, hateful voice. "Answer the fucking question. Own it. Or, so help me … " I advanced toward him.

His façade of chief and president at *The Daily News* collapsed. He was not a man interested in physical confrontation. Words were his arena.

"Yes! All right, yes!" he squealed, fear in full bloom. "She and I, we had a relationship."

The armpit of his shirt, the Van Heusen brand he always wore in the same eggshell color, betrayed a ring of yellow damp. What had that commercial said? Never let 'em see you sweat.

The face of the man who had cuckolded me throbbed on the edge of my vision and superimposed itself on Walter's face. Although I'd never seen them together in a compromising position, in my twisted version of events, he laughed at me while fucking Evelyn. That image continued to haunt me.

Didn't these swine have any notion of what they did to the people who lived in a marriage when they inserted themselves? Did they consider karma? I prided myself on my empathy, but I could not, would not, give them that benefit.

I sneered at him. "Is that what you call it? A relationship."

"We care about each other," he said in a small voice.

"That's easy to do when you don't have to live with each

other or support each other day in and day out. It's fun. Like being an aunt, who thinks because she comes over once a week to babysit, she knows what it is to raise a child. Marriage is a child. Yeah, you are a murderer."

Walter and Dana both stared at me. The stillness of my office, of the entire afternoon, felt like a pointed finger. I blamed myself for Evelyn's cheating. What more could I have done to make her happy? Lots. There was always lots more to be done. I still had to believe it didn't excuse her behavior. How else could I live with myself?

"So, what? Are you gonna marry that woman?" I said.

Walter's eyes were still wide as craters. He knew this went beyond his ordeal.

"Boise," he said.

Some of his bravado was coming back, his politician's mind sorted through options on how to get back to respectability. Walter couldn't exist for long without it. These few minutes were driving him mad. The fear that we would spread his disrespectability like a virus to the rest of his staff and the island.

He sat up a little straighter, his hands out in a plea. "Boise. Dana. I really do care for her."

"Shut up!" I blurted.

He slumped back.

"All right," Dana whispered. "All right, Boise." Her hands were out, spread like spiders. "Walter's going to help us with this. Aren't you, Walter?"

He limply nodded.

"See? Boise? He's gonna help."

My back was turned to both of them. A bush on the right in the parking lot brought me out of my trauma. A perfect hiding spot for someone wielding a bow and arrow. I opened the door and left it open, beelining to the spot.

"Boise!" Dana yelled.

Halfway down the stairs, I shouted, "Don't touch that door!

CHAPTER 17

Standing behind the bush, I scoped the angle. Why had it taken so long to spot this? It must have been where the shooter had crouched, which explained why I saw no one when I looked out the window. The bush was dense and had some vines crawling over it. I called Harold, and he drove to my office at a breakneck speed judging by the swiftness of his arrival.

We huddled behind the bush. Walter had scampered upstairs to the newsroom as soon as I was out of sight.

Dana wandered down and listened to my theory.

"We need you to stand in the doorway. I'll position her the way Kendal was that day. You figure out exactly where you would shoot from, but like I said, when you find a spot, use this towel to cover the ground. Maybe we can preserve some evidence if there's anything."

Harold slung the towel over his shoulder and waited for us to take up our positions inside the open door of my office.

Walking up the stairs, Dana tried to speak. "Boise, I…"

"Not now, Dana. I'm onto something. You deal with Walter. Clearer heads. It's not something … just shoulder it."

We reached the open door. "You're gonna be Kendal." I positioned her at the door, facing inside as if talking to me, her hand on the knob, ready to leave. I assumed my position and propped a chair where Junior had been standing.

"Wow, you were really this close to him when the arrow?" She made a stabbing motion into her chest with her finger.

"The head came through his chest like an alien. Don't move, I'm going down to talk to Harold."

Harold and I surveyed Dana's position. We found two nice openings in the leaves with enough room to pull the bow back. Harold commented that the second opening had better sight lines for center mass.

"How tough is this shot?" I asked.

"You'd need to be competent, but not necessarily brilliant."

Lifting the towel off the ground after Harold finished sighting on Dana, I snapped photos. There were no clear footprints in the browning leaves and dirt. No cigarette butts. No candy wrappers. So much for a stupid shooter. One leaf had some brown liquid dried on it. I inched my nose close. Cola. Coca-Cola.

I waved Dana down, then turned to Harold.

"How's about a trip to the archery range?"

"Today's the busiest day of the week. I like to go on Tuesday mid-day better."

"Perfect. Let's go watch folks shoot. Maybe you'll even introduce me to a killer."

***

Dana waved off, saying she wanted to keep on Walter. He'd agree to get more from the widow about Kendal's doings the last few months, or she'd expose him. When Dana had you in her sights, it was scary.

The archery range was full of adults on one side and teens on the other. We had texted Junior, and he'd agreed to meet us there.

Junior charged up behind us and did a mock tackle, shoving us forward. A couple other archers gave us librarian scowls for talking in the stacks.

"Who's the best shooter here?" I asked.

Harold and Junior gave each other a knowing look, then Junior said, "Him," and pointed at Harold. An attractive nineteen-year-old woman in a halter top dress sporting an African color pattern of gold, blue, and grey geometric patterns marched right up and kissed Harold on the mouth. He pulled away after an awkward moment.

"Hiya, Teysha."

"Hello, lover," she purred. "Brought your favorite." She handed him a can of Coca-Cola dripping with condensation. Eyelash extensions jutted from her eyelids. Everything about her screamed, *look at me!* And it worked. We were riveted. Harold popped the lid and guzzled some Coke.

She did a slow turn and pecked Junior on the cheek. "Where you been, J.?"

Junior blushed a little. "You know, school. I've been off in Georgia."

"You shooting?"

"A little."

She tilted her head and held out her hand, knuckles up. "I'm Teysha Collins. You are?"

"Boise Montague," I said, following her lead. "A friend of these guys." Her fingers were almost as hot as her stare. This was a woman who could make a man do things. All kinds of things.

"Strange we've never met," she said, looking pointedly at

Harold.

"Boise's been away a while. He just came back. Isn't that right, Boise?"

"That's right, Harold. So right."

"You a shooter?" she batted her eyelashes at me as if blinded by the sunlight dimpling through the surrounding trees.

"No, no." I waved my hands way more than I needed to. "Harold's shown me some basics, but I'm a full-blown beginner."

She smiled and nodded. "Harry's a good one to learn from, if you can get him to teach. He's never taught me shit about shooting arrows. We always wind up working on other things, right Harry?"

She had close-cropped hair and dancing brown eyes. More than that, there was a palpable sensuality in everything about this woman. But, for many men, and I believed Harold was one of them, the sleazy factor was crucial.

"Teysha Collins, get back here!" The holler came from a graying man wearing a shirt depicting Legolas, the elven warrior from *Lord of the Rings*. He had a leather weight belt wrapped around his waist and waved his bow around for emphasis.

"My dad wants me back. Ta-ta."

She sidled away, the dress swaying like a hula skirt.

"Woah," I muttered. "Who is that, Harry?"

"No, do not call me Harry. Only Teysha calls me that. Sounds strange coming out of a dude's mouth."

Junior had a sullen look on his face. It appeared that his grandmother's death weighed on him, but he was doing his best to take his mind off it for the moment.

"You okay, Junior?" I asked.

He ignored me. "I wish I could talk to girls like you do, Uncle Harold."

"It's a gift," Harold said without the slightest hint of irony.

Harold seemed fine, like his mother being gone mattered little. That said, everyone handled death in their own way and life really did go on. I'd laughed and cried alternately in the days after Evelyn's death, and I often wished my mother would go away. Maybe it was a relief to be free of that maternal shadow, particularly when it was as large as Francine Bacon's.

What really irked me was that Junior was asking Harold for a lifeline, a way for uncle and nephew to connect by having his uncle teach him a life lesson: how to get chicks into bed or at least to go out with you. Harold showed no interest. He watched Teysha saunter away, then eyed some of the other people, nodding hellos between sips of Coke. So, this was the real, real Harold. The persona that appeared when he was in a comfortable surrounding where he belonged. The alpha-male of the St. Thomian archery set.

"Hey, Junior, I'm happy to take you out or help you to meet women."

"Nah, that's cool, Boise. I'm good." He punched his uncle in the shoulder. "Hey, man, can we shoot?"

Harold looked at me. "Who do you need to talk to?"

"Anyone you think could legitimately make that shot through those bushes and into my office."

He pointed at one group in the middle that a bunch of other archers were watching. "Boom. The best ones are right there. We got some others scattered about, but these are the best."

"Then let's talk them up," I said.

We walked over, Junior trailing behind us. I'd never loved crowds. The place reminded me of recess back in grade school. People standing around, talking, laughing, playing games. Only here, everyone played one game: shoot a target with a deadly weapon. Who were these people kidding? They practiced the art of killing. Archery was not some country club sport like polo or golf. Archers trained day in and day out so they could kill things. Three archers turned, the same bulbous arrowheads held in their hands. They all grinned at me and their teeth were iodine red, like wolves after a kill. I blinked and their teeth turned white again.

"Hi," one of the women said. Her wolf eyes narrowed.

I tapped Harold on the shoulder and told him I was going to the restroom. After he pointed the way, I slipped into a stall and tugged a small flask of vodka I kept for intense encounters out of my pocket. The vodka felt hot going down, but then it settled in like an epoxy seal. My frayed nerves calmed. Since I'd walked into this den of wolves, the bloody tip of Kendal's murder weapon repeatedly flashed in my vision. Why all of a sudden? I didn't really care about Kendal. Roger's photo from his grandmother's album snapped into my vision, adding a macabre slideshow.

People died all the time. I'd solved Roger's murder months ago. It was a done deal, so why was that black space haunting me at this moment.

Bang! Bang! Bang!

"Hey, Boise! You in here?" Harold shouted.

I followed him out into the superficial sunshine after dousing my face with water.

"I thought you'd fallen in," he said as we trudged through the crowd. He crumpled the can of Coke and threw it into a wastebasket. The faces blurred in a fog of people. A dark bedroom, droning soap operas and solitude beckoned.

"Hey, everyone, this is the guy," Harold said as we approached the group. "He's the one who wants to know if any of you shot and killed a reporter last week."

"How many points we get for that?" a wise-guy hollered. A few people chuckled. Others looked serious.

"You a cop?" someone asked.

I cleared my throat. "Uh, no, I'm trying to find out what happened for the family."

What was Harold's play? Did he just like the attention? This was not helpful to the investigation, but I'd make the most of it. I started interviewing each of the archers, one-by-one while the others kept at their reindeer games. These people found the questioning exciting, even alluring. A couple of the women offered to give me their numbers after seeing my card that said, "Private Eye." Some kind of romantic notion from Raymond Chandler or James M. Cain of the dark, dangerous investigator and his seamy existence tripped their wire. If nothing else, I might get a couple dates out of this, but most of the women weren't my type, whatever that was.

One woman gabbed on and on about how she could make the shot I'd described. She had a blonde and green weave in her hair. A peacock, although she was not alone. Several of the women wore wild clothing. More attention-seekers.

"That shot. That shot is through a door and up a floor you say?" She had a slight British tint to her West Indian accent. Probably from Tortola or Jamaica.

"Yes. What do you think of that?"

"Piece of sweet potato pie." The words buzzed out of her mouth like bees making honey. "Watch this."

She nocked an arrow. Her equipment was also peacock-ish with swirls of color splattered over the shaft and head. Every feather was a different color. Horizontal primary colors striped the bow from pole to pole.

Her chest rose and fell twice, and I sensed her heartbeat easing into idle. Hand against the corner of her lip, sideways stance, elbow up, all the things Harold had demanded in our short lessons. Then one queer movement.

The arrow flew straight and true to the inner circle, only slightly off a dead-center bullseye. I gave a golf-clap. She bowed.

"When did you first take this up?"

"I saw a competition on YouTube one day. I was twelve. Eleven years, two months, and six days ago."

"What is that you did with your back leg?"

"You mean the toe-thing?" I nodded. "Yeah, that's a thing my coach could never beat out of me. Just wouldn't leave, you know. Totally wrong form. Terrible for balance. Too much weight here." She touched my left hip. "Not centered. Blah, blah. But, he finally gave that one up after the fifth year when I won the Pan American sixteen and unders."

I whistled my admiration. A man strode up beside me. He clapped sharply.

"Break time's over, Isabelle." He glanced at his watch, which appeared to be a Rolex, or a knock off. Like the girl, he dressed flashy and had oddly hairy arms. He had a Coke in his hand, as if he needed more caffeine. "I told you fifteen minutes. It's been twenty. Why must I always come looking for you?"

She started to answer, but he cut her off with a dismissive wave. She looked over her shoulder and gave me a sad smile before following him. Isabelle. Was she a woman or a girl? The math said early twenties, but the way that man spoke to her made it seem like she was a teenager. Sweeping my attention around the grounds, I noticed that at least five or six other people also drank Coke.

Harold put his arm around my shoulder. We broke away from the rest of the group.

"You sly devil," he purred. "I think Isabelle likes you."

"What's her story?" I asked as we headed for a table with a punchbowl atop a white tablecloth.

Harold scooped out two plastic cups worth of fruit punch, pieces of grape, pineapple, and mango floating in it. He raised his cup toward the girl and her coach.

"The golden hope. They are trying to prepare for the 2020 Olympics. She's a shoe-in to compete for the Virgins, but still has a ways to go before we can safely call her the favorite. I was her coach at one point."

"But…"

His expression grew remote as he watched her shoot arrow after arrow into a distant target. Was that love or lust I saw in his face? Harold had to be thirty years her senior. I was at least ten to fifteen, assuming she was early twenties.

His gaze broke. He went back for another scoop of punch. "But, nothing, man. I took her to the title, then he wanted her back. He wants the glory if she wins the real deal, you know, vicarious living. Those who can't do, coach their nieces."

"She's his niece?"

He pursed his lips, which were a bright red from the punch. "And the cash behind her run. My mother wouldn't finance some other rich guy's daughter, although I asked her to. Practically begged. Some sense of duty mama has about that. Thinks they're trying to take advantage of us. So, she had to agree to work with Uncle Douchy over there. Asshole has no panache. Brute force is all he knows."

I waited, thinking Harold would elaborate, but he again stared vacantly in Isabelle's direction.

"Where's that guy get his financing?" I asked

Harold patted his pocket. "'Scuse me for a minute, I gotta burn the lizard." He downed his punch and dumped the cup.

I continued to watch Isabelle. As fast as she could shoot the arrows, he handed her another. He timed her shots, using an analogue stop-watch. Perhaps her release or the time she had to nock and release. Were these things timed in competition?

After several minutes of continuous shooting, she put the bow in a stand and chugged water. He gestured and spoke to her in a rough manner, like he was commanding a dog who wouldn't behave. Her soft features remained impassive, but her eyes were attentive. With a curt nod, he gestured for her to continue. He raised the stopwatch. I raised my phone. As soon as he hit the button, I hit my button. This time I watched him and waited. When he hit the button again, I stopped the timer on my phone. Exactly one minute. She paused. He restarted the watch and timed again. He was timing how many shots she could release every minute.

At one point, Isabelle glanced over when her uncle went to pick up an arrow he'd fumbled. The stolen look was as fast as her shooting. She had a bit of playfulness in her. Uncle Douchy was all business.

The next set of shots took longer. Although I didn't time it, it seemed to take at least twice as long. I decided to time the next set. Sure enough, three minutes. This went on until they did a ten-minute set of shots. She aimed at three different targets. She was most accurate to the target directly in front. Next best was the right. To the left, her shots were sub-par by her standards.

The longer I watched, the more impressed I became, not only by her skill, but by her endurance. My shoulders were getting sympathy aches as I tried to imitate her stance and raised elbow technique. Even without holding an actual bow, my arms got extremely tired after only a minute or two.

She said something to her coach after almost an hour of continuous shooting. He nodded reluctantly, and she headed to the bathroom. Her uncle took the bow and began to apply something that resembled thick lip balm on the string.

When she came out, I "bumped" into her.

"Hey there, stranger," she said. "You need some more tutoring?" Nice smile, but colored by sadness.

"I was watching you train over there with your coach."

"Uncle, coach, flaming lunatic. Take your pick. He drives me like a Ferrari."

"That bad?"

"Naw, not that bad. Without him, I'd probably still be in the pack." She pointed over at the group huddled around the shorter distance targets.

"What about Harold?"

Twisting her head sideways, she flashed a twinkly smile. "What's that boy sayin' 'bout me and him? Nothing tawdry, I hope."

She violated my personal space. I backed away.

"No," I said quickly. "Nothing like that. He just said you'd moved on to your uncle as coach, but he used to have that job.

137

Looked upset about losing it. Maybe he suggested your uncle's a bit, oh, I don't know…"

"Jealous? Yup, Harold's right, the man was jealous. But, you know family. Can't say no. You gotta deal with them all flippin' day long."

"About your training. What are you doing?"

"Interval training. You know, fast for varying periods of time. He figures if I can pump out the shots non-stop for one to ten minutes, then I'll be flippin' awesome. Might be, he's right. New idea we've been on for a few months."

With that she wandered back to the shooting area. I had wanted to ask about the different targets. All the other archers were only shooting at targets directly in front of them.

***

I sat down on a patch of shaded grass where I could watch all the archers. I pulled up some Olympic competition videos on my phone. The competitors were engaged in straight-ahead targeting. The bows used had a pole sticking forward off the bow and two more sticking out to either side right below where the archers gripped. After release, I marveled at the eerie calm they showed while watching their arrow fly. These arrows didn't resemble the arrow sticking out of Kendal's chest. These were slight. Small feathers. Thin shafts that came to a point. The head on Kendal's arrow was wider, menacing. The competition arrows needed the small head so that the minute differences on the targets could be easily ascertained for scoring purposes. In the case of hunting, you either felled your prey or not. No scoring of points on a target mattered. Kendal was a deer, and he'd been felled by a hunter. Scrolling through my phone, I found the photos I'd taken and sure enough, I had a solid one of the arrow's head.

Harold was chatting up another woman, but I pulled him away and showed him the photo.

"Yeah man, that's a hunter's arrow. Not suitable for target competition like the Olympics. In fact, that was almost certainly shot from a crossbow. Compound."

"I've heard of crossbows, but what's the difference?"

"A crossbow is high-powered. You can set then release when you're ready to fire. It sets the string in place with a piece of wood or metal rod. Compound bows are for pussies. They use too much tech, but if you need a job done right in one swift blow, they're the sure winner. Accurate and easy. But they lack soul."

"I'm still wondering why anyone would use an arrow or crossbow or whatever. Why didn't they use a gun like a normal killer in modern society?"

"Flair."

"Flair?"

"Sure, why not. Man, it's a good word. Archers like to flair, do a little show-boating. It's why we're archers, not boring marksmen wearing camo and skulking around in the woods." He picked up a stray arrow on the grass nearby. People seemed to leave their arrows laying about. "See this." He flicked the blue synthetic feathers. "Panache. Bullets get the job done, but…" He shrugged and made a face like he'd just eaten a rotten egg. "A hunk of metal with some black powder rocketing through the air." He made a snoring sound and his eyes drifted shut. "Even worse, if you use one of these modern guns, you leave behind trash. At least a revolver didn't make a mess on the ground."

"What did you say about compound?"

He nodded toward a corner of the range where some guys were shooting much more complicated bows with pullies and multiple strings at animal targets.

"Bullshit tech. See her bow? Simple. One string. That's archery. Besides, the Olympics doesn't have a compound bow competition. Strictly weekend warrior stuff. Not for purists."

"What's the purist bow called?"

"Recurve. Same bow used by the Greeks thousands of years ago. The real deal."

He handed me the arrow. I examined the shaft. It did have an elegance to it. Lithe and supple. Definitely the ballerina of the weapon world.

"People still fence, right?" Harold asked.

I had no idea if people fenced anymore, but I seemed to remember seeing fencing in the last Olympics as I passed a television at a sports bar in Santa Monica.

"'Course they do. Swords and arrows and all that shit is dead meat compared to automatic weapons and bombs. So why use it? Style, man. What's life without some style? Panache."

Running my finger over the arrow, I flicked at the tip. "You mean to tell me someone used an arrow because it makes a statement?"

"Yup. No question. Shooting someone through a door from around fifty meters through those branches? It's impressive." He held up his hands. "Don't get me wrong, it's fucked up, but still…damn impressive. Also, the pressure. Jeez. Like the gold medal round. Massive cojones on that hombre if you ask me. Massive." He made the universal show of cupping someone's balls with his two hands. For a rich guy, Harold could use a few lessons from Lady Etiquette. "Crossbow is kinda cheating, but hell, still, not bad. 'Sides, you need something more maneuverable. Recurve is unwieldy for hiding and stalking. Still, I'd use recurve. More excitement. More of a game."

Thinking back on Kendal's demise, the arrow did make an impression. Not that him being shot wouldn't have, but the head coming through his chest. I'd been shot. And for sheer gore factor, the arrow won the day.

Harold held up my phone. He had blown up the photo and focused in on the arrow. "You see how this came clean through? That's some power. To pierce skin and bone and come out the other end. Damn. Serious power. Crossbow. Gotta be."

"Could Isabelle make that shot?" I asked.

He laughed, then he let it die as he watched my face. "Dude. You're serious? Dude, woman can't pull that kinda thing. No way."

"You mean you don't think a woman can kill like that?"

"Exactly. A dude did this."

"You mean a woman's emotionally incapable of killing?"

"Woman killers are rare, man. Rare. I mean, come on. What's there like one serial killer who was a woman? Lots of dudes, right? What about war? Women don't fight much."

"They weren't allowed in the past. I think that's changing," I said.

"Yeah, well. Why'd they want that? Shoot, they should be happy. No getting shot."

"In archery competitions, why are men and women in separate categories? It's a test of accuracy? Distances are the same, right?"

He nodded. "Yeah, but men would win."

"Why?"

"Longer arm, stronger pull with tighter string, and faster arrow velocity. Less arc." He curved his hand then straightened it. "Flatter path. Man, it's gotta give better accuracy 'cause wind has less effect. Just physiology, man."

"But for killing someone or for an individual woman, she could do those things. Right?" I countered.

"Hey man, sure, you could have some uber-strong chick with long arms and shit who could do whatever, I suppose. But, on average, they'd get smoked."

"But you're saying a woman couldn't have killed Kendal, not because she couldn't physically do it, but because of her mental makeup or emotions or something?"

"Now you're on it. Yeah, not their bag emotionally. Maybe if this Kendal dude cheated on her, and she caught him with his pecker in another chick. Then, maybe."

"Wow. Okay, glad we cleared that up. Did you and Isabelle date?"

He reached into his pocket, pulled out something small, popped it in his mouth and started chewing. "Yeah, we had a thing." He pointed at me with conviction. "But it was after she turned eighteen. Hey man, this killing talk has made me a bit tense. Waves at Carat are kickin'. I got a spare board. Wanna join?"

I needed to get away from this guy. Women were capable of killing. Sometimes for different reasons, but nonetheless, very capable. If I had to listen to any more of his bullshit, we were going to have another homicide.

"That's okay. I'll call you later."

Junior trotted over as Harold booked.

"Any news?"

I wanted to speak privately to Junior, so I asked if we could get some lemonade. We stood off to the side under a tamarind tree, sipping the sugared drinks.

"What's up?" he asked when we were alone.

"Do you know Isabelle?"

"Harold's student? Yeah, I know her. She's a babe who can shoot arrows better than any dude on this island. I had a crush on her when I was fourteen. Her dad and uncle keep her on a tight leash. Regimented training. Not for me."

"You know why she does interval training?"

He puzzled that for a minute, becoming a statue as usual. He came back to life. "You mean that fast shooting she was doing today? I noticed that, too. Not a typical competition archery thing. There are time limits, like two minutes to shoot three arrows, but it's nothing like what she was doing."

"Could it be something else?"

"What else? She's a competitive archer. Everything she does is to kick ass at hitting targets from distance. Her mission in life is to win the Olympics."

I smacked at the mosquito sucking on my neck. "You know about your uncle and her?"

"No, but I can guess. Harold's not shabby with the ladies. If he hangs out with a good-looking chick for long, it ends up one way. They love his surfer, archer vibe. Besides, he has that easy smile and perfect teeth."

True, Harold's teeth were bright as the white of a baby's eye. It reminded me that I was due for a trip to the bathroom to brush.

"Someone shot Kendal, and she's one of the best. From what everyone at the range was saying, that was a hell of a shot. You think she's capable?"

At first Junior's face contorted into a that's-ridiculous look of bewilderment, but then it shifted and he became still.

"How would I know?" he noted philosophically. "People kill people all the time and someone's gotta do it. She could make that shot. But so could Harold and a bunch of others on a good day. She's not the only one."

"How many?"

"How many what?"

"How many people around here could make that shot?"

"I don't live here all the time. I didn't recognize many of the people at the club today. I think you're better off asking Uncle Har."

My phone buzzed. An unrecognized number. I excused myself to the club's driveway to answer anyway. As I exited, I narrowly missed crushing a brown lizard with a white racing stripe down his back scurrying by on the concrete.

Leber.

"What can I do for you, Detective?"

"I'd like to share with you, if you've got anything worth sharing."

"Detective, you'll forgive my skepticism, but I've never, never had any police officer or detective offer to share anything with me unless they felt they'd get the better end of the deal."

He groaned. "I already showed good faith. You know something, you're too busy trying to act tough. You're not."

My turn to groan. "So, because you agreed to show us the crime scene, I owe you? I thought that was some agreement between you and Harold or his officer buddy."

"Eddie," he muttered.

A clattering erupted from my earpiece, then an expletive. Moments later, Leber said, "Sorry, damn phone case…slippery. Look, I need your assist. Can we meet?"

Cops hadn't given me a warm, fuzzy feeling since the sheriff in Los Angeles shut me down and threatened to arrest me if I didn't let go of Evelyn's case. They had my respect as a group. Individually, some were as bad as the criminals, and the bad ones didn't have a tattoo announcing "bad cop."

Tough? I didn't act tough. Fuck him. I'd ram one of those cop billy clubs up his ass. I didn't need Leber to like me. Barnes, either.

"Fine, we'll meet. Text me a time and place," I grumbled before clicking off.

Back inside, I found Junior intently focused on his phone. He pulled up YouTube and rapidly keyed in Olympic archery 2016. A Korean man named Ku Bonchan, whose skin looked cool as a rose petal, ran away with the gold, besting a French bloke who kept shaking out his hand like it was numb.

Junior tapped the screen and said, "Ku could have made the shot that got Kendal."

CHAPTER 18

Hillary drank the remainder of the white wine left on her bedside table from the night before, just to wet her dry palate, mind you. She then came downstairs to discover Herbie on the phone, blasting someone for calling so damned early.

The blasted phone had woken her again from a perfectly sound sleep. She needed beauty sleep. The cream would only keep the bags at bay for so long. The insufferable police wouldn't stop calling. They kept asking the same questions and wanting more information on her mother's life, finances, habits. What did she know of Francine's habits? Fact was, their mother kept all of them at arm's length with the business. As far as she could surmise, Francine's personal life was her work. She did nothing with them as children, and little changed once they became adults.

For the first time she considered abandoning the elegant, rotary-dial landline that sat on the end table. The antique had no off switch for the ringer, but Hillary liked that. She always feared she'd miss an important call. About what? The list was as endless and indistinct as the sky, although her nephew headed the list, that much was certain.

She next discovered Harold on the lawn coming unhinged. Harold yanked the arrow he'd just shot out of the target, dropped to his knees and violently stabbed the innocent grass, still moist with morning dew, fifteen times, as if the Bacon family quad were responsible for some grave misdeed.

From inside the French doors to the grand residence Hillary smirked at her anguished brother. Watching Harold like this brought her joy. He always tried to act so calm. He rarely let her see him totally lose control. If he'd known she was watching, he would undoubtedly have forced himself back under control rather than allow her to witness his inner demons at work. But at this distance, with the eastern sun reflecting on the French door, he was oblivious to her voyeurism.

Behind her, Herbie hung up the phone.

"Damned police. They want to know everything," Herbie groaned coming up behind her. "They woke you up again, right?"

"Um-hmm," she murmured, still watching Harold.

"They don't like that we are each other's alibis for the day mom died. They want to know more details."

"We gave them details. Harold backed us up. We're covered."

He strolled over and placed his hand on her shoulder. "Can we trust him? Look at him. He's weak."

She turned around and gazed into her brother's eyes. "He's kept it to himself all these years. Besides, he was alone, so he needs us as much as we need him."

Normally always clean-shaven except for his thick mustache, stubble had sprung up on Herbie's neck the last few days. She rubbed it playfully. He grabbed her wrists and squeezed her fine bones till they compressed. Her face contorted with a moment of pain, then a devious smile cracked her lips.

"Want to play?" she asked in a breathy voice.

Flinging her wrists away, he slapped the frame of the French door. "This is no time for games, Hill. Evans wants more money."

"I don't care if we give it to him. We can be pariahs for all I care. So long as we have each other." She held her breath after saying the last.

They looked out at the back of the Bacon Estate. Harold now lay motionless in the grass on the archery range, his chest rising and falling like a sprinter at the end of a race.

"Do you see this behavior? Does Harold look like he's holding it together? He's going to compromise everything. On top of that, how do we know he didn't do it since he wasn't with us and has no witnesses to his supposed whereabouts?"

Hillary's playful demeanor vanished. She growled, "We know because he is our brother, and even if he did do it, he's still our brother. No Bacons will go to prison over this." His eyes remained fixed on Harold's prone form. She inched closer, her breath hot on his ear. "Do you hear me?"

"I hear you."

CHAPTER 19

The bar at the Greenhouse glowed like honey in sunlight. Some kind of special paint had been used below the varnish to give it a shimmering appearance. The Aussie bartender, Willy, said some Russian artist named Vlad, who was hiding out from the mob, had agreed to paint it during the last renovation in exchange for a month's worth of chow.

"It was worth it," I said every time I showed up there and he turned on the overhead lamp. The special thing about this type of painting, which apparently was as secret as the Coca-Cola formula, was that it became brighter or darker depending on how much light shown on it. The glow made your glass of alcohol seem even more heaven-sent at the end of a long day.

As I slugged my first gulp, movement on the stool next to me. Leber. He clapped me on the back like we were old pals.

"Boise. What up, da man?"

I gave a weary nod. "You're in a chipper mood, Detective."

He put his finger to his lips and hunched toward me. "Let's be incognito tonight."

"Whatever, man." I chased my beer with heavily salted peanuts. "I'm not super-fond of police officers or detectives or anyone with a badge. What do you want from me?"

He ordered Bacardi and soda, then adjusted himself on the stool. "Preferred it better when the stools here had backs." He rubbed his lower spine and winced. "Some kinda slipped disc, my chiropractor says. You believe that?"

Willy frisbeed a green Heineken coaster in front of Leber and set his drink on it.

"You friendly with Corey Hart?" I asked.

"Who's that?"

"Never mind."

Corey Hart sang the hit tune, *I Wear My Sunglasses at Night*. I loved the song, but found that the real guys who did this were douche-bags. Luckily, most of them lived in Holly-weird.

Then Leber surprised me. "You makin' fun of my glasses?" He pulled them to the tip of his ample nose. His deep brown eyes peered at me over the rim. A predatory dog sizing up the enemy. "I got sensitive eyes. Work-related accident. Some bastard turned on a very intense light while enhanced-interrogating me a few years back. I see fine, but can't stand bright light or even faint light much anymore."

"That didn't disqualify you from police work?"

"You think competent detectives are coming out of the woodwork around here. The department's lucky if we can find anyone with a college degree and no record."

"Sounds like every cop I've been involved with," I said. "So, what is it you want?"

"Boise, drop the cop-hating act. I know you don't feel that way about folks trying to do the right thing and putting their lives

149

on the line." He waited while I silently acknowledged he had a point. He continued. "Pickering's being a hard-ass about Kendal's laptop. Says he doesn't know where it is. I could bring him up on obstruction, but I know him, he doesn't care about that."

Pickering had shown me the laptop only days ago, so I knew he had it. I wasn't going to divulge that to Leber. But neither would I lie openly if the question came up. Pickering was a good newspaper man. Any good newspaper person had spent time locked up for something they believed in. The guy was political, but I suppose he had his principles.

"What do you want from me?"

"You guys are buddy-buddy. I remember you solved those cases a few months back, got them lots of readers. Walter Pickering must love you."

He crunched on a piece of ice, which sent chills down my spine.

"He definitely doesn't love me. He's charging me for ad space after all that bump in readership."

Leber winced down a swallow. We were both nearing the end of our first round and ordered another.

"You want me to convince Pickering he should share information from Kendal's laptop with you, assuming he has it?"

He nodded.

"And why should I go to bat for you, Detective?"

"Francine's body, for starters."

"Not the same ballpark. What else? Can you give me a copy of the murder book?"

With a sideways look, he raised one eyebrow ala Roger Moore.

"Then tell me what you have. If we really are helping each other."

He proceeded to feed me information the police had recovered concerning phone records for Kendal. He'd been in contact with several people in Barbados, St. Kitts, the Dominican

Republic, and St. Croix. The same places the Bacons owned sugar plantations.

The offices and the mercantile operations were in St. Thomas because it had the best harbor and the most lucrative shipping, allowing Bacon Rum and their other sugar products ease of distribution. St. Thomas was also the safest place historically since the slave rebellion had taken place in St. Croix in 1848. The Bacon family had left managers at the various plantations while holing up in St. Thomas. Under Francine's leadership, much of the property had been liquidated or donated as historical sites with an endowment.

"She had a need to make amends if you ask me." Leber leaned on the bar. He looked like a wet newspaper in a windstorm.

"Why are you so clued in on Francine?" I asked. "What about Kendal?"

"Ninety-percent he and she are mixed in the same thing. This ain't a coincidence. Probably family. Am I right?"

"Hey man, you're the detective. I'm just a lowly investigator trying to make it in the man's world."

"You sayin' I'm the man?" He paused, then after another sip said, "There's two kinds of detectives: the kind who gather information and the kind who take that information and gel it into a good theory to catch the perpetrator."

I waited for more, but he seemed to want to fill me in on categories of detectives. When he didn't say anything for a while, I responded, "So, what are you?"

Leber started to lean back and caught himself. "See! Who likes backless stools? Who?" He yelled the last word and Willy glanced our way. Leber waved him off. "Boise, I need some more and your pal Pickering has it. Talk to him. Get him to spill on Lady Francine Bacon's plans. And what about your bosses?"

"Who's my bosses?"

"Junior and Harold. Aren't those the guys who're paying you?"

"Mind your business, Detective." I bolted the last of my Guinness, then wiped my mouth across my forearm and licked the residue. Cops made you feel like a whore for being in the free-market.

CHAPTER 20

It was late and I was exhausted, but I knew I wouldn't sleep. Pickering answered on the first ring. Guess I wasn't the only one running myself ragged. He agreed to meet me at a hole in the wall with no sign near Backstreet Pizza. Very covert.

As I walked, internal questions rained on me like confetti. What was Francine really up to with Kendal? What was Junior's role? The rest of the Bacons were dysfunctional, but killers? What of the inheritors, aka the descendants of the Bacon slaves? Could they be involved and if so, why? They were on the winning side of this thing. The lucky ones who would finally reap what their ancestors had sowed under lashes and nooses.

By most accounts, Francine appeared to be a stand-up lady in the community who decided to abdicate the throne. She was not mother of the year and she continued that trend by shorting her heirs, but the money was never theirs, not really. Least that's how I'd always looked at inheritance. Not mine to begin with; if anyone wanted to give me their hard-earned fortune, that was blind luck. There was no right, not even with spouses or children. Then again, if you felt you were being cheated, well, there's no telling what you'd do. I also never had a mother or grandmother with over one-hundred million to give.

The same mutt that begged in the morning near Market Square, ambled behind a parallel-parked car. I whistled, hoping he'd recognize me from the piece of chicken I'd given him the week before. He eyed me cautiously and seeing I had nothing in my hand, trotted away, his overgrown toenails clicking on the ground.

"I understand," I muttered, "you didn't survive out here all these years trusting bush-men on Backstreet in the middle of the night."

A voice came from behind me. "Boise, who're you talking to?"

"There was a..." I looked around, but the dog was gone. "Aw, forget it. You have notes?"

Pickering tapped his shirt pocket. I'll be damned if he wasn't wearing a tie, a button-down shirt and dressy slacks to meet in this dive.

"You're gonna stick out in here, you know?"

"Dress for success, Boise. Never be ashamed to look better than those around you any more than you should strive to be as gullible as the masses."

"I need a beer," I responded, holding the door for the lanky man, then continued holding until a wobbling woman on the arm of a grinning toothless man stumbled out. "You're welcome," I muttered, but they were clueless and unresponsive.

I tried to pull my hand off the doorknob and it came away sticky. I headed to the bathroom, which was really just a black hole with a toilet splattered with god-knows-what and a slippery floor that was stylish in the 1940s. There was no soap and no towels and only a trickle of water, so I wet my hands as best I could and wiped them on my shorts. Someone pounded on the door as I opened it.

A woman pushed past me with a whiff of cheap perfume and gin. She slammed the door to the men's room in my face.

At the bar, Pickering sequentially pounded two shots of whiskey. Cutty Sark must have been his drink. After I joined him, he called for something off the top shelf and retired to sip it in a dark booth. My stomach was too bloated for Guiness, so I ordered a light beer.

I filled him in on what Leber had told me earlier.

"So, Widow Bacon was what, a reparationist?" he asked.

"She sold off some of the plantations, but we're not sure who bought them or why. Maybe to liquidate so she had capital to distribute. You get anything from the computer?"

To my surprise, Pickering readily handed me a stack of hard-copies printed from Kendal's computer. He smelled of Jurgen's Lotion and starch.

He pulled three pages out that confirmed her plan to divest. Kendal even had one confirmation of sale of the plantation in Barbados to a land developer. My eyes grew wide when I read the name: Payne & Wedgefield.

A kidnapping case I'd worked involved the daughter of the man who owned the real estate empire. I hadn't heard nice things about him, but, Payne and Wedgefield were in real estate, so not that strange that they'd be involved.

"There's more, but I ran out of ink in my printer. I can give you more tomorrow."

"Why not go to the paper and print?" I asked. "This relates. It's gonna be a story."

"Nighttime at the paper. The place feels off. I don't know."

He tilted the glass to his mouth and finished it. He returned with two more this time. Off my look, he said, "What?"

I sipped my beer, a little less eager to keep pace. Dana had made me feel guilty with her question about attending an AA meeting. "Nothing," I said. "Go on."

"As I was saying, there's a lot here. He and Widow Bacon were working on something fairly monumental. If you look at that sales contract closely, you'll see that the widow had the land rezoned so that it had to be low-income housing moving forward with the plantation house turned into a museum about the history of sugar and slavery. The influence you can have when you own thousands of acres and millions of dollars. Do you know much about reparations?"

"Making amends for past wrongs. My grandmother used to talk about it in regards to slavery."

"Then you know slave reparations are rare birds."

I nodded. Reparations for slavery had been bandied about for years, mostly right after it ended in the U.S. Not a ton of talk about it in the Caribbean to my knowledge.

Pickering continued. "The only real example of an entire nation providing reparations for past wrongs was Germany giving billions to Israel after World War II. The very act of forming the state of Israel was a form of forced reparations to the Jewish people, but it didn't come out of Germany's hide since Germany didn't own the land used to form Israel."

Sometimes it was interesting listening to Pickering's historical diatribes, but tonight I didn't have the patience, so I eased him out of lecture-mode and back on track.

Pickering shook his head in disgust. "Fine, fine, a man tries to color the narrative. This is why folks don't like history, no patience for the payoff at the end of a good story anymore. You know, Boise, you could stand to gain some historical perspective about the racial divide that you're a part of. Do you even know if your African grandmother willingly married a white man? Did she do it for love or out of necessity or something more sinister?"

His eyes had that watery glass over them, so I cut him some

slack.

"Walter, what say we leave my dearly departed grandmother out of this conversation."

He raised his hands in the universal gesture for "sorry, man, I wasn't trying to offend you," a staple of drunken insults the world over.

"Point is," he spoke deliberately, enunciating each word like a scholar lecturing to his freshman English class. "I figured out their agenda and it might be," he coughed, "they both bought the farm for doing the right thing."

I threw back the last of my beer and got myself another. If I caught up with Pickering, maybe I'd understand what the hell he was trying to say.

When I returned, he asked, "You ever hear of H.R. Forty?" He still had his wedding ring on.

"No," I said, afraid what road this led down. *Patience Danielsan*, I thought. *Show patience with drunk lizard or all you catch is tail.*

"It's a bill introduced by Representative John Conyers in the House of Representatives to sturdy, er, study reparations for slavery and discrimination in our colonizers."

"Colonizers? You mean the U.S.?"

He slapped the bar. "Yes, goddamn it, the U.S.!" A couple in the booth behind Pickering, who were hunched together whispering in each other's ears, turned and glowered at us.

"It's a bar," I said, "not a library."

It was late and after only a beer and a half, my buzz was strong. This side of Pickering could be fun. As if to accentuate his irreverent attitude, he loosened his black tie and unbuttoned the top of his stiff shirt. The man looked like a Mormon on his mission to spread the gospel.

My second pint was suddenly on its last sip. My boozing was gaining steam. Seeing Pickering was getting low on gas, I ordered another round. I, feeling a mite peckish, ordered extra-spicy chicken wings for two to be brought over. Pickering probably needed food in his gut soon or I'd be cleaning up a mess. Some people couldn't handle the business of drinking. Pickering appeared to be one of them.

"There was a lot, lot in that computer of Kendal's. Thank heavens for the ravishing Ms. Kendal. Don't you think she's ravishing?"

"Walter, let's stick to the content of Kendal's computer."

Pickering resumed. "So, Conyers does this every year. Stubborn as a Taurus, and you know what?" I waited. "Nothing! Nothing happens. They won't even vote on the damn thing. It wallows. The bill doesn't even ask for reparations, it just asks to study reparations. Would you pasty white guys merely check it out and see if there's any merit? That's all he's asking. You believe that? All those old, supposedly reformed and open-minded congressmen afraid to even study it."

My worry that I'd have to convince Pickering to eat some of the wings dissipated when I placed them between us, and we jointly set upon them like wildcats. The blue-cheese dressing was exceptional, as was the spiciness of the wings. I went to get another ramekin as Pickering mindlessly double-dipped in the first one. A small glob of white dressing clung to his chin for over two minutes. A photo to prove the guy wasn't always immaculate would have been nice, but I resisted the urge.

"Did Kendal have something to do with H.R. Forty?"

Pickering sniggered. "No. Boise, Boise, Boise! He and the Bacon woman were old family friends, according to Savannah. Kendal had some affinity for reparations. Like a hobby. He was a student of the topic. Must have gone to her with numbers and tragedies." He waved a dismissive hand at me. "You got to know what I mean."

A bit of spice caught in my throat, and I swallowed hard. My eyes watered. Pickering crunched on a bit of ice from the water I'd brought back as a mandatory beverage with spicy wings.

"He convinced her to make reparations to the descendants of

the Bacon Family's slaves. They calculated a fair amount and located the people. They found around twenty-eight who live here, a couple in Barbados where their original plantation operated, and the rest scattered around." He ripped into another wing, exclaiming, "Spicy!"

CHAPTER 21

There it was. Pickering refused to entrust Kendal's computer to me, but in true investigative fashion, he'd pieced together the story. It was Kendal who'd convinced Francine to do the right thing and hand over the bulk of her fortune to descendents of former slaves, plus form a permanent fund to help anyone else who came forward later through an endowment. The family was abandoned at sea. Strong motive for offing their matriarch.

Problem was, killing Francine didn't fix the reparation issue. In fact, you could argue that the heirs should do anything and everything to keep her breathing. This would give them more time to convince her to change her bequests. Her demise actually benefited the Bacon Group most immediately.

"So, what does that leave for the Bacon family?" I asked.

Pickering laughed again. A giggly drunk. "I gave the trust instrument to a lawyer, who says they get to live in the house till they pass. Something called a life estate. The children each get $1.5 million in a trust with Kendal, Miguela Salas, and someone named Camilla as trustees."

"Well, that's not too shabby ... the money I mean, not what happened to Kendal."

He squinted at me like a father assessing his daughter's new hipster boyfriend. "You daft? If you'd expected to each get twenty to thirty mill and wound up with one-point-five, you'd think that was shabby."

True. To me, one-point-five million was a dream. To the Bacons, a nightmare.

"What about Junior? Does he get anything? Wasn't he the favorite?"

"The grandson stands with a trust fund of ten million."

Nineteen-years-old with ten million in the bank. Most would be lucky to see one or two million earned over the course of a lifetime.

Pickering excused himself to use the bathroom. When he returned, I could smell that he'd thrown up. His eyes were milky. So much for spicy chicken wings saving the day.

"You okay?"

He shoved aside the last Cutty Sark, only half-drunk, and downed a mouthful of water.

I pressed on although Pickering appeared ready to be poured into bed. "The kid gets the most. Guess he really was her favorite. What about the people in the Bacon Group?"

"What about them?"

"Have they been notified they stand to inherit a small fortune?"

Pickering's eyes blinked shut, then popped open again. He looked at me, absent recognition, then his eyes swam back into focus.

"Yes, they know. It was part of the story Kendal was working on. He interviewed members of the group for genuine reactions. I think he got a kick out of seeing the joy he expected it would bring struggling people who'd never had much."

"Who else knew?"

"The family was made aware not too long ago, except the grandson. What's his name again?"

"Junior. Well, Herbert, Jr., but everyone calls him Junior."

"She wanted him to have his degree before he became a trust fund baby. Until he's thirty, he only gets $40K per year."

"What happens at thirty?"

"Junior's allowance goes to $100K, then he has full access at forty. According to the notes, that's when she thought he would have the maturity to responsibly handle the money. Also, it'll force him to work and be self-sufficient in the meantime."

That's a long time to have a carrot dangled, but Francine was probably right, forty would be late enough to give him an appreciation, but sometimes knowing that money's waiting out there keeps a person from doing anything else with their life.

CHAPTER 22

The Bacon family dynamic nagged at me like a hungry mosquito. Up until now, my amateurish deductions had kept me dialed in on them as part of this murder. But my mentor's voice nagged that something wasn't right. Henry would have agreed that the family had secrets and that they had had a less-than-loving response to Francine's demise. But one thing I'd observed in myself and others who suffered the loss of someone close, it was damned hard to judge behavior in a room full of grief. People sometimes laughed at funerals or remained stoic to everyone on the outside while cheering on the inside. They clung to habits and behaviors that might seem heartless, but got them through each second until they were ready to process.

I'd spent hours riddled with guilt over my anger since I'd found out about Evelyn's infidelity the same night she was killed. Try dealing with hate and love and death in one melting pot of guilt and grief. Try getting the call that your wife's died of a collapsed lung from a hit-and-run driver, when you've spent the whole night stewing about her staying over at another man's house. Instead of worrying about her safety, I imagined the worst, most graphic sexual events as I drowned my sorrow in a bottle of not-so-cheap scotch.

I couldn't know what Hillary, Herbie, Harold, or Junior felt internally from the brief moments when I infiltrated their home. What I did have was the endless and confident loop of every base behavior immemorial—primal motive.

Henry liked to say, "When you lose track of the tiger's teeth, go back to why. Teeth are for eating, find the food." It always seemed like a weird metaphor, but the gist was pure and simple: motive solves cause. Cause narrows your suspect pool.

None of the family had a rational motive from a long-term perspective. That doesn't mean they didn't or couldn't have done it. It did mean if they did, their reasoning was flawed or they killed from an emotional place, which was entirely possible if they discovered her intentions to abdicate, tried to convince her to change her mind, and upon failing ended Francine's life in a mad rage. The obvious place for a family member to kill her would have been in the house with lots of privacy, but everything looked copacetic there. It seemed the person who knew every inch of the home, Wilma, had no inkling of anything untoward happening on the premises.

A non-disclosure document to Kendal that Pickering had shared with me, indicated Francine purposefully kept her children and Junior out of her business. This explained the bickering I'd witnessed when Junior asked about getting involved and Herbie put him off. Herbie had no access, but he didn't want the rest to know that was because his mother had kept her first-born out of the family business and nothing he could do would change her mind. The man had three business degrees, but they didn't matter. He would never measure up, because it wasn't about measuring up.

This feeling of inadequacy on Herbie's part would certainly satisfy motive. Being ignored by the one person whose approval he craved could drive anyone to engage in reckless, even lethal behavior. After all, once you cleared all of the hoops and still get nowhere, you might just want to see the whole thing burn, if only to see what would happen next.

From what I'd gleaned from the notes from Kendal's computer, Francine's motives were more altruistic. Consciously, Francine seemed to be trying to protect them all from the whole messy sugar business and to give them a life independent of the Bacon family's sordid history. Subconsciously, perhaps she really was not satisfied with any of her children and knew they could not cut it in the sugar world.

My phone buzzed.

Pickering barked at me, "Get over here to Kendal's now. Savannah came home to find the place ransacked."

Even in the shade of a coconut palm outside the house, the relentless heat pressed on my shoulders like a weight. A flock of sparrows exploded from beneath a festive bougainvillea bush. Bees circled and crawled between the magenta petals.

Kendal had a standard two-story job of cinderblock construction doused in white with gray trim. Thick tempered glass blocks wiggled between the cinderblocks to allow a diffuse light into the house. It wasn't the house I pictured Adirondack Kendal living in, but when I tried to imagine anything else, my mind drew a blank. Maybe a condo out by Aunt Glor in Bolongo Bay? Probably the wife picked this, which was more in line with a sophisticate like Pickering. The wife had the cash or one of them had family dollars. No newspaper guy in a small backwater could afford this pad on his salary.

"Boise, this is Savannah."

"Hi, yes, we met at the paper's memorial," I said, extending my hand. "How're you holding up?"

165

She shrugged.

Pickering eyed the yard and street with suspicion. "Does anyone know you came here?"

"The cabbie," I said.

After one more furtive glance around, Pickering beckoned me inside slamming the door and throwing the deadbolt in one fluid motion.

"What happened?" I asked.

Pickering looked at Savannah. "Is it okay I tell him?" She nodded and he continued. "Boise, this stays between us. Right now, I don't want Dana on this. I'm trying to send her back to Tortola, but she's being difficult."

"You didn't hire her for her tact."

He held up a video tape. I hadn't seen one in some time and it caught me by surprise. The bulky black plastic, the reality of our isolation here in St. Thomas, and the low-technology all struck me at once as very out of place; a time-warp.

"You should watch it," Savannah said in a whisper.

Kendal's basement had a bulky old television on a press-wood entertainment center that looked left over from a college student's dorm room. A dusty Emerson VCR with a blinking green display sat on the bottom shelf.

"I've thought about throwing this bulky electronic junk away so many times," Savannah commented before shoving in the tape.

The screen blinked to life, a blue field, then some static. From off camera Kendal's voice hummed through the speakers.

"I can only get it to record in black and white," he said in an irritated tone.

"Fine, fine," said an older woman's voice, then Francine Bacon filled the frame. She sat in a cushioned chair. She wore no make-up, but the poor lighting was kind. "Let's get this over with."

Francine Bacon stated that she'd been working for years in

secret to bring the sugar industry down to earth. It needed clearing up. Morals and ethics had long ago perished because of those connected to it who needed to maintain profit margins. She named the players and government officials from places all over the world, but mostly the local Caribbean officials who helped to perpetuate the growing and processing of cheap sugar through what she termed the twenty-first century slave labor. She was forming *"a sort of non-profit"* to beat the bastards at their own game by any means necessary. She made clear that Kendal and the other two trustees were in charge of carrying out the annihilation of this white, crystal industry by any means necessary. The kids and Junior, and any others who made a claim to the family fortune, would be cut out completely if they contested the trust or undermined the singular purpose of the non-profit. She admonished the trustees to remain steadfast in their primary objective. Whatever was left after sugar was brought to its knees was to be then used to continue an assault on any other industries that enslaved people in unfair and unsanitary conditions.

"So, where's this leave us?" I asked.

"I'm personally paying you to figure that out, remember? I'm struggling with my feelings about this." Pickering made a fluttering gesture at Savannah. "Kendal got on my nerves, but he was a damn fine reporter with a nose for news. Two reporters gave me notice yesterday. One is a senior guy nearing retirement with tons of contacts. I'd convinced him to stay on the last two years, because we already have too many greenies on staff and even free-lancing. Every blogger thinks he's a reporter these days. The experienced ones have more contacts and sources. They know where to sniff. The youngsters aren't …" He snapped his fingers as he searched for the right word.

Savannah tapped his other hand in a motherly manner that made me wonder how long these two had been carrying on. "Dogged," she said.

His eyes lit up, and he leaned into her. She held him off with a stiff arm. He cleared his throat and pulled back, an embarrassed look flashing across his face.

"Yes, dogged! They aren't dogged. Anyhow, the second quitter is a woman right out of the journalism program at a northeastern school at the second tier. Tufts, I think. No huge loss, but it's hard to recruit talent to leave a place like Boston or New York and come to this god-forsaken rock."

"And you're saying they split for fear of their safety? You can't convince them to stay?"

"Convince them? Great idea, then when something happens to them, not only will their families sue the paper, they'll sue me personally for telling them to stay on." He pursed his lips like he was dealing with an insolent child. "This leaves me shy three reporters on staff and scrambling for people to give me enough content. So, although I'd like to stay on this with you, as they say on Broadway, 'the show must go on,' and I need to get with my headhunter on this asap."

With that, Pickering rummaged in a cabinet and came out holding a pile of papers, Kendal's laptop, a zip drive, and a bag.

"I haven't even been through all of it." He settled the pile in my arms. "Good luck."

Savannah ejected the videotape and placed it atop my pile. "Walter says we need to trust someone who is not emotionally involved. Guess you're as good as anyone."

I looked at Pickering, a smile beginning to crack my lips. "I'm as good as anyone?"

He gave me his professorial stare. "I'll have you know, I don't trust easily and we've only been acquainted a few months."

"Half-a-year," I corrected.

"What I said."

"Okay, so by your non-trusting standards, I've breached the wall quickly?"

"Very," Savannah said, leaning into Pickering's side and

giving him a playful bump with her hip. "I'm still not sure he trusts me."

Pickering rubbed her shoulder. "I trust you with some things."

She playfully shoved him away, and he allowed a small smile. It vanished as soon as he turned back to me.

"This is all hush-hush," he said, pointing back and forth at himself and Savannah.

"Course," I said, "top secret, except one thing." I explained that some details would need to be shared with Leber the next time I saw the curious detective. We hashed out which details were appropriate for disclosure and which should be kept under wraps. Savannah got antsy and went to bed, saying she trusted us to make these life and death decisions so long as no one else tried to break into her home for any more of Kendal's secret mission notes.

A cab shuttled me back to The Manner as Pickering didn't want to leave Savannah alone in the recently ransacked house. He had arranged for a security company to come out the next day and install an alarm system.

The evening warmth felt good after being in West L.A., where there was almost always a chill at night, even in summer. Never needing a jacket. Never even needing to sleep inside unless it rained or the mosquitos were bad. Never needing to close my windows. The whisper of crickets floated on the wind from the grassy hillsides. You could get lost in that easy rhythm and never do anything productive again. As the cab passed over the hill, I spotted the sea, shimmering in the faint moonlight. Many days I felt like slipping into the breezy worry-free life so many islanders enjoyed. Waiting tables or selling trinkets to tourists would pay the bills and keep food on the table. Easier and safer. Apparently, not my bag.

CHAPTER 23

The pile of crap Savannah and Pickering had dumped on me littered my desk. The vastness of the information in Kendal's computer caused my blood pressure to spike. What was I looking for? His personal organizational system made no sense to me. I couldn't help wondering if Pickering had bogged me down to keep me from solving this thing in under a week just so he wouldn't have to make good on his bonus offer.

I started to call him and ask, but realized I was being ridiculous. The family was not giving me anything new. Another angle, that's what I needed. Then I remembered the picture of the slaves working in the fields. Sugar cane. Rum.

***

The Bacon distillery and warehouse had a tour starting at a little after eleven. I'd purchased a bottle in the gift shop and went along on the tour as they explained the process of distilling and bottling rum. Little plastic key chains in the shape of bottles with the Bacon pirate skull on them were given to each of us. I bought a pint and nicked away at it during the tour, then examined the grounds afterwards. The place had a garden with a patch of sugar cane growing for examination and a woman in a shanty selling hunks of cane if you wanted to suck on them.

A group of tourists gathered around, grabbing pieces and handing her dollars. There were ten kids and seven adults milling about, touching the cane leaves and tapping on the hard reeds. I thought again of the reed painting from Francine's room. "If not me, who?" A call to action that had gotten Francine killed. Then I remembered the second half of the quote: "If not now, when?" Indeed.

"You want a piece?" It was the woman selling the cane. She was holding one out like a baton in a relay race.

"Sure."

I fished a dollar bill from my pocket and handed it to her. The sweet juice bathed my tongue as I gnawed on the bark. All the Caribbean markets sold sugar cane. I had often begged my mother to buy me a piece, and she often complied to shut me up. It back-fired in the end, because I wouldn't stop stammering on about the toys I wanted or stupid observations about other cars and pedestrians I spotted as we drove home. The sugar rush turned me into a prattler.

"How long have you worked here?"

She squinted at me. She had almost no teeth, probably from sucking sugar cane. "I been here since da start."

"Since 1969?"

"Yes sir. Since 1969 when dey open dis place."

"What can you tell me about it that is more interesting than the tour?"

171

Her eyes twinkled.

"You want sweet juicy stuff?" Her lips curled in a mischievous smile. "I can smell you been," she leaned her head back and forward like taking a drink. Out of nowhere she produced a highball glass and wiped it out with a yellow handkerchief. I poured a shot into the glass, took my own taste.

She sipped the rum. "What you want to know?"

"Anything you know about this distillery and the rum business. I don't know, hit me with something interesting. Here." I handed the remainder of the pint to her. She slipped it under the counter without hesitation.

"All right. I tell you one t'ing. All them casks in there, they just for show."

"There's no rum in them?" I asked.

"There's rum in them. In the real storage. This place was open for tourists, but this ain't the real operation. Not for making rum. This place for distribute da rum. They put these here mostly for show. They agin' them, but have much more other places. Mostly here is for shipping and tourists. Gift shop is the money."

"Is the rum business not good?"

"Nah man, I ain't say that!" She swatted at the air. "What I sayin' is St. Thomas got all the people."

She waved her hand around at the surrounding area. People bustled about.

"Don't they have sugar production in other places? Puerto Rico, St. Kitts. That's what the website says."

"Sugar. Ha. Don't know what happenin' there. Don't know. Rum good. Who care where you get sugar? It all the same. No?"

"This seems like hard work," I said. "Do you pick the cane and cut."

"Yeah, I do it. This my sugar patch."

A machete stuck out of a chopping block that had a couple reeds of sugar cane laid out, ready for the next customer.

"But you can't cut da cane too early or it dry out," she said.

"All this fresh dis morning." She dipped a hunk of the cane into her rum and sucked it off. "Like celery in a Bloody Mary, mi son."

A man walked from behind the sugar cane patch. He had a neatly trimmed beard and wore a black shirt with Bacon Rum printed on the breast pocket. The woman dropped her glass into the large trash can along with the piece of cane.

"Florence, what have I told you about drinking the rum?"

"What rum, sir?"

He reached into the garbage can and fished out the glass. He sniffed it. "This rum. Florence, if I report this, it will be your third infraction. Do you realize what that means?"

Her head bowed in shame. "Yes sir, I do. Would you like I should pack up me t'ings now?"

"The rum belonged to me," I said.

The man turned to me slowly, a pained grin on his face. "And you are?"

"A tourist. I was on the tour and bought a pint. I insisted Florence have a drink with me and she was just obliging. The customer is always right, right?"

He looked back and forth at each of us. Florence did not raise her head. I stared straight ahead, still gnawing away on my piece of cane.

"Florence. Did he pay for that cane?"

She nodded solemnly.

"I wonder, what compelled you to share your rum with this woman, sir?"

"Common courtesy and the desire not to drink alone, sir. I was very keen to try your spiced rum as this was my first visit to the distillery, and this fine woman agreed to drink with me. Is that really so bad?"

He steepled his fingers in front of his lips, then said, "Very well. Seeing as you were complying with a customer's wishes. Florence, please go back to work. I see some more customers approaching. Remember, I'm watching you."

Her head bobbed quickly up and down. "Yes, sir. Yes, sir."

"Good, good. Now, sir, may I walk you around a bit? I mean, you appear to be very interested in our rum."

He was pigeon-toed but had an athletic build. The man worked out.

"Oh terribly," I said. "Are you the manager?"

"Yes, you could say that. Foreman, manager, whatever you wish to call the person in charge of the day-to-day operations of this facility. What brought you here?"

"An interest in your rum, but also, I'm assisting Junior in an inquiry."

He stopped in front of a discarded barrel someone had propped up. A sign was posted on the barrel: Rain Water.

"Do you mean, Herbert Bacon, Junior? Francine's grandson?"

"Yes, him. And his brother Harold."

"Now I'm curious. Is there something you need from us here at the distillery?"

"To be honest..." I paused.

"Gilroy," he filled in his name.

"Gilroy. I'm at an impasse. You know about Francine, right?"

"Terrible news. It's why I wore my black shirt all week. She was a fine woman. Don't know what we'll do without her."

"Was she hands-on here?"

"You know, Mister?"

"Montague. Boise Montague."

"Yes, Mr. Montague. Do you mind if I see some identification?"

I showed him my license. He pulled out a cell phone and made a call. He stepped to the side while reading my name off the license to someone. I presumed either Junior or Harold. After a minute of whispered exchanges, he returned my license and ended the call with a, "Thank you."

"Harold confirmed you work for them. I hope you

understand, I must…"

"Please, Mr. Gilroy, no need. I completely understand."

"Francine Bacon was very active in all areas of her business enterprises. She believed in this business and the people working here. I am trying to uphold her standards, hence the strict policies you saw me enforcing on Florence."

"Sure, sure, I get it. No drinking on the job. Makes sense, but kind of ironic, wouldn't you say?" I laughed.

He forced a thin smile. "Of course, but we do serious work here and people drinking can be dangerous, even if it is our business. Wouldn't you agree."

"Yes, yes. Safety first. Can you tell me what kind of wood you use for these barrels to age the rum and give it such a great flavor?"

A huge grin burst from his face. "Ah, my area of expertise. Our spiced rum is aged a minimum of three years in oak barrels."

We now stood inside a storage area that was not part of the tour. I tapped gently on one of the barrels. "Three years seems short. I mean higher quality whiskey ages ten, even twenty years, right?"

"It is the minimum. Aging happens faster in the tropics, so we cannot age as long as they do in places like Tennessee or Kentucky or Scotland."

"The heat?"

"Evaporation or what the Brits call *The Angel's Share*. While those producers lose two or three percent annually, we are bound to lose up to eleven percent. We cannot afford for all the product to evaporate."

"How long have you worked for the Bacons?"

"A long time. My family has worked for them since the eighteenth century."

At this point, my antenna rose like a shirtless wrestler's nipples in a blizzard. I wasn't sure how to ask this question delicately so I let it tumble out, my inhibitions lowered by the rum

I'd imbibed.

"Were your ancestors slaves?"

Ahead of me he had been walking, the rubber soles of his black shoes lightly echoing in the large space. He stopped. A monstrous silence reigned as if all the workers, tourists, even Florence, had frozen in place in anticipation of Gilroy's reaction to my incendiary inquiry.

The wedding band on his left hand glinted, catching some unseen source of light. Somewhere a compressor hissed. The sweet smell of liquor and wood permeated everything. What did Gilroy's wife think every night when he came home smelling of booze? Did she accept this as his job? Why would anyone keep working for someone who had enslaved your family? I didn't quite have the nerve to ask that question.

"I'm sorry, but what is your name again?"

Had he really forgotten my name after viewing my driver's license and asking Harold about me?

"Boise Montague. Did I say something wrong?"

"It's a delicate subject."

"Slavery or your family?" I asked.

He continued down the passage, passing cask after cask until we came to another area where the bottling took place. There were barrels set on their sides and tapped. A woman filled the bottles by hand and placed them on a conveyor belt that sent them along and sealed the caps.

"Here is where our spiced and select dark rums are bottled by hand, as the label states." He pointed at the bottom of one of the bottles that had just come off the conveyor and was being placed in a cardboard box by another woman. This woman wore a mask over her face.

"Why the mask?" I whispered.

"She has a cold. That's why she's not pouring today. We don't want any contamination. Bottles are already sealed at this point, so we're safe. She needs the hours, right, Yarey?"

"Hello, Dad."

"This is your daughter?"

"Yes. The next generation. We are proud of our association with this fine distillery and getting prouder all the time. We built this place." He raised his hands like a preacher in his pulpit on Sunday morning. Light filtered through a ventilation opening high above. "I want to keep it going for the future. I am teaching Yarey each of the jobs so someday she can oversee things."

"Oversee," I muttered. "Interesting term."

"Excuse me?"

"Nothing, nothing. You never answered me, Gilroy. May I call you Roy?"

"No, you may not. I don't like that moniker."

Touchy. This guy was going along, but I wasn't sure why at this point.

"Are you receiving reparations from the Bacons?"

We were now headed upstairs to his office. "Before we go any further with this interrogation, I have a phone call to return. If you'll excuse me."

"No problem here. Do you have a vending machine?"

He directed me to a room with cheap cafeteria-style tables and three machines. Peanut butter crackers and a bag of Cheetos, the cornerstone of any nutritious meal. Back in the office, Gilroy was finishing up his call. The place smelled like a banana factory, but I saw no fruit anywhere.

"Harold says I should tell you whatever you want to know." He took a swig from a gold flask, then capped it and dropped it back in a desk drawer. Next, he pulled an e-cigarette out of his shirt pocket and puffed away. The vapor smelled of banana. He blew the smoke directly toward me. No regard. Passive-aggressive. All right.

I'd go along to get along, but I couldn't help a tone of annoyance entering my voice. "Yeah, so what about your ancestors and the reparations I asked about?"

He sighed and pondered the mess of papers tacked to a corkboard. To the left was a large window that looked down on the floor below where the workers milled about; ants on an anthill. A laminated card specifying workers' rights and the current year's minimum hourly wage was tacked to the wall adjacent to the corkboard. One of those motivational posters showing a breaking wave hung above his desk.

On the opposite wall, behind me, was a giant canvas of what appeared to be an original painting. A landscape of a plantation. In the center bottom of the vast, green expanse of sugar cane stood a white woman wearing a sun hat tied around her chin. Next to her a black man, no doubt a slave, shirtless in pants held up with rope. He on bended knee holding something, perhaps a piece of sugar cane, up to her as an offering. While the background of the painting gave one a sense of oneness with nature, like the feeling from William Wordsworth, the foreground snatched that away, forcing you to face the grim reality of human relations. I suspect that was not the painter's intent, but there it was.

Some of the articles I'd happened across while researching the years of slavery in the Caribbean alluded to this idealized world that the wealthy landowners tried to propagate through art and literature of the mid-1800s when abolitionists attacked with fervor the sale and torturous nature of the slave trade in gory detail through leaflets and other propaganda. Until the public outcry back in France, England, and other European nations could no longer be ignored.

"Yes, I come from slaves. I do not enjoy discussing this with people outside those close to me. My tribe as it were. What are you, Polynesian?"

Here we go again. "No, I'm white and African."

He threw me a skeptical look, then continued. "Fine. Yes, I'm from slaves, but my family was always keen to maintain their pride and quickly rose out of that life once given a chance. It was difficult as those of African heritage were always kept down by the

Europeans, but intelligence eventually won out and we rose to managerial positions. We have passed along our knowledge. I am lucky my offspring wish to continue to learn what turned out to be the family business. It was destiny. A long, slow bend to justice. I intend to own my own distillery. Rum from the Caribe region will always be sought after and small distilleries are becoming more and more fashionable with the wealthy tech-savvy crowd. I have already been doing small batches in my yard and selling much to Silicon Beach."

Silicon Beach was a region along the coast of West Los Angeles that had grown in recent years into a smaller version of Silicon Valley. Many wealthy, young men and women with technology backgrounds had moved there, frequented the watering holes and had so much disposable income, even with the sky-rocketing housing costs, they could spend freely on luxury items like craft beers and aged cheeses from around the world. Spirits would apparently join the fray.

"Sounds like you have a conflict of interest here," I said.

"No," he said with a smirk. "I am insignificant when compared to the commercial prowess of Bacon Rum. See, what Francine and the Bacon family have are deep pockets. I have no such luxury. My business loses money every month and probably will for years. It is for my children and grandchildren, so they have access to the means of production. So they do not have to rely on others for work. That is my dream."

A dream can get you into trouble. He had a determined look. The face of a man on a mission to better his station. Sometimes, the cost could be one's soul.

"You still haven't answered my other question. Are you part of the reparations that Francine Bacon decided to pay on behalf of her family?"

"Yes, I was interviewed by a reporter about my family history."

"Was his name Adirondack Kendal?"

179

"Yes. Kendal. I told him that Francine Bacon knew my family history in the business. Mr. Bacon made sure everyone knew the deal, especially when he was dying. He wanted to make sure nothing happened to our position in the company."

"You are referring to Francine's husband, Dominic Bacon?" I had read about him in the notes from Kendal, as well as in some of my research online. "Sounds like you miss him?"

"Dominic was a complex man. He was hard, yes, but fair. Yes, I suppose I miss him."

He gazed out the window at the storage area and the bottling going on below. Something wasn't right. There was a sadness in the man's eyes, like the golden rays of the sun. Some kind of personal connection Gilroy didn't want to discuss. Perhaps Dominic Bacon was more of a father figure to Gilroy than he wanted to let on. It would explain why he stayed here.

I plucked a business card from the holder on the corner of his desk. It read: "Gilroy Antsy, Operations Manager."

"Is there anything else, Mr. Montague?"

"Do you know the status of your reparations payment or what you expect to receive?"

"There are rumors circulating around between those of us who have a, shall we say, history here. They apparently located others but most of the payments are going to workers. The family has a loyal following."

"Despite the fact that they were slavers?"

"They were not slavers. They were only doing what everyone at the time did. A lot of money and resources were tied up in the laborers purchased. Freeing everyone nearly bankrupted this company and many others. Our loyalty and patience are finally being rewarded."

"Forgive me, but I'm just having trouble understanding why someone like you would stay."

"Pardon me? Someone like me?"

"You are well-educated and in a managerial position. I bet

you've had this position a long time, correct?"

He nodded.

"Is there anywhere to go from here in this company?"

"Not really. Owner of a distillery and as I've said, I'm already doing that."

"Yes, but you make no profit and you cannot truly put your energy into it. To me, you should own this distillery." I stomped my tennis shoe lightly on the floor. "Wouldn't that be fair as your reparations? You could have asked Francine for that. She seemed to be in a very generous mood the last couple years. Any idea what brought that on?"

He stood and shoved both hands into his pockets. "I'm not interested in owning Bacon Rum."

"Why not?" I asked. "You mean if Francine Bacon offered you Bacon Rum you'd say no?"

"Don't be ridiculous. That is not a possibility. She is not offering me Bacon Rum. She is not offering...her offer is fair."

"Oh, so you do know what the reparations entail?"

"I think half-a-million is the amount or the total value. Might not be all cash. That's a rumor."

"Lots of rumors floating around. The others are dwelling on this a lot apparently."

"Of course they are," he said, raising his voice. "It's more money than any of these people would ever see in two lifetimes. It would change everything or maybe nothing. Most of them are still stuck in a slave's mentality. They don't have the emotional capability to break out no matter how much money you hand them."

"I understand. And you deserve to have things change. Right? You've put in years of service to both Francine and Dominic. You know what to do with the means of production."

He spun around and slammed his hand on his desk. "You're goddamn right I have! My sweat is on every conveyor belt, shelf, and plank in this place. My sweat and blood!"

"And now Yarey's too, right? You let her become part of this."

"That's what it takes. It's what we know. We are distillers. She can learn from me, not waste money on useless college degrees or thoughtful platitudes. I read. Books. On my own. I learn with these and these." He held out his hands and pointed at his eyes. "In the real world you are learning every second if you pay attention. I don't need anyone to give me instructions or a syllabus to become a better man. This is the best there is. There is nothing out there." He pointed emphatically at the window.

"Right, right. You're right. Most college people don't know shit about the real world."

"Yes. That is right. That is right. Yes. You understand. I'm surprised. They don't know anything about reality. About pain. About love. Schools cannot teach you that. And this singing."

"Singing?"

Now he was making eye contact and speaking with the authority of an expert. He was in an arena where he was in charge. Like a bull, he plowed ahead. These were his deepest convictions, vocalized to a stranger. Sometimes strangers were the only ones people felt comfortable talking to.

"Yarey. She's got this thing about singing." His hands were on and off his hips with each new declaration. "She has a performance at Reichhold Center tonight. She does silly gospel music and sings in a choir."

He now stood at the window looking below. I seized the opportunity to read some of the stuff tacked to his cork board and glance at his desk. All of it related to molasses production and distilling everything from rum to whiskey to sake. The way he spoke now shoved me far away, like the man was talking to himself while I wore earplugs and listened from the closet.

He mumbled something indecipherable, then more forcefully said, "Time to put childish things away. She's twenty-one. I was already a father at her age."

He turned around and I twisted in the chair, acting like I'd leaned forward to crack my back. He didn't seem to notice or care. My stomach was grinding away on the alcohol and the crackers weren't enough to soak it all up. I'd been here a long time.

"Can't she have a hobby and still move forward in her work?" I offered.

"You sound like my wife. That's not an option. This money is not enough for her to become complacent. And she makes no money from this so-called hobby. She thinks she's going to be another Susan Potts."

I had no idea who Susan Potts was, although I had a vague recollection of seeing a talent show with someone called Paul Potts.

"Do you only get money as a family or do each of you get money?"

"Direct descendants. She gets it and I get it. My wife's not part of that lineage."

"It seems like there would be a lot of people who were part of this lineage, but from what I know it's under fifty."

"That's an easy answer: most slaves who worked on sugar plantations died. These islands were brutal to my people. Tropical diseases and immorality run amok. Brutal. They didn't procreate, they didn't have families, they just worked and died."

He paced from his desk to the window and back. "Do you know what tonight is?"

"Your daughter's show?"

"Wednesday."

"Yes."

"Do you know who plays at The Reichold Center on Wednesday?"

I shrugged, not sure where he was going with this. He emphatically wagged his finger.

"Exactly. Nobody plays on Wednesday."

CHAPTER 24

Junior Bacon wanted to go out, but he could hear his father's voice ballooning out of Aunt Hillary's room. He was halfway down the spiral staircase, when curiosity got the better of him. Returning to his room, he came out with a glass he'd used for water before bed the night before. He checked for Wilma, but she was not up here. Probably in the kitchen.

Whipping out his phone he texted Boise that he'd be running late and to order his meal to go. Something vegetarian with fries. Beans and rice would also be good.

Stuffing the phone back into his pocket, he creeped to the thick door to Aunt Hill's room and gently, ever so gently, propped the mouth of the glass against the wood. Moving the glass around slowly, he found a spot where he could make out some of their conversation.

"We are not to discuss that and are not discussing that when he's here," Herbie said. "Do you understand?"

"Ow! You asshole, that hurt. You better watch out. I'm not Junior. You can't manhandle me like that."

"What are you gonna do about it?"

After that the room got silent. He supposed they'd stopped talking or had started whispering. He could hear harsh tones from his father and Hillary laughing.

"...drunk?" Herbie said. "What has gotten into you? You are becoming more and more like one of these islanders."

"You aren't an islander?"

"Not anymore. Not if we don't stop this mess. What got into her?"

Hillary laughed, then snorted. "You could never control mama. She controlled you. You were always a little boy to her. Hell, we're all still children to her. She's controlling things even from the grave."

Suddenly, a yell came from downstairs. "Miss Hillary, Mister Herbie! I have your supper ready. You want me to serve it?"

Shit, Wilma, was yelling for dinner. Before he could move, footsteps approached the door. Junior tried to palm the glass, but it crashed to the floor, shattering on the tile. He let out a startled yelp as his father unlocked and opened the door, filling the doorway.

"Hello, Junior. Why are you breaking glasses outside Aunt Hillary's bedroom?"

"Uh, sorry papa. I was...uh...taking this glass back to the kitchen from my room. I had a glass of water last night and I was going to tell you that I'm leaving for Yarelle's performance."

Herbie licked his lips. Junior could see every pore on his father's face along with each individual hair going backwards from his receding hairline. He wiped perspiration from his upper lip, then stammered on. "Be careful, Papa. Let me get a broom, and I'll clean this up."

Wilma came to the top of the stairs. "Oh goodness, look at this mess. Mr. Herbie, stay in the room, you are barefoot."

At this Hillary shot up behind Herbie and bumped him forward. "What's happening? Oops!"

Herbie howled as he stumbled and stepped on a sliver.

"Papa!" Junior cried.

"Son of a…" Herbie's face contorted in pain as he hopped backward into Hillary's bedroom and dropped on the bed, his foot raised. Blood flowed from the small gash. Upon seeing the blood, Hillary swooned and fell to the floor. Junior's breathing accelerated as thoughts of his last brush with blood flooded his memory, the arrow protruding from Kendal's chest.

Wilma entered, calmly crossed to the bathroom and returned with a wad of toilet paper. She plucked the sliver from the wound, then staunched the blood. Herbie howled again, slamming his fist against the headboard.

"Hold that," Wilma intoned, taking Herbie's hand and placing it around the toilet paper.

"It hurts!" he cried, then lowered the pitch of his voice. "Goddammit! Hillary, what is your problem?"

"Miss Hillary is on the floor. She unconscious, Mr. Herbie."

The anger left his voice. "What? Is she okay?"

Wilma leaned over to check Hillary's pulse and breathing. "She fine. She faint."

At this Herbie rolled his eyes. "Again?"

"Yes, she faint again."

"Junior?"

Junior's eyes drifted far away, his legs bunched against his chest as he rocked.

"Junior is just sittin'."

"What do you mean, just sitting?"

"He sittin' on the floor. Just sittin'."

At this, Herbie started to sit up.

"No, don't sit up. You need to keep your foot raised. I don't

186

think you need stitches, but you want to keep it raised till the bleeding stop."

"Fine," he muttered.

He turned his body so he could see off the side of the bed, while still reclining. His foot stuck in the air and swayed like a palm tree on a beach. Junior continued to rock, and Hillary looked peaceful. Thankfully she seemed to excel at fainting on rugs, away from hard objects.

Wilma straightened out Hillary's leg, then gently, but firmly gripped Junior's shoulder. "Junior? Junior?"

"Just yell at him! What kind of crap is this? He causes this mess then checks out like some kind of baby?"

"He ain't acting like a baby. He's in shock or having some reaction. Me don't know why," Wilma said, now rubbing the young man's back. Slowly, Junior's eyes returned from whatever far off place they'd gone.

He squeezed Wilma's hand, then stood and approached the bedside.

"Papa, I'm sorry about that. I dropped that glass."

"Junior, that boarding school is making you soft. What were you doing sitting there and rocking back and forth?"

"I don't know, sir." Junior looked at his phone. "It's getting late. I've got to go. I'll clean the glass."

"No you will not. Wilma, get to cleaning that glass."

Wilma, who had been trying to revive Hillary, rose and pivoted. "You a rude man."

"Because I asked you to do your job, I'm rude?"

"No, you rude because you rude. You talk down. Mrs. Francine, does not talk down."

With that, Wilma left the room. Hillary groaned. Junior helped her into a chair.

"Auntie, are you okay?"

"What happened?" she asked, shaking her head.

"You fainted again," Herbie spat. "You need to get a hold of yourself."

Junior, sensing the rising tension, excused himself and rushed downstairs. Wilma had the broom and dustpan in hand, but Junior would hear none of it.

"I got it, Wilma. My mess."

She patted him on the cheek, "You a good boy. Not like them. You are lucky to be away at the boarding school, you know that?"

"Why's that?"

"You don't have to live every second in a house fill wid all these secrets and lies."

CHAPTER 25

The box office at The Reichhold Center for the Arts sold Junior and me two tickets to Yarey's show. They were good seats and not expensive, which made me think that perhaps Gilroy was right, this was not a way for Yarey to make a living. But, he was wrong in that without arts, many people felt lost, and that feeling could be as bad as poverty.

Junior and I milled about, admiring the romantic feel of the amphitheater. The evening was surprisingly cool and a light breeze tickled my skin. Junior had been late so I'd brought his food in a to-go bag that we took in the cab he showed up in. It filled the car with the enticing smell of fried fish and fries. On the way, I glimpsed Patrick Roberts' law office and thought about Roger and Elias again. Father and son. Dead and alive.

Before things got even more strained between us I needed to call Elias. After shooting a quick hello-text to him, I turned back to Junior as he examined a message on his phone. Elias was right. Junior's eerie stillness could be unnerving. At first, I chalked it up to his beyond-his-years maturity, but now it started to strike me as a primal freeze, as in fight, flight or freeze. Besides, when he argued with his family about getting into the business and his behavior around his father in particular, he didn't strike me as all that mature. He was stuck in some emotional loop, probably caused by his father's overbearing nature and lack of compassion.

"You believe he said that?"

He looked up. "Huh?"

"Gilroy. He said that. What're you doing on your phone?"

"Nothing. Oh, right, Gilroy." Junior pocketed the ticket he'd bought. "He used to be cooler, but something changed. The guy got more intense the last few years, you ask me. They used to be friendly, but Harold doesn't like him anymore. It's all business with him now."

"All business. That's accurate," I said, rubbing my stubble.

"You know there's an art exhibit down below?"

"Aren't you hungry?" I asked. "We can sit now and you can eat."

"I want you to see this. I'm fine. I'll eat during the show. Thanks for the food, but remember I'm vegetarian?"

"You from here and don't eat fish? Really?"

"I'm allowed to eat whatever I wish, Boise. I'll eat it since they're already dead and battered, but I texted you what I wanted."

"They didn't have any beans and rice. I did what I could."

Junior led me down to an art gallery on the lower level. We ambled through the African Art section, then circled back up in time to take our seats.

A tall woman with her hair wrapped in colorful dressings sat in front of me.

"I'm always the lucky short guy," I grumbled.

The woman's tiny daughter sat in front of Junior. He leaned

over and whispered, "Bummer, dude."

Using both hands, she adjusted the mass of fabric and hair. I wondered if carrying all that around on your head all day was healthy. Did she get headaches? My hair follicles ached at the end of the day from my hat, but it only weighed a few ounces.

I removed my hat to make it easier on whoever was behind me. Leaning towards Junior and scrunching down a bit gave me a better angle. He smelled faintly of weed.

"You smoking with Harold today?" I asked in a hushed tone.

He shook his head. Lying about something that small, especially when I'd seen them do it before also struck me as immature if not outright deceptive.

The show lasted about an hour and twenty minutes. The choir was fairly standard, but one singer who performed a solo had range, hitting some high notes with feeling. She was also physically stunning: Alicia Keys eyes, braided locks, a high forehead and shimmering skin.

After the show, my luck held as we found Yarey standing next to the solo-singing beauty in the stone courtyard, meeting and greeting the assembled masses as clouds slipped gently over the full moon. When the crowd died down, we made our way over to the pair.

Yarey hugged Junior and commented on how much he'd grown up since she last saw him.

"You never come by the distillery anymore. I thought it was your passion."

"They shipped me off to boarding school," he said with a shrug. "So much for passion."

An awkward silence settled before Yarey turned to me. "You look familiar. Did we meet recently?"

"I was with your father today at the distillery."

"Oh, right, the investigator."

When she said this, Alicia Keys turned from speaking to an older man and eyed me with her sultry, half-closed lids.

"What do you mean 'investigator?'" she asked. Her red and black dress spun around her full hips in a wide arc, making her even more angelic. She looked to be about twenty-five.

"I'm a private eye," I said, extending my hand. "You have a lovely voice." I sounded like an idiot, but forced myself on. This was only the second woman I'd taken real notice of since Evelyn passed. Eventually I needed to get back out there.

Yarey laughed. "Yeah, it looks like it's her voice you like."

I blushed, and the singer patted my cheek. "You are cute for an investigator. You sure the criminals are gonna take you seriously with your baby face?"

"You've got a point there," I said. "Not much I can do about that. I'd like to think underestimating me would be an advantage."

"You could get in a knife fight and hope for a gash across the bow here." She ran a long fingernail along my left cheek. An electric jolt shot through me. She pulled away, her perfect lips parting. "Sorry, it's just, being an investigator must be exciting and dangerous."

"Being a singer entails some excitement, right?"

"It has its moments, like this. But most days it's standing alone in a room practicing notes, drinking honey and tea, and making sure I stay healthy." She squinched up her nose and leaned close. "I had to quit smoking entirely. You believe that shit?"

"You don't have to do anything, do you?"

She laughed. "No, I don't." she said. "You have a light?" She pulled a menthol cigarette out of her purse.

"Hang on." Spotting a woman behind her smoking, I procured her lighter.

"Thank you," she sighed through a stream of smoke.

Junior and Yarey continued to talk. I vaguely remembered that my real purpose was to pump Yarey for information, but I couldn't tear myself away from this beautiful woman, who in some shocking plot development bothered to speak to me.

Holding up the program, I found her photo and a brief

192

description of her training and other performances. It seemed she preferred jazz and hip-hop to gospel. Her name was Anna Lynn.

"Yeah, but a good singer doesn't pigeon-hole herself, right? I'll bet you investigate more than one type of crime."

"Is Anna Lynn your stage name?"

"Wouldn't you like to know," she giggled, sipping on a plastic glass of Chardonnay.

"This is nice," I said, referring to the refreshments and cheese plates. "Do they always do this?"

"Are you kidding? This cheap-ass place normally does nothing, but my manager's trying to class up the joint when I perform. My latest contract demands that some kind of beverages and food, not in a bag, be served following any performance. That's how you build a following. See that brother with the iPad?"

She pointed through the crowd at a forty-something-year-old mustachioed man shaking hands with a white couple. The woman wore a black sequined gown, the man a tux.

"Those two are some of the richest art patrons in the islands. They actually know a lot about the history of jazz and gospel. Getting them on board could launch me into orbit."

"Do you write?" I asked.

"Both lyrics and music. I play the piano."

"Another Alicia Keys, huh?"

She rolled her eyes and nudged Yarey. "He just went there."

Yarey laughed. "I hope you didn't just compare this unique flower to that singer with all those Grammys."

"What? You mean you dislike being compared to beautiful people who are extraordinarily successful. My apologies."

"How'd you like to be called Tom Selleck all day long?"

"I like Magnum, P.I. That's a worthy comparison."

She pushed her hand into my face. "Uh-huh. Believe you me, it gets old. It's like your better-looking, more successful sister who always overshadows you. No can do, my brother. You can make it up by getting me another glass." She turned her wineglass-shaped cup upside down

Her manager wandered over.

"This guy's an investigator," she said, taking the drink and patting her manager on his muscled shoulder. The guy's mustache and hair were perfectly groomed. He bowed slightly and shook my hand with a wide grin.

"My pleasure to make your acquaintance. I'm Oba. You have a great look, brother. I like the hat. What do you drive?"

"I'm not much of a car guy."

"Ah yes. Keeping it simple. I like this."

He sounded like he hailed from a West African nation. His accent flowed with a natural cadence that loosely resembled the Queen's English.

"You're Anna's manager?" I asked.

"I'm that, and more." He leaned over and gave her a thick kiss. Anna didn't kiss back with much enthusiasm.

"What did I tell you, Oba?"

"Yes, yes, my queen. No public displays, I understand, but when you look so ravishing, how can I resist?" He grinned again and her demeanor relaxed.

"I want to be taken seriously as an artist, which means we must be…"

He turned to me and asked, "Artists are passionate, no?"

She walked away, typing something into her phone.

"I'm not sure my opinion carries much weight," I said.

He bowed again and said, "A pleasure again, Mr. Montague." He kissed Yarey on her hand. "And you, Miss Yarey."

When he was out of earshot, Yarey said to Junior and me, "That guy's such a tease. You have to watch him. And, he's not discerning, if you get my drift."

Junior looked lost, so I said, "He likes men and women."

"Oh. Riiiight," Junior intoned.

"He's okay with either, both, or trans too."

I turned back to her. "He likes trans? What about nonbinary?"

Yarey snapped her fingers. "Look at the big brain on Boise! You down with the modern sexuality."

"I lived in L.A."

She nodded as if this explained everything.

"Where?"

"The westside, a little south of Santa Monica."

She continued nodding. "Very cool. Why are you here?"

I explained briefly my reasons for returning, mainly the death of Evelyn and how I was from St. Thomas. I left out salient details that might scare a young lady upon meeting me for the first time, like the fact that the sheriff in LA County was on the verge of arresting me for interfering in an official investigation.

I continued, "I guess to get away from the craziness. I don't know. Run back home?"

"St. Thomas makes you feel safe?" she questioned with raised eyebrows.

"What's that mean?"

"There's a lot of death here. A lot of crime. Not enough work or opportunity."

"For a crime-fighter like myself, it's perfect, right?"

This made her smile, and what a smile it was. Gentle as the tide on a warm summer night at Magen's Bay. Perhaps I'd overlooked Yarey's understated beauty.

"What about you?" I asked.

"Me. I'm boring," Yarey said. "From this rock, and I still here."

"Don't insult my home," I said. She laughed. The theater crowd had dwindled. "Didn't your dad come?"

Her face plunged. "Could we not talk about him?"

"Sure, sure," I said. "You sounded great." Too late. She had that far-away look people got when thinking about loss. In her case, she had lost her father's pride. He didn't even come in faux solidarity, just to show he cared. Being right was more important to Gilroy Antsy than showing his daughter he loved her.

Junior patted her awkwardly on the shoulder. She stared down at the floor for a moment, then said, "I'm going to go change."

"Yarey ... " Junior intoned.

She waved him off and headed backstage. Still looking at her phone, Anna soon followed. When they came out twenty minutes later, Anna scolded us.

"Wha'd you idiots have to ask about that man for? Which of you fools asked?"

I sheepishly raised my hand. Right then, Yarey skipped out and exclaimed, "So, where we going?"

"Hey, Yarey, I'm sorry."

"Forget it!" She exclaimed, rubbing her nose. "Let's go, I'm ready for some real music and dancing."

We piled into Oba's SUV and he zipped through the streets with practiced ease. We arrived at Mojo's, a surf shack and nightclub not far from my office in the Port of Sale Mall. The place was already going strong, Calypso music bouncing off the walls as ladies ground their hips suggestively around drooling men in shorts holding Corona bottles aloft like mistletoe.

Oba insisted on buying the first round and I elected to have whatever Anna recommended. In short order I was gulping down a rum punch, heavy on the guava juice. Not typically a keen dancer, after two large glasses even my hips loosened and we all gyrated. Everyone except Junior. Not even Yarey's pleas could get him out of his chair. He sipped his drink and excused himself outside. When he returned, he stunk like a skunk and Anna asked if he had any more. They ventured back out. I followed, mostly to keep an eye on Junior, which Yarey insisted was sweet.

"He could use a big brother," she announced to Oba, who spread his patented grin.

Junior was stretched out on a thick stone wall, watching a chubby guy in a bowling shirt and flip-flops, argue with his cauliflower-armed wife about whether he was sober enough to drive. Anna lounged behind him, contemplating the dark storefronts of the mall. Somehow, she managed to look elegant smoking a joint on a stone wall outside a divey surf bar.

Yarey trailed me out. She refused a toke. I decided to stick with my rum buzz as well, but settled down next to Anna to enjoy the earthy smell of the weed. Yarey giggled at something Anna whispered. I asked what was so funny.

"Nothing. She just said something about my dad having a stick up his ass like a scarecrow, but you know what?" She paused, then said, "Of course you don't know, silly, how could you! I've never seen a scarecrow. Least ways not for reals. Aren't they in corn fields in Kansas?"

"I suppose they could be anywhere you want to scare birds away from messing with crops." I pointed at the joint. "Probably good for keeping pests away from marijuana crops too."

She laughed. "You call yourself a detective. What would birds want with weed? You don't eat it."

I wanted to tell her to go fuck herself for questioning my detective credentials, but she was right, birds didn't eat weed. A piece of advice from my estranged uncle when I was eleven: don't insult a beautiful woman until after she sleeps with you. He was a church-goer.

Anna continued to stare at the buildings, a sobering expression playing on her face while Junior people-watched the crowd milling about the entrance. The place was packed for a Wednesday.

"Is tonight some kind of ladies' night?"

"Nah," Anna said. "Just locals started coming here after eight a couple years now. Shit, this is quiet."

An island breeze swept through, drying the light, yet constant film of moisture on my skin. The hairs on my arms prickled, and I knew it was time.

"Yarey, can I ask you about your dad?"

Anna piped up. "Shit man, you're killing my buzz." With that she got up and went back inside. Junior rolled over and gazed at the sky. Even in this well-lit parking lot, you could see more stars here than in the darkest recesses of Los Angeles. That was one of many things I'd taken for granted when I lived here, the immense natural beauty, real darkness, and genuine, almost noisy silence. The kind of silence that made you believe you were hearing the last remnants of the Big Bang.

"What about him?" Yarey asked.

"Did Junior tell you what I'm up to?"

"I know a little. I mean you don't have to be a genius to know when an investigator is helping a family after someone died suspiciously."

"Bingo. Your dad said you and he were both part of the reparations package Francine put together."

"Yes, far as I know we are."

"Has he given you instruction on your share?"

"If you're asking whether he has designs on my money, I think he wants me to invest it in his distillery and stay in that business. Is that what you mean?" She looked confused and unsure how much to tell me.

"Listen, Yarey, I'm not trying to pry into your finances, but I need information on people who were financially involved with Francine because that's always a potential conflict with the victim and might lead me to the killer."

"How can you be sure she was murdered? I heard she drowned."

"You think it was just an accident?"

"Isn't it possible?" she posited.

Junior listened, then chimed in. "Yarey, you can help Boise. I hired him to figure this out. If he's asking, it's to find out what happened, even if it was an accident. How'd she get out to the water and drown? I'd like to know, and so would Harold."

She snorted softly. "Funny you don't mention your father or

aunt."

Junior looked at me, his bloodshot eyes drooping under the weight of the THC. "Guess I'm not sure they really care. They're interested in moving on. Taking care of themselves."

"My dad wants me to learn the distillery business so I can take over someday and build this empire he imagines. Always on about the means of production, whatever that is. I read Cliffnotes on Marx. Still don't get it. But, he's probably right, I should just stick with what our family knows. I've learned a lot and understand the process all right. I've worked there since I was eighteen."

"You can work at a distillery at eighteen?"

"Sure, you just can't drink any of it. Least not out in the open."

"Sounds like you would do it because it's the smart thing, but what do you want?"

She opened her mouth and released a gentle note, like a finch flitting out of a golden cage.

"I could make a record. Move to a city. Get started." She hung her head a little. "But, that's not smart. It's a pipe dream. The odds are astronomical."

"Astronomical. Like the stars," Junior said wistfully as he blew smoke into the night. "Me, sometimes I think I'd like to be part of the darkness between the stars. You know, just disappear from all of it."

The smoke dissipated while I looked into the darkness between the stars and considered whether I'd ever had a fantasy career that lit me up the way Yarey was lit by her dream of being a singer. My path had been much more practical and survivalist. If my parents had given more practical guidance—really any guidance, perhaps I'd feel differently. My father yelled at me mostly in a drunken rage and my mother maintained an iron demeanor of passive resistance to all of life's minor tortures. We existed in a permanent state of crisis until he died and she flitted off to be free of his anger, yet ruled by it.

Freedom was my dream, and now I was living it. I'd left my mother behind by coming back here. She hated the islands and had sworn never to return. When I came back, she cursed me under her breath, like a woman curses her child's killer as she watches him hanged on the gallows.

"It is astronomical. Dreams are like that. High risk, high reward investments," I said.

I wanted to continue and tell her something you'd hear at a commencement address about setting the world on fire with your passion. That nothing could stop a will that's true. Like an arrow. But none of that came to me and if it did, I didn't really believe it anymore.

"Your father has big plans for that money and for your family."

"He's been like this the last few years. He got it in his head to strike out and create one of the dynasties like the Vanderbilts or Rockefellers. You know that story about shirt-sleeves to shirt-sleeves in three generations?"

"No," I said.

"It's some kind of saying about families who inherit wealth lose it all because the kids are spoiled. Dad was obsessed with that idea. He wanted to build it and for me to grow it. He loves to say, 'that's what it takes, Yarelle.'"

"How was his relationship with Francine?"

"He was devoted to her, but mostly to suck knowledge from her. The Bacons amassed wealth. Not Rockefeller wealth, but they did well. Dad didn't like how they did it with slavery. He respected what she was trying to do to repair damages."

"You mean the reparations."

"Yes, those. But there was something else."

Junior leaned up on his elbow and offered her the joint. She tugged and puffed, then handed it back.

"What was that?" he asked.

"He didn't trust kindness. I don't know how else to say it. He thinks people are untrustworthy and kindness is a disguise to get something or use you."

"That's a dark position," Junior said. "I don't think my grandma was like that."

"I don't know about that, but she was trying anyway. She didn't have to do anything," I said. I looked back at Yarey. "Right?"

"I want to sing, that's what I know. I also know that your grandfather wasn't such a great guy. He was all about holding on to that wealth for the family. Your grandmother was giving it away and rich people don't stay rich giving it away. It went against everything your grandfather believed."

Anna reappeared from inside and took a drag from Junior's joint.

As she handed it back, Junior said, "My grandmother was her own person. That's what it means. But that doesn't mean she was right."

"Maybe she died for being so…" I couldn't think of how to say it. "…I don't know…herself?"

A pearl-colored Mercedes pulled up in front of us. The passenger door shoved open and there was Gilroy.

"Get in!" He barked at Yarey.

She, like Junior, had a frozen look as she walked over zombie-like and got into the car. Her father glared at me a moment. Before the door slammed shut, all I saw was the reflection of Mojo's surfboard sign in the dark tint.

"Does this happen often?" I asked Anna.

"Yeah, it happens. Shit happens. These men." She jumped up, threw the remainder of the joint into an ornamental hedge and declared, "Let's get back to it." She took my hand and dragged me back inside where we danced and drank.

Mojo's closed at eleven. We went to Junior's house and snuck into the backyard. It was so quiet you could hear the ants digging holes.

"Your family turn in early every night?" I asked.

"No, but recently everyone seems to be doing their own thing. Whether they go out, isolate in their room, or whatever. Harold's probably out with some girl."

He went to the kitchen and brought out a bottle of brandy. We sipped it and watched the stars in the impossibly black sky. Anna dozed off on a lounge chair, her hair gently swaying like a palm in the ocean breeze. The perfumed scent of a flower drifted by.

"Wasn't Herbie sending you back to school soon?" I asked Junior.

"He threatens." He looked like he wanted to say more, but stopped himself. "He's not a good guy," Junior mumbled in a drunken, half-asleep tone.

"Your father?"

"Gilroy, man. He's…I don't know…not right or something and I should know."

"I'm gonna need more than that."

"Well, just last few years really, he got hotter."

"Perhaps he was always like that, just got less interested in hiding it. Frustration can do that."

"Frustration?"

"I get the feeling he was promised something by one of your grandparents that he never got."

"Like what?"

"You think Harold or the others would know?"

"I'll ask and get back with you tomorrow."

***

Back at The Manner, Lucy lounged on the enclosed porch upstairs. She shuffled cards absentmindedly by the light of a kerosene lamp. It reminded me of an old painting housed in the

The Getty Center Museum of a philosopher-scientist studying the orbits of the planets with a compass by a single candle.

"You're up late," I said as I cut through to get to my room. She nodded. I stopped. The breeze buoyed me as I leaned against the wooden railing. Crickets chirped in the light breeze of dark morning.

Below us, Charlotte Amalie spread away to the black sea at Waterfront. Even in a small place like St. Thomas, there were always lights dotting the hillsides or peeking out of buildings at all hours. A stripped metal awning extended over the porch that could be lowered during hurricanes for added metal protection from the cataclysmic winds.

Strangely, I felt comfortable here with my landlady, amongst the chirping crickets and soft shuffle of her Bicycle cards. Lucy and Marge hosted a friendly poker game on Wednesday nights for the guests and a few close friends. Lucy dealt and Marge filled drinks and food orders. The bar-restaurant had recently begun to get busier with non-guesthouse patrons as word spread about the happy hour and good food at reasonable prices.

"This private detective from Georgia asked about a poker game this week. Should I have sent him over?"

Lucy shook her head. "No. We got da people we like. Might be we need to hire a cook or a waiter," she said. "Marge don't like that idea."

"Why not?"

"She like it just be us."

"I get that," I said, shifting my weight awkwardly from one foot to the other. My knee ached from dancing.

"But we growin' and I tired of doin' everything myself. This business ain't easy, you know."

"If you want my opinion, hire a bartender or waiter, not a cook. You and Marge are already too good at that."

She smiled, never looking up from the cards in her lap. "That's nice for you to say, Boise. But cook is the cheapest.

Besides, I don't want give up tips."

How could I argue with that? I was tired but not sleepy. Too many factors rattling around, and I still didn't have the hold on things I had hoped to have by now. Was it the family? Was it someone in the business? Was Francine's killing simply an accident followed by Kendal's because he had figured something out? If that was the case, why hadn't he gone straight to the police, rather than set up a meet with Junior. All illogical, but then again, human beings were illogical. The killings had to be related.

"Me don't like the night," Lucy said above the quiet din of her shuffling.

"Why don't you turn on some more lights? It'll feel less like night."

Lucy did a thing where she fanned out the cards and popped one out of the deck. She could do things with cards like some of the magicians.

I was about to ask where she learned to do that, when she said, "Lights don't take away the night. Trying to pretend it's not night impossible. I don't see the night, I *feel* the night. It heavy. Me don't like it. It's why I can't sleep. I sit up, waiting for it to be over."

CHAPTER 26

The mixed drinks at Mojo's were made with cheap liquor. Really cheap liquor. I could usually drink any damn thing and a lot of it. My eyes felt like there were tiny strings with tiny dumbbells hanging off the tiny strings pulling down on my eyelids. It felt like that all damn day. Coffee didn't help. A cold shower didn't help—it may have even made me sleepier.

Slapping myself only made my eyes bulge, causing Lucy to comment that I looked more intense than usual as I walked through the lobby on the way out. Despite having still been on the porch shuffling cards when I went to sleep the night before, she was chipper as a cheerleader. Some people never seemed to get tired. I envied those people.

The sugar in the doughnut from Island Bakery helped slightly, but the stifling tropical heat countered the positive effect.

Relentless sunshine—oh the humanity. Tugging my hat lower, I had to squint under the brim to keep from walking into people.

I trailed a tour group into the Bacon Distillery, breaking off as we approached Gilroy's office. At the bottom of the stairs someone hollered my name. Yarey. She had dumbbell-eyes, too.

"Long night?" I asked.

"Amen. Fun, right?"

"You're fun," I said playfully. "When's your next gig?"

"I'm supposed to sub in as a singer at The Normandie next Friday, but he … " She nodded up at the office above. " … said I gotta stop this nonsense or else."

"Else what?"

"Probably kick me out."

"Is he up there?" I asked.

"Probably. I haven't been checking. I'm fed up. Anna said I could come stay with her. Problem is, he might be right. Singing isn't much of a living, but what if I'm one of the lucky ones?"

Gilroy was right to be concerned. Yarey wasn't even the lead singer at a local concert last night, so how the hell was she going to make it in an ocean of talent like New York or L.A.?

Gilroy didn't look pleased to see me when he opened the door. He reluctantly waved me in.

Sitting down, he slid a book that had been open on his desk to the side along with a small length of rope tied in a knot.

"What you want?"

"Your daughter is talented."

He remained impassive at this comment. After a time, he said, "She's throwing her life away."

"It's hers to throw away, don't you think?"

"If you came here to lecture me on the importance of letting children experiment and follow their dreams, you can save your breath. Here," he held his arms wide, "we live in reality. We need money. We need to build something. That takes time and at my age you become aware how little time there is. If she goes off…"

He banged a fist on his orderly desk. "What do you want? I have work to do." He pondered his watch. "We have a tasting in twenty minutes."

"Then I'll keep it short," I shot back. "Were you promised something by Dominic before Francine took over the business?"

Having worked for lawyers in Los Angeles, I'd picked up a couple of interrogation techniques. Most of the time, the attorneys I worked for asked questions in their own clients' offices or the opposition's office or home where the person being deposed felt most at ease. A less formal atmosphere resulted in fewer guardrails or preparation. If you could show up unannounced and get answers, all the better. Divorce cases, my firm's bread-and-butter, involved a ton of lying.

The best way to spot a liar, contrary to popular belief, was not knowing the tells. Tells were nice, but could be misinterpreted. A common tell is when the person won't make eye contact, then most times there's a lie or half-truth going on, but on the other hand, some people are exceedingly shy and hated making eye contact, even when being truthful.

The ideal scenario was to know the answer to the question you were asking. In the courtroom, this rule supplanted all others on cross-examination. "Don't know answer, don't ask question."

I waited for him to answer the question, but Junior had already called me with the answer. Junior had done his own snooping and he had a lot more access to his grandparent's inner workings than I did.

"I don't know what you're talking about."

"So, Dominic Bacon, the owner of this business, made no promises to you prior to his demise that weren't fulfilled by Francine Bacon?"

"No. Francine has been fair and generous. She's giving me half-a-million dollars and doing the same for my daughter."

He picked up the bit of rope that looked like it was tied in a slipknot and dropped it into a drawer, then stood up formally. He didn't look at me, which reinforced what I already knew. The man was lying, but why?

Once outside, I called Junior.

"Are you sure Harold knows what he's talking about?"

"Yes, Harold's sure."

From a stump in the shade I watched a butterfly flit about in the hazy heat. The grassy area behind the distillery was littered with hedges that hadn't been cut for too long. The areas in front and on the sides were properly mown and trimmed, probably because of the tours. No one came back here except workers, as evidenced by a bucket of sand with dozens of cigarette butts protruding from it.

Who kept an eye on Gilroy Antsy now that Francine Bacon was out of the picture? Was there a new CEO who took over upon her demise? There must be some kind of contingency in the case of illness or death, although this was a closely-held company, so they could presumably do whatever they wanted. And there was nothing like the Securities and Exchange Commission to hold them accountable. On top of it all, we were on an island notorious for poor governmental oversight.

If there was no one new in charge, that left Gilroy to his own devices. He would manage things until someone else was brought in. Francine must have trusted this man to leave him in charge of the rum operation, although that was small molasses compared to the sugar. Then again, if the whole thing was now for the reparations, what did it matter? Would it be dismantled? There were a lot of moving parts in Francine's life, a lot of people with things to gain and things to lose upon her death.

Movement on the side of the building. Gilroy came out and moved into a corner of the property where a pair of saw horses stood at the ready. A board was propped against the wall along with a hand saw. His back was to me.

Sneaking closer, I positioned myself behind a pillar with hunks of brick protruding from ancient, powdery plaster. He pulled out a measuring tape, consulted a slip of paper from his pocket, then marked a length of the board and proceeded to cut. Once the cut was complete, he measured the board again and sanded the rough edge for a couple minutes.

He walked back to the parking lot and dumped the wood into the back of his sedan before re-entering the building. Less than two minutes later he exited again, hopped into his sedan and raced off.

Sprinting out to the main road, I hailed a cab that had just dropped off a group of gawking tourists. He sure had an odd way of preparing for a tasting.

"Follow that pearl Mercedes," I yelled.

"Hold on, da man," the cabbie said casually.

I blew out an annoyed stream of air as I waited for him to make change and collect his tip from the previous fare. Out on Veterans Drive I directed him to turn right, but the sedan had already disappeared into traffic. We caught the first light.

"Where's the nearest marina?" I asked.

"Marina? Mi son, I don't know nothing about marinas. I look like a sailor? Where we going?"

Looking around desperately, I had him pull over. I searched in my phone for marinas. The closest one was only about a mile away where Veterans curved inland as you left the waterfront. There were seven others.

***

We stopped at Yacht Haven Grande, which was located in Havensight. It moored large yachts for the most part, hence the name. According to the security guard at the gate, they typically didn't take boats. They took ships since they could accommodate up to four-hundred feet. They were also very prestigious because of their proximity to downtown and the main harbor.

"Everything is close. You go out to Sapphire or Boat Hawk, you'll find more of the local flavor. Is this guy major league?"

"What's major league?" I asked the muscular guard sporting a flat-top.

"Is he a hot-shot business guy or Brad Pitt?"

"No. He's a guy who works and lives here with an upper management job making rum."

"That's guppy-class. I put him at Sapphire or Fish Hawk. Under fifty feet and maybe barely six."

"Six?"

"Figures. You gotta be high six or seven and up for these real places."

We headed for Fish Hawk. The place was dead. A couple of drunk sailors lounged around in a hut that passed for a bar at the end of a poorly maintained dirt and gravel road. Four small boat slips were occupied by vessels of dubious seaworthiness, all badly in need of barnacle scraping. One appeared to be taking on water.

I watched and waved to a dingy that motored through the channel between the mangroves and the shoreline, then asked one of the bleary-eyed loungers if he had seen a Mercedes come by. This elicited a toothless laugh followed by an extended fist, which I dutifully bumped.

We slalomed along Bovoni Road to Red Hook where the ferry for St. John anchored. I paid the cabbie and dismissed him since Red Hook had taxis on every corner.

Before combing the area for the Mercedes or Gilroy, whatever came first, I bellied up to the bar, ordered my Guinness and their Cheeseburger in Paradise with onion rings. I doused everything in ketchup and chugged the beer. As I got up to leave, I spotted him at one of the tables, his back to the door, as he chatted up an angry man who looked vaguely familiar. Where did I know Gilroy's table-mate from? I suspected it was his outfit. Gilroy's companion wore some strange glasses that looked like goggles ala James Worthy and a knit cap. Whoever he was, he appeared to be undercover. His baggy attire, made it hard to determine a body type. As I considered the companion's identity, I realized I'd made a mistake not wearing my own hat for the first time in weeks.

Slipping out, I jogged across the parking lot to the Marina Market and purchased a St. Thomas baseball cap and four-dollar Ray-Ban knockoffs, all the while watching to make sure they didn't disappear on me.

Feeling suitably concealed, I perched on a different seat at the bar that offered a better view. I pretended to take a selfie with the Duffy's Love Shack heart logo hanging on one of the wooden stanchions, but snapped Gilroy and his friend instead. The light was poor, so the photo could only serve as a general reminder, perhaps a means of getting an ID on Gilroy's companion later. It certainly wasn't worthwhile evidence in any criminal proceeding.

Don't get ahead of yourself, I thought. This might be nothing more than him meeting a friend in the middle of the work day just to hang out.

The bartender, a small woman with an emo hairdo, cutoff jeans, and a plaid, sleeveless shirt, sauntered over. She had the gait of a cowboy in chaps who'd dismounted from a horse five minutes earlier.

"Are you Boise?" she asked.

The disguise didn't seem to be working. Whatever the two men were discussing, they were engrossed. I shifted position so I could look at her and watch Gilroy out of the corner of my eye.

"That's my name. Who are you?"

"I know Irene."

"Who's that?" I immediately regretted the question.

"I'm gonna tell her you say that," the bartender said, her hands positioned on her hips like Wonder Woman and her voice rising.

I pulled her closer, realizing people were starting to pay attention. "Sorry, sorry. You mean *that* Irene."

"That's what I say."

I shook my head apologetically. "My bad. I thought you said Ilene."

"Serious? You think I dumb?" She pulled out her phone and started texting. "I going tell she about you. What you doin' out here?"

Her theatrical volume was drawing more and more attention from patrons in the bar. People loved to watch a man and woman fight.

"Hey, uh…" I searched for a name tag, but Duffy's was too casual for that, "…Miss, please don't tell Ilene, I mean, Irene, you saw me. Please."

"You do that to me friend after she put herself out to you and you expect me to respect your wishes? You can't treat a woman like that." Her head was shaking back and forth so rapidly, I wondered how she didn't get dizzy. Over her shoulder I saw Gilroy's eyes narrow as he studied my countenance. Even with sunglasses and a hat, a hint of recognition crossed his face and then blossomed into full realization.

"Shit," I whispered, ducking my head and shrinking behind the irate bartender. Gilroy pointed and said something to his companion as they dropped money on the table and hurried out.

"Excuse me." I slipped around the furiously texting woman. As I moved past her, she gave me the finger.

"Yeah, you best run! Loser!" she yelled as I exited.

Now, I know it sounds like I'm some kind of womanizer, but in my defense, I haven't had an ounce of sex since stepping foot on St. Thomas six months ago. During my last investigation, I had one date that Dana set me up on by losing a pool game at the Normandie, but it didn't go so well, mainly because I forgot to show up.

Bartenders on St. Thomas all knew each other, at least the females seemed to, because Duffy's and The Normandie were about as far apart as two businesses on this rock could be. Did they have a bartender's union or something?

Once outside, my thoughts quickly returned to the crisis of the moment. Gilroy and his buddy had split up and were speed-walking across the parking lot in opposite directions.

Gilroy found his car, ripped out of his space and sped away. The other guy was nowhere to be found, so I headed to the boat slips in hopes of finding Gilroy's boat, if indeed he owned one.

Having nothing whatsoever to go on, I helplessly scanned the marina. One of the St. John's ferries motored in, a mixed crowd of natives and tourists dotting the deck. The wind caught one man's baseball cap and sent it flying into the face of a woman behind him. She laughed and handed it back.

Swinging my attention back to the parking lot, I spotted Gilroy's companion, who gestured feverishly as he shouted into his cell phone. Anticipating he would leave soon, I hailed a cab and waited. We sat in the lot, the meter ticking away, while the gray-templed man continued his heated conversation.

He ended the call, then hopped on a motorcycle parked outside Duffy's.

The cabby dutifully took off in pursuit of the bike on my command.

There was little traffic going out of Red Hook, so although his bike was fast, the cabby, once I promised a generous tip, kept pace. After a while we circled back around up the north side to the small road that led to only one place: the archery club Harold and Junior had taken me to.

The cab let me out at the end of the road. It was quiet and green. The only noise, the distant sound of a car motoring up a steep incline and shifting gears. My mind also shifted as I switched my focus from the Bacon family to the Bacon family business.

I couldn't enter the archery range without a Bacon in tow, and I didn't want this suspect to know I'd followed him. That's what I told myself. The reality was entirely different.

CHAPTER 27

The Normandie hadn't changed much in the thirty-three years I'd been around, and probably hadn't changed much in fifty. A large plaque bearing my father's name should have been mounted on the wall for being a lifetime donor.

Irene stood behind the bar, pouring Bacon Rum and shooting Coke from a soda gun into a glass. She plopped a skinny straw in and stirred it expertly before placing it in front of a fat guy with slicked back hair and his ass-crack showing.

"Belt's not working," I said before sitting two stools away.

"What?" he slurred.

I shook my head, then repeated myself.

"Hey, man, fuck you!" he said, but remained seated. "I'm too tired after a hard day or I'd ... "

"You'd what?"

Irene slapped the bar. "Boise! What the hell? What you want?"

"What do you think?" I said.

She watched me a long moment, then turned and poured a perfect Guinness from the tap.

"Eight bucks." All business, as expected. "I better collect now or you might forget to pay."

She made change, and I left a couple of ones on the bar. She picked them up and dropped them into a glass pitcher full of bills.

"So what, buying a beer and a twenty-five-percent tip supposed to make up for what you done?"

"No, but I've also apologized."

"Yeah, once, over twenty-four hours later. How's that make a girl feel, you think?"

"I'm an ass, what can I say." The Guinness tasted good. "But your girl out at Duffy's, that was uncalled for."

She poured some whiskey into a glass for another guy at the far end, then came back.

"I can't stop what people do," she said.

"Oh, so you think that's funny?" I muttered. "Real funny. I was working. That bitch ... jerk ... blew my cover. I lost my mark."

She was doing something behind the bar which forced her to lean forward. She wore a loose-fitting tank top and her cleavage nearly smacked me right between the eyes. I maintained eye-contact, barely. What was it about this woman? Thank God for peripheral vision. On the top of her left breast, I could make out a small red butterfly tattoo.

"Boo-hoo, what you want me to do? You be nice and shit like this don't happen."

"I got caught up with work. Time got away."

"I don't go on dates much. That was the first in two years."

"You won the bet," I said. "I still want to honor it."

"You still hanging around with your little red-head?"

"Dana? We still friends, but she off on some assignment. I'm more on my own this time."

"Good. I no like she," Irene sneered.

"Don't worry about her. What about you and me?"

"I liked you better when I baby-sat for you, but I always liked your father. You have his nose."

Here I was, trying to make time with a woman who only liked me because she had some power over me and I probably only liked her because when you're a ten-year-old boy, of course you fantasize about having sex with your baby-sitter. The ten-year age difference didn't feel so significant anymore. Something about her having been my first crush, I couldn't let it go.

The case was important and the iron was hot, but right now, I wanted this more. I had forgotten about the dough and the family and Pickering and Kendal. Things were primal tonight. I wasn't even thinking about a date, I wanted to consummate, but I'd never been smooth with women. I was a slow-roller, not a close-out.

I dumped some more beer down my gullet. It didn't help. Stuffing my hands into my crotch below the bar was the only way to keep them from shaking.

She came and went like a bad radio signal for the remainder of the evening. Sometimes it felt like reception was clear, then the next time nothing but static. I talked about our shared past, but that was cheating and it made me seem like a kid, not a man. Things had to move away from that tip. Away from my father too.

She was now at the corner stool, talking to a guy who kept jerking his stubbled chin at me and making a dangerous face.

"Hey! You Terry's kid?" the guy yelled down the length of the bar at me.

Ignoring him, I sipped my whiskey. I'd switched in hopes that the harder, leathery color and flavor would harden my nerve. Balderdash. Those bullshit sayings about liquid courage—they only worked if the drinker was able to completely let go. That

216

wasn't me.

When Irene was getting off, I walked her to her car, but really, she walked me.

"Honey, honey, you gotta hold your liquor better if you want to hang."

The oppressive night weighed on me. My damp shirt clung to my skin.

She asked if I was okay, but it sounded like she was at the other end of a long tunnel. My head hung low as I leaned against the cool metal of her car. The door opened, and I tumbled into the backseat.

Lights flickered through the windows. From the front of the car, Irene said, "Don't you hurl in my backseat, mi son!" Roger Miller's *King of the Road* filtered out of the speakers.

"Stop the car." I jerked up, unlatched the door, and poked my head out as we lurched to a halt. Everything gushed out of me into the gutter bordering the road. Tropical places had gutters, deep and wide. As a kid I used to straddle the v-shaped cesspools on my walk to school. A gross game of dare. If you lost, your shoes wound up covered in god-knew-what, running out in the brown water.

A bazooka joe wrapper was trapped in my throw-up. Joe's grin and indecipherable words above his ever-jeering expression. We were in front of the cemetery where Roger and my grandparents were buried.

"I gotta go see someone," I said, getting out and pushing open the gate.

"Boise! Where you going?" Irene said. "This is enough. Come back in this car. I'm tired. I'm going home. You can crash on my couch, but I'm not coming in no ghost-yard after midnight, you hear?"

A sad headstone read "Roger Black" along with his years of life and death. No one cared to write something meaningful to remember him by, like "Beloved Son" or "You will be missed."

Roger would not be missed, except by me. Did his Auntie Glor even miss him? I remembered our sleepovers and yelling for him to come out and play through white, metal louvers. Two powerful emotions gripped me: a longing to have my friend back and the need to piss.

Scanning the yard, I tucked into a corner and pushed up against the mildewed barrier wall. It burned a little coming out, but once it was over, I sighed with relief. Irene was so close behind me, I nearly bowled her over.

"What the fuck, Irene!" I said, still zipping my fly.

"What did you say to me? You are in the corner of a cemetery after midnight pissing and you asking me 'what the fuck?'"

Pissing had sobered me up slightly, but I figured I should play up the drunk thing a little longer otherwise this conversation would dump into serious-ville mighty fast.

"Yeah, well," I waved my arm over the silent expanse of greenery and death, "they don't much care."

She watched me a second, then shrugged. "I suppose you right. So why we here?"

"I thought you were frightened."

"I'm not scared, but I ain't been in a cemetery at night since I was messin' round as a teenager."

"So, about the time you were sitting for my parents?"

She got a thoughtful look on her face, the past running behind her eyes like a light show. "Yeah, I guess I come to the graveyard once or twice when I knowing you."

Suspicions and questions rattled like the bones of the dead.

"With whom?"

"You wanna know who I make out with in a graveyard? Don't remember."

"There were that many?"

"You are a little fuck, aren't you?" she said with a devious grin. "What you really want to know? Just ask, mi son."

The dawning sobriety got the better of my bad judgment.

There were questions you didn't ask. They flung a relationship off a cliff. Most times, relationships wore away, the steady erosion of waves pounding against limestone, until one violent day, the rock crumbled for seemingly no reason. Between the two, I preferred slow erosion, but if I asked this question, the limestone would snap off and tumble into the sea.

"Nothing. Forget it," I said.

"That's what I thought. All bark. You always been all bark, Boise. You haven't changed that much."

"You calling me a boy."

She shrugged and started back to her car. I yelled after her, "I'm not the one who's afraid of graveyards!"

We were parked in front of The Manner, her car idling roughly. "You wanna come up?" I offered. My shame had no bounds.

"I like you, Boise."

"Don't say you like me. Don't say that."

"But I do," she said, her voice getting slightly higher with faulty insistence. "I always have. You were a cute kid."

"Here it comes."

"I have to get home. It's late. We're really not supposed to even be out here."

"What, the curfew? They don't do nothing about that," I said thickly. "I been out after midnight so many nights."

"You not a woman."

"You could…" My third eye watched me from above, cynical and judgmental. "You could stay here. I promise to behave. Dana stayed before, you can ask her about it."

She sucked her teeth at the mention of Dana.

"Are you jealous?" I asked.

"Jealous? Ha! Mi son, I ain't jealous nobody. Out!" She shooed me, scraping my skin with her fingernail.

"What time do you work tomorrow?" I really was never this persistent.

219

"Five."

"Five. Then what's a little more time out with a friend. I bet you've known me almost as long as anyone. We go back, what twenty-three years?"

She bit her lower lip, then said, "You really are cute, just like your old man. But you look like you ten. You got some other habits from him too."

"Oh please, you serve the shit, don't start."

"I do, so I won't. You right. I even drink my share. But Terry, he could put it away."

"Don't say his name. Between you and that asshole at the bar, that's two mentions in one day."

She muttered something indecipherable.

"What?"

"Nothing. I have to get up at seven and take my little brother to school. My mom has a doctor's appointment. You happy now? You have to know."

CHAPTER 28

Harold, Junior and I arrived at the archery range at ten the next morning.

"What's that smell?" Harold asked, getting out of the car on the still damp dirt. "One of you dudes fart or something?" He waved his hand in front of his nose. Sometimes I wondered how old Harold was.

I sniffed the shirt I'd slept in. Yup, I stunk. "Dunno," I muttered, "don't smell anything, but I'm not much sensitive to smell."

"Me neither. You live in a dorm, you learn to breathe out a lot," Junior said.

Junior's red face was peeling, and he rubbed at his skin. A thin, sugary snow drifted to the ground.

"Maybe your skin's rotting," Harold said, grabbing Junior in a playful headlock and knuckling his scalp.

The guy was a fun uncle. Driving a Rav-4, rough-housing, I always wished someone had done that with me. My father's version of roughhousing wasn't fun. He'd try, but in his drunken anger, he'd always wind up hitting me for real before long. In general, I avoided contact. Handshaking was one of the physical ways of connecting I had painstakingly worked on over the years. It was a safe zone; a connection with little danger.

Inside the seven-foot-tall walls that resembled a medieval castle, the outdoor archery field looked like it had been freshly mowed the day before. Harold clapped everyone he met on the back and was greeted warmly. We rode his coattails. Junior was more like me, formal but awkward. He'd get better over the years. At least, that was my hope for him.

After the meeting and greeting and grabbing a beer each from the adjacent indoor shop and lounge area, we went back out to the range. There were a few familiar faces amongst others I didn't recognize. One face eluded me. Gilroy's accomplice.

The flirt came up, waving an arrow around.

"You back," she said to me. She didn't wait for my response before whapping Harold playfully on his ass with the arrow. "Hey, love. Where you been?"

Harold leaned in, loving the attention. "Nowhere and everywhere, baby." These two were made for each other.

Scanning the rest of the shooters and their companions, I found no one that resembled the man who'd met with Gilroy the day before.

"Hey, Harold."

Harold was whispering something in her ear. Whatever he said made her open her mouth in a large "O" and slap him lightly on his shoulder. Two slaps so far, arrow and hand. Harold took her wrist, and they headed into a small grove of banana trees in the corner of the large yard.

Continuing to survey the scene, Junior tapped me on the shoulder.

"That who you're looking for?"

It took me a moment to spot Isabelle sauntering out of a door to my left. Her distinctive hair had changed color since last we met. Today, it was a very tasteful purple and black combo.

"Where's that she's coming from?" I asked.

"Members call it the smoking room. A lot of the guys smoke cigars in them high-backed chairs you see in rich dude studies with buttons and paisley patterns. They got lots of bookshelves with books about archery. It's kinda pretentious you ask me."

Isabelle moved past us, eyes distant. Moments later, the man Gilroy had met at Duffy's the day before also emerged from the smoking room. I knew the guy looked familiar yesterday, but with the goggles, hat, and loose-fitting clothing, coupled with my having never seen him outside this archery range, he'd managed to fool me.

"Clever," I muttered to myself.

"Sorry?" Junior said.

"That's her uncle and coach, right?"

"Yup, he's everything."

"Name?"

"Jermaine."

The man ignored Junior and me, although he passed within two feet, close enough for me to dial in on his thinly shaved beard and the faint scent of metal. Today he wore tight-fitting athletic-ware and nothing on his eyes. The eyes were the giveaway. I wouldn't make the same mistake again. Isabelle's coach-slash-uncle was involved. Jermaine. His features were burned into my memory.

"What's that guy's story?" I asked without taking my eyes off the stern-faced man. He pointed at the target, punched a stop-watch and she commenced shooting again. Like some kind of archer machine-gun turning right then back to the front over and over.

"He was a champion-level dude way back they say, but his

temper got the best of him. In one competition, after he lost a lead, he took his quiver and broke every arrow. The ref wouldn't let him borrow arrows, so he was d-qued. He was the favorite to win the Pan Am Games that year. He never competed again. Now he trains her like she's his second chance. I shudder to think what he'd do if she quit or fucked up, you know?"

"Sounds like a prince."

The man had the focus of a cat tracking a bird. Every movement noted for improvement later, or maybe so he could justify his coaching position and take credit for her skill.

Personal trainers and coaches were mostly bullshit. In California these leeches infested public spaces. *Bro-dudes* seemed to be everywhere, puffing their chests and spouting new-agey crap about positivity from every orifice like they were the fifteenth Dalai Lama. Since they didn't actually do anything, they constantly justified their existence with trite advice and intense scrutiny.

"Does she really need a coach?" I asked. "I mean, how complex is shooting an arrow, really? Strategy?"

I could feel Junior doing his thing, staring at me as that thoughtful stillness engulfed us. Finally, he said, "You don't respect my sport?"

"I thought cycling was your sport."

"So's this. Do you play a sport?"

"Darts."

"Darts? Not a sport."

"What's the difference between archery and darts? They're virtually the same in every way."

"Archery is outdoors."

"That makes it a sport?" I asked incredulously.

"Yup. Sometimes you have to track something or move on terrain or even run and shoot. Some people do archery competition while skiing. They ever do that with darts?"

"Okay, granted. But what's the difference between target archery like this," I gestured at the people shooting at round, stationary targets, "and darts? You really think being outside is the distinguishing factor?"

"Dude, it matters. It definitely hurts darts that the only place it's played is in a bar, usually by people holding a drink."

I had no comeback for that. In fact, I wasn't even sure why I was arguing at this point since I didn't think either of them were sports. Well, maybe the one on skis or if you were chasing deer through the brush like Davy Crockett.

Isabelle had stopped shooting. She and her uncle were engaged in a heated discussion. She flung her bow down and stomped away, her locks whipping back from her face as the wind picked up and some dark clouds rolled in. In the distance, lightning flashed.

Harold appeared, solo once again. "What you guys finding out?"

"Nothing," Junior said sullenly. "Boise's got the hots for Isabelle."

"Where is she?" Harold asked.

Junior pointed out the main entrance to the driveway beyond. Her uncle picked up the bow and wiped it off. Then he nocked an arrow and shot it, straight and true.

"The guy's got great form, even if he is an asshole," Harold said. "So relaxed, like nothing could shake him." He nudged me with his elbow. "That's why competition's the real test. Guy couldn't hold his shit together when the pressure was on. See it all the time."

"Go challenge him," I said.

"Ha! Me?"

Junior and I waited and stared.

"That'd be fun to see, uncle."

"Yeah, uncle," I repeated playfully. "Show us how this sport is done."

Harold looked around like a wallflower nervous about asking the prettiest girl in the room to dance. He acted so in control, but that was when things were on his terms.

Suddenly, Junior hollered out, "Hey, Jermaine!" Isabelle's uncle jerked his head and locked eyes with Junior, who pointed at Harold. "My uncle wants to challenge you. Three shots. Best total from seventy."

A jackal's smirk appeared on Jermaine's dark face. He hollered back, "How much?"

Harold didn't look happy. His Adam's apple bobbed.

"Fifty," I yelled, joining the fray.

"Make it one-hundred," Jermaine retorted.

"Done. Let's do it," Junior said, a jubilant grin breaking across his face.

Isabelle returned a few minutes later, no doubt after someone informed her of the contest. She marched up to Junior and me.

"What is your problem? You know my uncle shouldn't be doing this. He has high blood pressure."

"And a temper," Junior snickered. "Come on, it'll be fun!"

"You don't have to live with him. He hates to lose."

She stomped over to her grinning uncle and tapped him pointedly on the shoulder. He was now having fun, she the stone-faced coach.

As Harold walked by, he threw us an annoyed glance. "I haven't even shot today. You guys are fucking stupid."

Harold asked for twenty practice shots.

"I don't think so," Jermaine intoned. "These," he looked Junior and me up and down, "boys said you were ready to compete. Let's do this."

"Come on, give him the practice. You've been here all day," I said.

A flash of anger crossed the thin man's countenance then vanished. "Fine. No Bacon excuses today." The smirk reappeared. I could picture the man biting the head off a cat as he feasted on a fresh kill.

I wandered over to Harold as he finished his last practice

shot. "You know, Harold, it would be really great if you busted this guy's marbles."

"Oh, yeah? How come that's suddenly my job, man?"

"Look, just relax and shoot like I know you can. You got this guy." I clapped him on the back.

Harold pursed his lips like he was ready to say something, then he shook his head and pushed me aside as he took his spot next to Jermaine.

"What the hell are you guys up to?" Isabelle hissed at me as the men lined up. "Is there something more going on here?"

"Friendly competition. I like your hair," I said.

"My uncle doesn't need this shit. Boise, you seemed like a nice guy, but you're just like all of them. No one understands him. He's socially awkward."

"Your uncle competed, right? He trains you to compete. He must have an understanding. What's so bad?"

She looked off at the approaching rain clouds. "It's hard keeping him focused."

I was confused. Every time I watched them together, the guy seemed to have laser focus.

"On what?" I asked.

"Me," she said.

With that, she went into the shop and plopped down on a cushioned chair to pout. I could see her through the plate-glass windows. The jackal had stolen the peacock's limelight.

An angry yell brought me back around to the match.

"What! What did you say?" It was Jermaine.

"Not feelin' it, man. We're not doing this." Harold had his bow and arrows stowed. He was walking in my direction.

"You get back here this instant!" Jermaine was talking to Harold like he was an obnoxious teen. Harold ignored him and kept walking. "Bacon!"

As Harold approached my position, he smirked at me, then whispered, "You wanted him off his game."

Jermaine threw down his bow and started toward us. I stepped between them.

"Jermaine, is it? I'm Boise." I stuck out my hand. "Pleased to … "

He shoved me aside. The man was stronger than he looked. Harold was about to open the door. Jermaine grabbed his hand and spun him around. He punched Harold in the face. Blood exploded from Harold's nose and lip as he stumbled into the door.

Isabelle burst from the lounge area, yelling, "Stop! What are you doing?" She bent over and cradled Harold.

Without hesitation Jermaine yanked Isabelle to her feet and dragged her toward the parking lot. We needed to follow. Someone gave Harold a wad of paper towels. Junior and I lifted him and hustled to Harold's car. I hopped in the driver's seat just as Jermaine and Isabelle peeled out in a cloud of dust.

"Shit, shit, shit! Get the plate!" I yelled.

"Can't see. Too much dust." Junior protested.

From the backseat we could hear Harold's low moans.

"Do you have Advil in this car?" I asked.

No answer.

"Harold! Advil?"

"Yeah," he whined. "Glove…"

Junior popped the glove box, found Advil and gave it to Harold as I motored down the gravel road.

"Do you know where that asshole lives? Anything?"

The Rav-4 groaned as I smashed the accelerator. After almost careening into a small palm heavy with earthy coconuts, I righted the car.

Harold moaned something.

"What?" I asked.

"East."

I headed east. Before long, we caught up with them as they slowed briefly, then blew through a red light on Bovoni Road adjacent to a housing development. A car honked a long blare before moving cautiously through the intersection. I swerved around and blew the light. The bleat of a siren, then red and blue flashers filled my rearview mirror. From the side of the road, I watched helplessly as Jermaine sped away, up an incline and out of sight.

"You don't have a local driver's license and your California license is expired!" Junior said.

"I been busy," I said as I stared at the enormous ticket I'd just gotten. "Why'd he nail us and not them?"

"'Cause, that's how it works."

We returned to the Bacon pad. Harold snored on the couch, a gel ice pack mounted on his face. Junior and I slouched outside to smoke a joint. Did I want to involve Junior further in this mess, or leave him blissfully ignorant? Knowledge about murder could be dangerous. I'd previously endangered Elias when investigating Roger's death. I didn't want that on my conscience. Someone else needed to know what I knew, but Junior couldn't be my confidant.

Excusing myself, I composed a text to Dana outlining my suspicions about Jermaine and Gilroy in the deaths of Adirondack Kendal and Francine Bacon. This, too, was risky. Dana liked to stick her nose in where it didn't belong, and she wasn't especially keen about keeping things silent. She also had a personal interest in both Kendal and her boss.

It was getting late, my chance for a bonus from Pickering dwindling, the weekend about to begin. I didn't know much about Jermaine and couldn't waste time there. My best move now: go smoke out a suspect. The problem: I could get my ass killed if I pushed the man too far. Killers didn't mind killing to keep their kills secret.

On the way to the distillery, where I hoped to find Gilroy, I stopped at Backstreet Pizza, had three slices and a Pabst to wash it down. My pants stretched against my thighs and the button dug into my lower gut. Evelyn's voice rang in my head. "Boise, you keep eating like that..." After Evelyn died, my mother picked up the refrain. Playing darts didn't qualify as exercise and even if it did, I knew deep down what science kept confirming: weight loss depended more on diet.

As these thoughts pinballed through my brain, I made a radical decision. No crusts. That had to account for at least a hundred calories. While there, I glanced in back, but Tony and Little Nicky were nowhere to be seen. Gina was in a salty mood, so I let it be. These jokers had connections on the seedy side of the island. They'd helped me find a kidnapped girl several months ago.

Walking down Backstreet, I kept the crusts wrapped in a napkin and when I got to Market Square, there was Jeff, the mongrel I'd befriended the day Dana and I had met in March. He trotted up, breaking away from the shade of a concrete vendor table littered with fresh veggies. A clump of dried mud clung to his golden coat. I scraped it out as he nuzzled my hand for the crusts. He preferred hand-fed small pieces. He would just stare at the chunks if I dropped them on the pavement. Picky for a homeless dog.

He gave my hand one last lick, nuzzling every bit of pizza oil, before trotting back to his shady spot. The woman whose table it was waved and yelled, "All right!" a favorite greeting among locals.

The pizza made me sleepy. I craved more beer. I made my way to The Normandie where Irene served me a Guinness perfect as the sunset. The asshole who hated my father made another comment.

Irene came to my defense. "Shut up, Norman! He's a paying customer. If you ain't notice, I need dem."

Norman shot back, "I'm a payin' customer too. Doesn't change the fact that this guy's pops was a prick."

I downed half the pint, wiped my mouth with the back of my hand, got off my stool and stalked over to Norman.

"So, you didn't like Terry, huh?"

He looked up at me, his eyes yellowed, stubble sticking to his face like miniscule grains of rice. We had a short staring contest, then he turned back to his drink and cigarette. I leaned over and whispered in his ear, "Me, neither."

Our solidarity shut Norman up from that day forward, at least about my old man. He was still prone to engaging in ill-tempered conversation with anyone who happened to be in the vicinity, however, he resisted badgering me.

Irene poured the surly Irishman another round of cheap whiskey. Upon returning, she asked, "What you say to him?"

"Nothing worth mentioning."

"I don't like hearing he talk bad about Terry. I like your father."

"That's nice. Can we stop talking about my father?"

Four more beers. Darts and pool. Irene played pool like a fish swims. At five dollars a game, my wallet was taking more of a hit than I could afford. I asked if I could get it back playing darts, she said no chance. She remembered how good I was, even as a kid, and wanted no part of that. When hanging out in a bar there were only a few things for a kid to do: play darts, play pool, or play one of the video games. My parents wouldn't spend money on video games and I was too short to play pool, so darts occupied hours of my time every day.

She offered me a ride home. I slurred my acceptance. Irene didn't go in for perfume. She didn't need it. Her scent was a combination of strawberries and sage. She'd always smelled like that. Her sitting on the edge of my bed reading a Hardy Boys book aloud as I dozed off. I'd peek out under my drooping eyelids at her brown cheeks and the swell of her breasts. In my dreams we kissed lightly, like I'd seen in censored movies shot through a filter.

"Aye, Boise! We here."

The West Indian Manner loomed over us from the top of the hill. The black fence, spiked with arrow-like tips flashed me back to Kendal's bleeding chest. The romance was dead and I was fading fast.

As I stumbled out of her car, she said something indecipherable. Gripping the railing, I pulled myself up the first set of stairs, then I lost my verve, but I held myself steady until her taillights disappeared at the end of the street. At the base of the first palm tree in the yard, I passed out.

CHAPTER 29

A hard slap shot me out of my stupor. It was still dark. Two people had me by the arms. Fingernails dug into the fleshy skin above my elbow as they led me down The Manner's steps and shoved me into the back of an idling car. My head bumped the edge of the roof on the way in, adding to my already considerable alcohol-headache.

One of them got into the backseat with me, ramming me to one side.

"Wha … " I muttered.

"Shut up!" my seat-mate growled. I tugged feebly at the door-release, but the child-lock was engaged.

A hand gripped my hair hard and pinned my cheek against the glass of the car's window.

"Ow!" I moaned.

My mouth tasted horrible. I hadn't brushed my teeth for almost twenty-four hours. They probably weren't going give me any floss no matter how nicely I asked.

"I say 'shut up' or you get some of dis." The whites of Jermaine's eyes glowed at me in the semi-darkenss.

Three inches from my eye he held my raven-colored can of pepper spray. He loosened his grip slightly, and I nodded. It wasn't a gun, but if you've ever had a dose of pepper spray in your eyes, you'd understand my compliance. It wouldn't kill you, but you'd wish you were dead for a while.

He let go and slid to the other side of the seat. The driver glared at me in the rearview mirror for a moment before returning his eyes to the road. Gilroy Antsy.

Outside the windshield the vegetation trembled in the mounting gusts of wind. Stars beamed down from the clear sky, but the wind acted as if a storm were brewing.

The man next to me was exactly who you'd expect. Jermaine the Jackal. So many questions. I couldn't help it. My mouth sometimes had a mind of its own.

"You killed Francine?"

No hesitation. Jermaine sprayed me, directly in the face. I squealed. The sound reverberated, bouncing around the car. My breath hitched in and out as burning, stinging, searing pain racked me. My eyes watered. I clawed the seat. I wanted to rip the skin off my face and scoop out my eyes. Anything to make it stop. Curled into the fetal position, I slipped to the floor behind the driver's seat and moaned.

"I told ya to shut up!" Jermaine hissed. "Now you in pain, little man. Why we can't just kill he?"

"I told you why. Stop asking to kill everyone. This why we in this mess! Because you got to kill."

"You shut your mouth!" Jermaine leaned forward.

"I'm driving the car, you want to crash? Keep cool, man. Cool."

Through the tears and pain, I heard the seat groan as Jermaine reclined and sighed. The acidic stinging wouldn't stop. I keened and keened, praying for relief. Jermaine pulled me up onto the seat and pried my quaking hands away from my face.

He laughed and laughed and laughed. Every time I moaned or whimpered, he laughed, his rancid breath bathing my face. After an eternity, the agony went from ten to eight. Tears flowed still, but I was able to bring my attention to bear on the situation. No way to open my eyes. They teared relentlessly. These men hadn't nabbed me for a bachelor party at Frenchman's Reef.

"Where're you taking me?" I snorted. My question probably wasn't decipherable outside my head. Mucus dribbled down my chin. I hacked phlegm. As the pain diminished, exhaustion took its place.

"What you say? What's he saying?" Gilroy seemed genuinely interested.

"I dunno." Jermaine leaned close to my ear and yelled, "What?"

Even my eardrums were sensitive. The nausea began in my toes and crawled its way up my legs until it erupted in my stomach. Vomit spewed. I was happy to let it out all over Jermaine's loafers.

The man started vibrating. He kicked me away as an endless stream of brown liquid and pizza plastered the carpet.

Luckily, it was my vomit, and I couldn't smell anything. The car swerved to the shoulder and shuddered to a halt as red dust billowed in the faint half-moonlight.

I was sprawled across the backseat, my face planted in the leather, moaning, writhing. My feet pistoned into the door frame as if trying to run from the pain. Sweat poured from my hot brow, but with the pain down to a manageable seven my thoughts cleared a little more. Gilroy and Jermaine hadn't killed me yet. There must be a reason. Probably they wanted to know what I knew and who I'd told. I recalled that I had texted Dana about these two. I didn't want anything bad to happen to my friend, but I was grateful that someone with balls knew about my suspicions.

Another assumption I'd been trained to make: if two were involved, there could be more. It was similar to the cop rule that you always assumed a suspect had one more weapon hiding somewhere on their person. Find a gun in the belt, check the ankle. Find a gun in the ankle and belt, check for a knife. Find a knife…well, you get the idea. Were these two the whole thing or could they be working with others who were among the people looking to inherit more from Francine than they deserved? Could they be working with someone in the Bacon family?

A push-up got me to a slumping, yet seated position. Outside, the men argued, Jermaine jabbing the air with exclamations about ripping my guts out and eating my heart, while Gilroy coolly stated the obvious: not worth it. We need this fool alive, for now.

Jermaine muttered a derisive "fine" and marched over, leaned in the open door, closed his eyes against the stench and punched me in the face. I lulled, barely maintaining consciousness. Gilroy pulled him out and told him I'd be harmless for the remainder of the ten-minute drive to the boat.

"Sit up front with me and lean out the window. Listen." They were on either side of the hood now, moving to get in. "I need you to keep it under control. We're almost home free. You okay? You took what you need, right?"

Jermaine slapped the roof.

"Yeah? How you know? If we almost home, why we keepin' him breathing?"

The lunatic had a valid point. They lacked all the information, otherwise why keep me alive.

After we'd been driving for ten or fifteen minutes, we bumped to a stop. The dirty-white awning of a storefront peeked down through the window. Jermaine dragged me to my feet. Red Hook Marina. The stinging had been going on long enough to become background noise. I was the guy who had driven drunk so many times, being sober made me more dangerous. Come to think of it, I was still a little drunk, which maybe lessened the effect of the pepper spray. Score one for the drunken. Then again, if I hadn't passed out in the yard from boozing, I wouldn't be in this mess. If I weaseled out of this disaster, I'd try sobriety.

Yeah, right. Evelyn tried to make me get sober. If I couldn't do it for her, I certainly wasn't doing it for myself.

Everything hurt. My face, my chest where Jermaine stuck his foot into me, my shoulder, and my knee. A welter of blows. At thirty-three, I felt like I had the body of a retired pro wrestler who'd been whacked with chairs and slammed to the mat hundreds of times. Except none of mine got me any fame or fortune. All my injuries came from stupid mistakes.

I was so out of it, I hadn't even checked to see if my phone was still in my pocket. I patted the back of my shorts where I stashed it earlier that night.

Gilroy held it in front of my eyes. "You looking for this? You are going to unlock it, now."

Jermaine seized my hand and pressed my thumb to the home button. The screen glowed. Gilroy walked ahead, scrolling through my logs, probably searching for a starting point.

The filthy marina water lapped gently against the boats, *whap, whap, whap.* Street lights crouched on the hillsides like fireflies waiting to take flight. One house in the distance had a light on in the window. I'd always loved to imagine what those distant home-dwellers did in the light, while outside, darkness concealed their transgressions.

I thought of screaming. No doubt someone would hear. There had to be someone who slept on their boat in this marina. But what could they do for me, except get killed?

Be patient. Wait for an opening.

Gilroy, apparently satisfied with whatever he'd found in my phone, dropped it into his pocket as he stepped onto a boat. I couldn't make out the name of the vessel, but took a quick look around to ascertain its location. Third dock to the left of the dockmaster's shed, second from the last slip. A fishing boat, in the thirty-foot range, white, two-tiered.

Jermaine shoved me onto a cushioned bench and plopped next to me. This time he pulled out a gun.

"I thought you only used arrows," I said.

The cyclops abyss gazed at me, unblinking. A short trip to a long goodbye. Glocks were so sinister. No style, all business. Typical Austrian attitude.

I needed to piss. Badly.

"Hey, Gilroy, can I at least piss over the side here?"

"Let him piss," he said to Jermaine, clearly tired of my whining.

"You know, that gun is loud," I said as I walked aft.

Jermaine stayed right behind me, the gun trained at the back of my neck. When I tried to piss, nothing came. My full bladder could not overcome my fear.

"Hey Gil!"

"I told you not to call me that," Gilroy said through clenched teeth.

"Can I shoot him, for being disrespectful to you?" Jermaine asked.

"Jermaine, stick to the plan. I don't need the respect of such a man."

Holding up the gun, Jermaine continued to complain. "He's right, this gun is loud. Inelegant. I want to use my proper weapon."

Gilroy sighed. "Fine. Give me the gun. Your precious weapon is under the seat."

Gilroy trained the gun on me with one hand and held the steering wheel with the other.

From under the seat, Jermaine pulled out a crossbow and loaded it. Gilroy returned his full attention to steering the boat, setting the gun next to the steering wheel.

Jermaine moved the arrow inches from my head.

"Hey, could you back up? You're making me nervous."

He didn't move. I stood a while, the wind whipping my shirt. Finally, I started to flow. I made sure some of my urine blew onto the side of the boat.

"Nice ride," I said, working hard to sound nonchalant, despite my shaking hand and still stinging face. My legs banged against the rail.

Jumping was an option. I could swim, but in my state, I wasn't sure I'd make it. Even in the half-light I could make out foam on the tips of the waves. We were already far from shore, as Gilroy didn't seem too interested in following the posted speed limits or the "no wake" signs. We passed the first marker, and tilted to starboard, heading to the same place Francine was found.

"You taking me to the harbor like you did Francine?"

Jermaine attempted to remain impassive, but islanders aren't naturally poker-faced, especially homicidal-maniac islanders. What I needed to know showed in the glint of his eyes. The man wanted to kill me so badly, he had the giddiness of a teenaged boy on the way to getting laid for the first time.

Right there, standing on the edge of the boat after urinating, I had a quick image of me and Yarey. Her tongue probing my lips as we kissed, wet and passionate.

"Hey! What da fuck, man!" Jermaine was not happy. "Put dat thing away. Hey, Gilroy, dis man got a coconut tree."

Gilroy grunted. Did he ever laugh? The quip made me chuckle. It relaxed me. Jump-started my mind. I began churning through new possibilities.

Always act as if you'll get away; that was one of Henry's rules. If you got away, you still had a case to solve, which meant you kept working the case. Was this the same boat they'd taken Francine on across the river Styx? Had to be.

Everything shimmered in the iridescent light of the setting half-moon. One spot in particular on the rim of the boat glowed like bleach had been used there recently.

Although I'd never been a homicide investigator, Evelyn's death had motivated me to learn a bit about covering up a murder. If you were going to get bloody, you kept bleach handy. Otherwise, you made it easy on the cops. Jermaine stared at me and didn't waiver. I was getting more comfortable having a crossbow trained on me. Henry used to say the reaper's always there, waiting around every corner and every decision. Waiting for his job to matter.

Although diving off a moving boat had its advantages, mostly it had disadvantages, like drowning, predators who loved to eat at night, and drowning. Did I mention drowning? If my mother's biggest fear was collapsed lungs, mine was drowning. I didn't much like holding my breath. A fear of drowning made jumping off a boat into deep water very challenging.

Although I was a competent swimmer, ever since I'd been caught in an undertow and held down until I passed out, drowning had come in at number one on my top-forty list of least favorite ways to die. A fellow surfer had pulled me to the surface, because my father had been drunk and unaware of his ten-year-old son. I forget what my mother was doing, probably yelling at dear old dad.

Diving off the boat drifted into the "last recourse" column. For now, they weren't questioning or physically harming me, so the status quo wasn't all bad. I slowed my breathing. After sitting back down for two minutes, my jack-hammering knee took its place.

"Stop that," Jermaine snapped.

"What?" I asked.

"That." He pointed the tip of the nocked arrow at my knee and poked me in the knee cap. A dot of blood bloomed on my skin. I stopped.

"You guys make me nervous." I immediately regretted the revelation. This was no time to overshare.

"So, how's your niece coming along getting ready for her competition?"

"You trying to be funny?" Jermaine asked.

Keep him talking.

"Sure, I guess. Is that funny?"

"I'm her trainer. Since I got her away from that Bacon fool, I'm finally getting her technique right. Six months of focus and she's unbeatable at all of it."

"All of it? Is there more than archery?"

The boat bounded over the wake from a cruise ship churning to port. The moon was all the way gone, leaving us alone with the dark water and the white stars and the floating hotel.

The few times I'd gone sailing in Los Angeles, the air always had a nip because the water was so goddamned cold year-round. It actually pissed me off. I'd slept comfortably on the deck of boats all my life. You couldn't do that on the Pacific coast of the U.S. The salt smell and the warm coolness of the tropics at night couldn't be matched. It made me like being on the water again. This would have been a welcome sojourn, if not for the weapon pointed at my head.

"Yeah, I've got plans for Isabelle."

"What kind of plans?"

"Big plans. She's going to do special t'ings in this world."

"Wow, sounds super important. You must be proud."

He slid closer, his pants like sandpaper against the vinyl seat. He pressed the arrowhead against my temple until my ear touched my other shoulder. A trickle of blood or anxious sweat snaked from the point of contact. I was beginning to feel like a pin cushion. An ache rose in my skull as I squeezed my eyes shut. I hoped to see something promising in the blackness. Gilroy didn't seem to care much what Jermaine did.

"What are you doing?" Gilroy yelled. I opened my eyes. He stood right behind Jermaine. "You crazy bastard, I need him alive. I need to know who he talked to and what he knows. I told you to control yourself. Just like at Kendal's house, you are too loud, too uncouth, making all of this more difficult."

"You just want to know if he doing something with Yarey. Your precious Yarey."

Gilroy started to reach for Jermaine's shoulder, then thought better of it as Jermaine bared his teeth. I expected him to growl like a sabretooth beast, but he only made a soundless face, which somehow made it more menacing. A flicker of madness lit his eyes as he pulled away. Gilroy returned to the wheel.

"I be proud when she do as she told," Jermaine said, shaking his head as if he were trying to shake water out of his ear.

Making it out of this night was beginning to look about as likely as a bloody cat out-swimming a hungry shark.

We stopped dead in the water. Streetlights and houselights twinkled from Charlotte Amalie, but the place seemed as distant as the stars above.

"You see him?" Gilroy pointed at the still twitching head of Jermaine. "This is what he lives for. He does the dirty work. Oh, yes. He does that."

"He killed Kendal?"

"The reporter? 'Course. I don't go in for that sort of thing."

"You aren't worried about controlling him?" I asked, genuinely concerned, but also wanting to drop an ounce of doubt on the deck for later should things go that way.

"Control is an illusion. Just ask Francine. All that money and good intentions didn't save her, did it?"

"Did he kill Francine?"

Jermaine piped up, "Yeah, I kill she."

"Shut up, Jermaine. You got a big mouth. She wasn't supposed to die. We were supposed to keep her alive and convince her to make a better…dispensation. I wanted her to do what Dominic Bacon wanted, not some half-assed, two-hundred-years-too-late crap."

"You could have dove in to save her," Jermaine chirped. "She needed it to be real or she wasn't gonna listen. You say to scare her."

"Dumping an old woman into the ocean a mile out wasn't what I had in mind, you idiot. Do you understand when you kill the person you are negotiating with, it defeats the whole fucking purpose! 'Hold her', not drop her is what I said," Gilroy barked. "Enough. We're asking questions, not you. Who else knows about us?"

Gilroy had wanted Francine alive long enough to get a better deal. To convince her to give him the distillery. That had to be it. Is that what Dominic had promised? It didn't much matter that he didn't intend to kill her, he'd still go down for felony murder. These were very desperate men.

"What is it Dominic Bacon wanted?" I asked Gilroy.

"Who else knows about us?" he repeated.

"Are you two a couple?" I shot back. My bravado seemed to be swelling after moments ago thinking it was all over but the clean-up.

Gilroy snatched a handful of my shirt and yanked my head downward in a fierce arcing motion.

"You feel that? Control. I have it. The rest of them are fools. In the end they'll get theirs. So will you. Now, talk. Who knows about you seeing us?"

"Harold, Herbie, Junior, Pickering, I think a cop named Leber. Oh, the sister, what's her name? Hillary. She probably knows, too. You know what they say about secrets, right? Once two people know. Well, you know."

He let go. As I straightened up I noticed a small, lightless vessel approaching from port. My captors were too busy interrogating me to notice anything else. Besides, who would expect to see a rowboat out here at this hour?

"You didn't share with all those people, that's bullshit. You're the lonesome type who likes to gather before showing anyone anything."

He was right. "Not true. I'm a sharer. Those people are paying me. They want constant updates. It's brutal."

I needed to keep their attention on me. Jermaine seemed preoccupied with his crossbow, not a good sign either. Was he talking to it?

"You know, Boise, you shouldn't play cards, ever. You're a terrible liar. Although I'd like an excuse to torture you…"

"There's no need for that."

Torture wasn't high on my list of fun activities either. Maybe it was time to reassess my negative opinion of drowning.

"Jermaine!" Gilroy said over his shoulder.

I threw another look to port. Nothing there. Maybe I was hallucinating. Maybe the grim reaper was in the row boat.

"Jermaine!" Gilroy repeated.

Jermaine reappeared in my line of sight, behind Gilroy. His mouth was still moving in that baring and unbaring dance between his lips, teeth, and nose. There was a rhythm, like a song played in his head. He had the crossbow held at the ready.

The gun. The gun wasn't next to the steering wheel anymore.

Gilroy threw a disdainful look at Jermaine, asking, "What is wrong with you?"

Jermaine shot Gilroy through the eye. The feathered end of the arrow tilted up as Gilroy collapsed. Blood splatter bedazzled the white seat and the deck around the steering wheel as the body dropped in time with a swell. A gunshot resounded from somewhere in the darkness. I tensed my legs, feeling only a twinge in my bum knee before diving into the black ocean. I struck the chilly water. The waves battered my legs as I dove under the choppy surface.

Darkness swallowed my body. Images of seaworthy, nighttime predators flashed in my mind as I desperately breast-stroked under the boat. Twice I started to surface only to find I was still under the hull. The second time I scraped my scalp on a barnacle. I burst to the surface on the other side. The frantic need for air and my disorientation had sent me to the edge of panic. Although probably only a fifty-foot swim, it felt like I'd crossed the English Channel.

My head banged against the underside of something else in my panicked need for air. I stifled a yelp and flailed at the surface as crest after crest of the deep, relentless ocean battered my face. I twisted in a circle trying to find purchase.

After rotating hopelessly several times, something thumped me on the head again. In the dim, a snakelike object swirled in the water next to me as I dipped into a liquid valley between swells. The hull of a small vessel bobbed on a whitewashed wave above me.

My name drifted in hushed tones from the far side of the boat. I knew that voice. He yelled something else, but the wind whipped the words away. Concerned about the eel in the water, I started to swim in the other direction.

The voice yelled more forcefully, "Grab the rope!" I thrashed at the water. My limbs were losing feeling. Rough fiber brushed across my cheek. I grabbed the rope and held tight.

"Boise! Boise!"

A slap to my face brought me back. For once, Leber wasn't wearing sunglasses.

CHAPTER 30

Jermaine's left elbow burst in a shower of muscle and blood as he raised the crossbow. The harsh sea wind carried his howls away. The pain was not physical. It was the agony of being rendered helpless.

The instinct to continue his onslaught on these men, his enemies, rose up in him like lava boiling through granite. Voices swirled in his head, a hurricane commanding him to kill. To never stop killing until he was at the top of the mountain.

He'd eliminated Gilroy already. Who had shot him? He hadn't been able to make out a face in the hazy, half-moonlit darkness. Did it matter? Everyone out here was going to die. He'd kill all the sharks, all the fish, all the whales. All of it.

He braced himself against the helm of the boat, gaining purchase and rising to his knees. Using his good arm, he propped the butt of the crossbow against his shoulder. When the shooter came over the gunwale, he'd bury an arrow in the bastard's eye, sweet as a flower in a lapel. He was the best shooter in the region, maybe the world. No, not maybe, he was the best. They just wouldn't let him compete. Soon, they would pay. He had set a machine in motion that they couldn't stop. No one would suspect a thing. No need to outwit security, they'd be the ones letting her into the arena.

A *thump* on the side of the boat brought him back to the task at hand. The games were seven days away. He had to deal with this problem first.

CHAPTER 31

"Did you hit him?" I asked from my prone position on the soggy bottom of the row boat.

My breath came out in labored gasps. We pitched and rolled so violently, it was hard to believe we weren't capsizing.

Leber gazed at the bobbing fishing boat as he answered. "I'm pretty certain. Question is, did I put him down for keeps?"

Leber had to be one hell of a shot to hit someone on a swaying boat while this rowboat we occupied also pitched and rolled in the nasty swell. My time in basic training had made me a competent shot, but nothing special. Maybe he'd just gotten lucky. Leber struck me as the lucky type.

I sucked oxygen in nose, out mouth, trying to calm my jangled nerves. My body shivered badly, the gusty conditions weren't helping. When you got far enough away from shore, even near the Equator, it got chilly. Add having a crossbow and a gun stuck in your face for hours on end, and a little shock was understandable. I tried to forgive myself for not being tougher.

"Just take a second. He's hit, I'm sure of it."

I shook my head like a wet dog as a spray of water doused my face from more whitewater slapping the side of the hull. "You don't understand. This one's like a guy on PCP. The bullet's likely to make him madder."

Leber stared at me a while, then pulled a gun from his ankle holster. "I suppose you'll need this if you're gonna be any help." I took the weapon and nearly fumbled it into Davy Jones' Locker.

Leber put a large hand over my shaking ones. "Can you do this?" he said, his face serious as stone.

I nodded, stilled my convulsions and clenched my teeth. "What choice do I have?"

He pushed the gun that I'd been pointing in his direction downward. He clicked off the safety. "Just point and shoot…at the bad guys."

"There's only one," I said as he steered us alongside using the oars.

"I saw two men with you, one at the wheel and…"

"That was Gilroy Antsy at the wheel. He's dead." I quickly explained Gilroy's demise.

"So he's using a crossbow?"

"I think so. He likes arrows."

The rowboat bumped the side of the fishing vessel louder than we would have liked. Leber remained impassive. I re-engaged the safety and tucked the gun to climb aboard. My face and body ached from the beatings and the pepper spray and the hangover. Shit, maybe I was still a little inebriated.

Leber secured the rowboat to the side of the larger boat as he hoisted himself up and lay down on the inside of the railing, just out of sight of whatever waited on the other side of the raised gunwale.

I clambered up beside him and we positioned ourselves on

the edge, our noses inches apart. I slipped off one of my soaked sneakers. Leber nodded, liking the idea. He pointed to the left and pointed at his chest, then pointed right and at the shoe in my hand. Finally, he pointed at me and straight up. After staring at him blankly for a couple moments, I nodded my understanding.

Gun out. Safety off. I flung the shoe to my right, then both of us popped up, Leber going over to the left and I went straight over the top, guns out. We fired. Our bullets both entered harmlessly into the deck. Blood was splattered everywhere. Gilroy Antsy lay in the corner, a trickle of blood and that iron stench coming off him despite the gusting wind. There was another splatter of blood on the far gunwale. It appeared that Leber had indeed hit Jermaine.

"Shit," I muttered.

Leber put a finger to his lips.

We climbed down to the deck. Other than the wind and water, no sound. I started shaking again. Where was he? There weren't a lot of places to go. I ticked off the options. Did he go over the side? Unlikely. Did he circle around the standing shelter to the bow? Possibly, but from the gunwale I hadn't seen anyone there.

Leber's head rotated side to side, like a lighthouse beacon, scanning the deck, running calculations. Then, I saw it.

"Hey, he's not here. Can we fire this thing up and get back to shore? I think he went over. The guy's fish food."

Leber looked at me. "You sure? You think he just went in the drink?"

"Nut job like that? For sure." As I said this, I pointed at the non-descript white bench that comes standard in every fishing boat to hold various nautical supplies like a fish bat, rope, flares, and life preservers.

Leber leveled the gun at the bench and crouched, maintaining balance as the waves continued to rock us. "Yeah, yeah, ok, Boise. You get 'er started, I go make sure my rowboat's secure."

Without looking away from the bench, he nodded me toward the steering wheel. I went and started the engine. It fired up on the first turn, idling and sputtering as it kicked water and dirty fumes.

Leber continued the act, boldly climbing on top of the bench, then getting up on the gunwale again where our boat continued to bang against the side of the fishing vessel.

"Not quite secure, Boise," Leber said, making sure it was clear to anyone hiding that he was now behind the bench with no clear shot. "I'm gonna tie it tighter."

I smiled and turned around, knowing that Leber was signaling we were both preoccupied and using our hands, therefore not holding guns. The lid inched open and the tip of the arrow peeked out, pointing right at me. I saw a reflection in the whites of Jermaine's eyes,

"Freeze, motherfucker!" Leber demanded.

"I got your boy in my sights," Jermaine said. His white teeth glistened as he grinned. "You ain't faster…"

Leber shot him twice from above through the lid of the bench.

I hustled over and yanked open the lid. Leber maintained his position, gun still held by both hands in a classic shooter's stance. Along with a shattered elbow, Jermaine now sported two red wounds center mass. His eyes and his mouth were all open, but neither recognition nor breath lived there any longer. The glock he'd been holding earlier was beside him, a back-up weapon in case he missed with the crossbow.

CHAPTER 32

After retrieving my phone from Gilroy, I found it was drenched. I started to mash the power button.

"Don't try to use it. Put it in dry rice for at least a few hours," Leber said. I stuffed it back in my pocket and extended my hand. He pulled out his phone. It slipped out of his fingers, plunking into the ocean.

"Shit!" Leber yelled, his hands trembling.

"Probably no reception anyway," I said.

"Goddamn case," he growled.

"By the way, how did you find me?"

***

I dry heaved over the side three more times on the way back to shore. My stomach was as dry as an Englishman's sense of humor. We got back to the guesthouse and demanded a whiskey after pounding on the bar to get Lucy's attention.

Lucy shuffled out of the kitchen. "Is seven in da morning, Boise. You need coffee, not whiskey. Maybe eggs."

The thought of runny eggs almost sent me into dry heaves again.

"Lucy, after the night we had, I need a whiskey. Single-malt."

"I save your life once already today. I ain't doin' it again."

She was right. The only reason Leber had even known I was kidnapped was because of Lucy, sitting up late on the porch again, playing solitaire. She'd spotted Gilroy and Jermaine shove me into their car and take off. She found Leber's business card on my bedside table.

"The only place I could think to go was right back to where we'd found Francine. Crooks are so unimaginative," Leber said.

"In a rowboat? In the dark?"

"I row before sunrise in that harbor every morning."

"Lucky me," I said.

I pulled out Leber's ankle gun, a Kel-Tec PF-9, and handed it to him. He studied the gun, then handed it back.

"You know how to shoot this?"

"Sure, I can handle a basic weapon like this."

He handed it back. "You keep it. I just acquired another."

"Aren't you worried about the registration?"

"Nope, but you'll have to get your own ankle holster," he said.

I pocketed the gun right before Marge popped up from behind the bar and poured me a Balvenie, two-fingers neat. I clutched her wrist and tilted another finger's worth. The golden medicine warmed my gullet as I slumped over the gouge in the smooth surface made by a bullet years ago.

"One day you're gonna have to tell me the story of this bullet hole," I said. "They all have a story, right?"

Silent Marge proceeded to run water into a sink under the counter.

Hours later, I dozed on the couch under the check-in desk where Lucy slept when expecting a late night or early morning arrival. I hadn't had the energy to trudge up the stairs to my room, and Leber was too drunk to carry me when he'd left. I rolled over to find Lucy's knees at eye-level. She was greeting a guest; I waited patiently for her to conclude the transaction.

When I tapped her knee, she leapt back, cawing like a crow. "Boise! Watch those hands."

She shooed me into the kitchen where Marge pulled an icepack from the freezer and placed it in my hand before gently pressing my hand up to my black eye. Marge held up ten fingers, closed one hand and opened another five fingers, then pointed at the egg timer. It ticked.

Fifteen minutes later, I forced myself to plod upstairs. I brushed and flossed for nearly ten minutes, chasing it with a warm shower. When I tried to shave, the hot water burned my raw face.

Moments after I was back in my room, my landline rang. Lucy patched the call through. Dana.

"Do I get an exclusive?"

This woman had a one-track mind.

"You back?"

"No," she said in a pouty voice. "Fucking Pickering wants continuing coverage. They've got television here, too. Something to do with Jarl. It might involve the governor."

"Ours?"

"No, silly, the one here in Tortola. Anyway, this story's good, but nothing's as good as murder. I hear you've got the killers."

"Yeah, we got 'em. Problem is there's no trial. One killed his partner and then a cop killed him."

"Which cop?"

"Leber. You know him?"

"Yup. A bit unconventional. I like him." I could hear Dana

grinning through the phone, her own teenaged giddiness. My cell phone buzzed from a bowl of rice in the corner.

"Gotta go, Dana."

"When can we do this? Pickering wants a story."

"You're doing it by phone?"

"Yup."

We arranged a time later in the day after I got some shut eye. I had already spent hours giving the cops my story and helping Leber fill out paperwork. He had helped it move along, but a fuller statement was in the offing. She said Pickering wouldn't like it. I told her to call Leber in the meantime and to let Pickering know that Gilroy and Jermaine were the ones who ransacked Savannah's house looking for Kendal's notes. She said she'd tell him.

By the time I hung up, I'd missed the cell call. Sleep first, call back later.

It turned out my ordeal was enough for Pickering to bring Dana back to interview me in person, as well as to work on some other story cooking here in St. Thomas.

"It's not a big deal," Dana grumbled. "Tortola's twenty miles away. There's a bridge in Louisiana that's longer. Besides, you're worth it."

The Greenhouse was quiet, as the brunch crowd had already deserted and, for whatever reason, the televisions were on the fritz, so no football to entice people into drinking in the middle of their Sunday afternoon. Dana had selected a table in the far corner, away from prying ears.

"Love you, too," I said, giving her a hug.

"You hug me like I'm a guy. Why is that?"

"I don't know what you're talking about. That's how I hug."

"No, I've seen you hug other women without the pat on the back and the closed fist between." She proceeded to demonstrate, puffing out her chest and deepening her voice. "Hey, dude Dana, what's up? Hug. Hug. Pat. Pat."

I laughed in spite of myself. "I do that. It's my way."

"Uh huh. Well, just 'cause I'm a lesbo doesn't give you permission to treat me like a dude. I'm fem."

"Hmmm ... " I extended my hand and made the kinda-not-really gesture.

"The point is, I'm a woman, so hug me like a woman. Now, here's your beer. Start talking."

"Did you order a burger, too?" I said hopefully.

"With fries. Bloody as hell, all the fixings. Anything else, Sugar Ray?"

She licked tomato juice off her top lip after taking a sip of her Bloody Mary. I always worried about the celery stalk going up my nose with those drinks.

"I want more free ads for bringing Pickering another paper-selling story." Dana just stared, so I back-tracked. "Nope. Perfect, right down to you nagging me. Did we get married?"

"You are so much a part of the patriarchy." She glanced at her watch. "Okay, let's get down to brass tacks. What happened?"

She tapped record on her phone. I relayed my tale, leaving out anything I deemed irrelevant or embarrassing to my clients. She got what counted, the abduction and my escape ala Leber. It would read like an action-adventure. I also omitted that I was passed out when they snatched me. Instead I said they'd grabbed me as I was walking up to The Manner and knocked me out.

"You have a concussion?"

"Don't know," I answered, licking some Guinness foam off my upper lip.

"Get it checked."

"Doc said I'm fine. Pepper spray has no lasting effects."

"Doesn't Leber have a partner?"

"Yeah, Barnes. I got the feeling Barnes is a nine-to-fiver. Leber, he's a lifer."

"A man after my own heart," Dana said.

The waitress bopped over and swept away my empty plate. I

ordered my fourth beer. Dana put a stop to things after two Bloody Marys.

"That's it, huh?" She pursed her lips and hit stop on the recording. She typed something into her phone, then gave me a serious look. "Boise, I'm worried about you. You really don't look good."

I shifted in my seat. She had this nasty habit of pop-analyzing my psyche out of nowhere on occasions when I was in no mood for it.

"Ouch."

"Don't give me that. You don't really care about your appearance, or you wouldn't have on that sweat stained tank-top and flip flops."

"Jesus, Dana, what's with the harsh judgments?"

"I'm worried about the way you're conducting yourself."

"I didn't ask for you to intervene. I'm doing fine. Yes, I'm a little burned out. I got careless."

"You left a couple things out of that story you just told me."

I shook my head. The hot needle was rising. Who was Dana to start patronizing me? When we'd first met, she slathered some bullshit pop psychology on me about Evelyn dying and my depression.

"I have clients to protect."

"Not what I'm talking about. I understand if you protect sources and clients. What I don't understand is exactly how those thugs kidnapped you. That part doesn't make a lot of sense."

She stared at me. I squirmed, a beetle under a magnifying glass on a sunny day. My beer tasted good and cold. Not cold enough, but I remained pinned to my seat. Heave-ho.

"Power-drinking another beer isn't going to scare me off." She waited. "Neither is the silent treatment. Boise, talk to me. Where's your head? Is it Evelyn? What about that flyer I gave you?"

My eyelids drooped. Sleeping in this chair in this bar on this island seemed like a lovely idea. Out on the waterfront, a wave crashed on the breakwater then receded, leaving only an oily slick on the gray, shell-laced concrete. I stood shakily. My shorts puckered to the back of my legs.

"You got this?" I asked.

"'Course, it's on me. Your payment was the story." She smiled, trying to emotionally backtrack. "Boise, you know I'm your friend, right?"

"I'll see you later, Dana." I couldn't help asking one more question. "Do I have a burning need to be liked?"

Dana smiled, held her drink up, "Yes. Did Leber tell you that?" She watched my face. "Yeah, he fancies himself an amateur profiler, but really he's only good at lame observations about regular people like us. Serial killers go right over his head."

Evelyn had accused me of being too nice during our relationship. I often wondered if that's why she cheated, because I wasn't dangerous enough.

I walked out to the waterfront and headed west. My head needed clearing. Part of me hoped a passing car would swerve and knock me into the water.

CHAPTER 33

Lindberg Bay lay southeast of Cyril E. King Airport. Since returning to St. Thomas, the small beach had called me back time and again. The ancient dock that seemed to weather every storm had the worn look of driftwood.

In my youth, I'd spent days lounging and playing here. The airport was sleepier then. The memories of relaxing afternoons fishing with Roger and Lucas gave me a sense of peace.

On the way, I'd picked up a spool of fishing line, a sinker, some small hooks, squid, and a bobber. Flies buzzed around the purple cephalopod carcass next to me as the line plunked into the turquoise water.

The sun beat down, baking my skin like a cookie. I wasn't much of a sunscreen user, being partly African, I figured I was good. Stupid, I know. Everyone can get skin cancer. I fished a length of floss out of my pocket and threaded it between my teeth. A hunk of hamburger popped out and bobbed in the water above my bait.

On the beach, broad sea grape leaves waved in welcome or warning. A plane shuttled down the runway and roared into the sky. Further down, a couple wearing bathing suits exited The Beachcomber restaurant and grabbed two lounge chairs. They laughed about something.

Dana had no business in my business. Drinking was my business. I was good at it. I wasn't good at much.

"Fuck her," I muttered in the direction of the cheerful couple, who were now walking toward the lapping blue water hand in hand. "Screw Dana, and screw Irene." Then I thought, *Yarey on the other hand…she's not so bad…yet.*

A foul mood descended after these cases. One thing seemed to have an overarching effect on all relations: avarice. Gilroy wanted the distillery because, as Leber had informed me, he and Dominic Bacon had been lovers. In numerous love letters they'd found in a shoebox under Gilroy's bed, Dominic had promised to leave Francine and give the distillery to Gilroy. He'd never made good on that promise.

Presumably, he had tried to use those love letters to convince Francine he should get the distillery, but how did he reason killing her would achieve that end? Stupid, Boise. He didn't. I recalled the argument between Gilroy and Jermaine. She wasn't supposed to die. Neither Jermaine nor Gilroy could control Jermaine's bloodlust. He drowned her. He was only supposed to scare her. Hold her over the edge and let her blood drip into the water from the cut on her arm in the coroner's report. Probably promised sharks would come. Instead of holding, he dropped her. She sank like a bullet.

Critical thinking became a casualty of avarice. I'd seen it before, bad judgment heaped on bad information. Garbage in, garbage out.

Instead of being grateful for what he was getting, a half-million dollars, or whatever it finally came out to be, the man wanted more. Believed he was owed more. Maybe he was. From Kendal's notes, it appeared that half-a-mill was all Francine Bacon was willing to give to anyone involved. She wanted to be equitable without being taken advantage of. "An equitable bitch" was the term Kendal had written in the margin notes.

Francine was as tough as granite and her calculations on present value of work done appeared to provide minimum wage level reparations. That's all she was willing to do. Furthermore, via Kendal's notes, she argued, and on this front, Kendal had agreed, that Gilroy Antsy had personally been paid quite well, among the best salaries in the rum business, for his position over the past seven years. The sufferings of his ancestors were his in a sense, but not entirely. At least that's what she appeared to believe.

A valid question in all reparations discussions always raised hackles: where does the guilt stop? Sins of the father and all that crap.

It all seemed so obvious now, like I should have known it was Gilroy. The fact that the man received half-a-mill made me doubt his resolve. Problem was, I viewed his motives through my eyes, and probably the eyes of all the other people being compensated who had expressed gratitude when informed of the attempted generosity of the Bacons. Gilroy Antsy's ambitions fueled self-righteous thoughts to action. At that point, all he needed was someone willing to carry out his plan.

Enter Jermaine LaGrange, a man who opted to finance his niece's dreams by becoming an assassin. It turned out he was wanted for questioning in two other jurisdictions. He already possessed the skills, why not put them to profitable use. Gilroy really only wanted a credible threat. What he got was bloodthirsty action. It made no sense to off Francine, but renegotiations required brinkmanship and real brinkmanship required risk. Nothing more risky than bringing a psychotic killer along as your partner in crime.

I whispered Gilroy's words again. "She wasn't supposed to die."

A couple of things still gnawed at me. Why was Isabelle LaGrange training on that timed targeting Jermaine made her do on the archery range? You are not timed in any pressing fashion in archery competition. This question nibbled at me like the little fish that swam around picking dead skin off your feet in shallow water. Dead skin. And Jermaine had mentioned Isabelle being unbeatable at "all of it" and doing special things.

On a completely different tangent, would Isabelle continue competitive archery without her maniacal uncle pushing her? She had a competition, The Virgin Islands Archery Championships, the finals scheduled for Saturday. They were outfitting the Emile Griffith Ballpark near the seaplane ramp since it had the best location, parking and capacity. I intended to be there.

The small-gauge fishing line tugged gently against my finger, yanking me out of my thoughts. I tugged back, careful not to pull the bait away before the fish was hooked. Tug-tug, tug-tug, then nothing. I pulled the line out. A naked hook.

"Nicely played, fishy friend."

Staring into the crystal water, I searched in vain for the culprit. Can't see well through water, even when it's this clear. Three dark shapes circled above the silky sand. There was no way of knowing which one had taken the bait.

Shooing away a patch of relentless flies, I dropped the remainder carcass into the water, packed up and propped myself against the crook of a palm. My tilted hat blacked out the bright afternoon. Siesta time.

***

I stirred a few hours later in time to see the setting sun blast orange stains over the clouds near the horizon. A bunch of people had gathered in various locations on the beach, including a young girl and a man I hoped was her father. Then they kissed as he caressed her back. Not her father ... I hoped.

What I'd really been fuming about finally hit me. I needed to talk to Yarey about her father, and I wasn't looking forward to that conversation. Yarey had been subbing for Irene in my latest fantasies.

Upon leaving Dana, I'd turned off my cell, knowing she'd be relentless. I wasn't wrong. Switching it on, I discovered eight missed calls. Five from Dana, and three from a local number that looked vaguely familiar.

It turned out to be the landline from the Bacon residence. The last call had only come in moments ago. The message was from Hillary.

"Boise, I need to speak to you. Please. I know you have no reason to help me, but I need your help. Just come to the house when you get this. I hope it's not too late." For a change, she sounded sober.

***

Hillary answered the door when I arrived. Her dress leaned to one side, like it might melt off her body from the heat of her distress. The wrinkles that she covered with foundation poked through the caked make-up. There was no hiding her age today. Even stranger, she didn't seem to care.

"Thank God! Where have you been?"

"Nice to see you, too, Hillary."

She held a glass of white wine and took a gulp before pulling me inside. Her calling me was way out of character, but the wine gave me hope that some sense of normalcy remained. The sounds of angry voices boomed from the kitchen.

"What are you waiting for? Get in there before they kill each other." She shoved me forward into the hallway outside the kitchen. Daryl and Herbie were in each other's face.

Daryl shouted, "You bastard! It's the least you owe to me and mine. The least. It's the same arrangement I had with Francine."

"I do not owe you or that woman anything," Herbie spat back. "Besides, my mother was a fool to pay so much for what? A babysitter? You know it wasn't about a real job."

"Herbie!"

"Her name is Gertrude and by all that's holy you owe her more than you could ever pay, but I'm giving you a number … "

"HERBIE!"

Both men turned, their faces burned red with seething anger.

"What the fuck is he doing here?" Herbie demanded.

"I called him," Hillary said. "We need a third party for this negotiation."

"We are not negotiating with this man," Herbie said, moving toward Hillary while pointing back at Daryl.

"Hey there, Boise," Daryl said pleasantly.

I nodded at him. "Daryl. Herbie. I'm not sure why I'm here, but if I can help … "

"You can't," Herbie said while staring at Hillary. "What the fuck, Hill? How clear do I have to be? No more outsiders. We already have this fool making waves and now you want to spread our business to this one? What's to stop him from blackmailing us too?"

"Blackmail?" I asked. "Whoa, what is happening here? I want no part of any illegal activity."

"See, Hill? He wants no part. This here involves this man." He again pointed at Daryl. "Blackmailing us. Blackmailing Francine. This one … " He jabbed a finger in my direction. I was getting sick and tired of all the pointing. "This one, he doesn't even know the truth about Harold the day our mother died."

"What truth?" I asked.

"Herbie, shut up," Hillary shouted.

"Harold was not with us when Mama was killed. We lied."

This hit me between the eyes like cold water, but I had no

time to shake it off. I wasn't sure it mattered. They had lied, but I already knew who the killers were and Harold wasn't involved, was he?

"How many times I gotta tell you? I worked for your mother," Daryl said menacingly.

"He's a degenerate gambler who's on the run from someone you don't want to owe money to. So, goodbye, Boise. And it wasn't nice knowing you. Shouldn't you go interview Harold and do your fucking job?"

Daryl grinned. "You see how they is, Boise? They look down on us. They always looked down, even when my Gertrude was helping him with his problem. Now, we want help. It ain't blackmail. It's what we're owed."

"Is that right? You are owed. If anyone is owed, it's Gertrude. Does she even know about this?"

At this, Daryl paused. "Naw, she don't know."

"You see. She doesn't even know. And, if I know her, she doesn't want any part of this. She wants to stay out of the Bacon family forever. Right? In fact, she probably told you to steer clear. Where'd you say you were going when you left to come down here?"

"I didn't tell her."

"What was that?" Herbie demanded.

"Nothing. I didn't tell her nothing. But that doesn't matter, 'cause I'm the one askin'. I need it."

"I knew it." Herbie said with I-told-you-so glee.

Hillary had finished her wine and was getting more out of the fridge. "You see why I needed you here, Boise?"

"I'm still not clear."

"I'll crystallize it for you, Detective," Herbie said, sarcastically. "This man knows something and to keep quiet, he wants us to give him money so he can pay off another gambling debt he's incurred. Our mother was paying him and now that she's dead, he wants us to keep paying. Understand?"

"Is it important that this information remain private?" I asked.

Hillary swung around with a bottle in hand. "Oh yes, very important."

"Hill, what's to stop him from doing it again? He's got a problem. He kept our mother paying for the rest of her life. He'll do the same to us."

She stood next to the open refrigerator. "Do you think Junior will ever forgive us?" she asked, panting like a gazelle fleeing a lion.

"Forgive what?" Those two words cascaded through the room as all four of us turned in unison. Junior had asked them.

"I thought you were gone for the night?"

"Papa, don't change the subject. What won't I forgive?"

"This is not your concern," Herbie uttered impatiently. "Leave now."

Junior didn't move. The boy and the father stood, one in hall-darkness and one in kitchen-light. After a moment, Junior stepped out of the hall and into the kitchen, joining the rest of us.

I felt as out of place as an oboist auditioning for a reggae band. Part of me wanted to go, to let them work whatever this was out, but the other part, the part that had once witnessed a police beating with equal parts disgust and fascination, wanted to be right here.

"Boy ho boy, you just like ordering everyone about, don't ya?" Daryl said, his twang rising alongside his outrage.

"Who are you?" Junior said.

"Never mind who he is," Herbie said. "I told you to leave. The adults have to work some things out."

Hillary emitted a sound, like a bird choking. She slumped to the floor, leaning against the cold bottom shelf of the refrigerator. Crazily, I thought about what a waste of energy keeping the door open like that was.

"He's Daryl Evans," Hillary said.

Junior blinked rapidly. "Evans?" He turned to Herbie. "Isn't that my mama's last name? Gertrude Evans. The one who left you?" He turned to Daryl. "Are you related to me?"

Hillary piped up again, but this time her whining had been replaced by what can only be described in retrospect as years of repressed pain and silence, voiced in a single sentence.

"No, he's not related to you because that woman is not your mother."

Junior's face remained impassive. "What are you talking about, Aunt Hill?"

"Shut your mouth, Hillary. I'm warning you. Shut your mouth!" Herbie headed toward his sister. Daryl and I stepped in front of him.

"How dare you!" Herbie yelled at both of us, but he stopped. He was not imposing despite his height.

Hillary sniffled once, then rose to her feet. She put her glass of wine on a shelf in the refrigerator and shut the door.

"Hillary! Stop!"

Daryl shoved Herbie into a chair and we stood over him while Hillary walked over to Junior.

"I've wanted to tell you this forever. I've wanted to be true to you." She now held Junior's shoulders.

"You can't take this back, woman. Once you let this out."

Daryl leaned over the thin, distinguished man, put his hands around Herbie's neck and whispered, "Stop talking or so help me God, I'll stop ya. Just gimme a reason, little man."

Herbie's adam's apple bobbed once and fell still on top of Daryl's thumb. Daryl released him and said, "Now tell it to him straight, Hillary."

"He's gotten to be your father, but you've been told by all of us for years that Gertrude was your mother and she abandoned both of you. That's a lie. She agreed to it at first, but couldn't live with it, so she left. And she was right to leave. It's unendurable to live with a lie this large. I believe it's killing me, or I'm killing me

267

because I can't live with it anymore either. If leaving would make it go away, I'd do it. But that won't work. Only one thing can make this pain stop. I have to tell you." She looked down as if scanning her soul for the right words. Finally, she just said it. "I'm your mother."

Herbie put his face in his hands and shook his head back and forth. "That's not true. Junior, don't listen to her. She's lying to you."

A tension left Junior's face then. A lifelong yearning banked away into the abyss as he took in what we all knew to be truth once voiced. The truth that his parents had been right here all along and somehow, deep down, we'd all participated in the lie, because the truth was too stunning, too real.

CHAPTER 34

The next morning Daryl Evans and I cruised to the airport.

"What are you going to do?"

"I'm not entirely sure," Daryl said. "Herbie's right, I owe some people money, and they ain't the most patient folks this side of the Mississippi. I thought the Francine gravy-train would go on and on. Then, she disappeared."

"Was it all a lie?"

He licked his lips and spit into a bush. "You mean was I really working for Francine and keeping an eye on Junior? That was true. She'd said since she was paying me, to make it look real, I should actually work for her so nobody asked no questions."

"Francine trusted you even though you were squeezing her?"

"Trust might be a bit strong, but Francine had the dough. That broad was tough. I'd call her a realist. She blamed herself for what her kids done, for how they felt about each other. Turns out she was even more scared of the truth about them than them."

We loitered under the awning outside the terminal. Taxis dropped off travellers and sped away.

Talking to him now, it all seemed so logical and yes, what a realist would do. So I asked why he didn't do what a realist might do next. "Why not run?"

"Gertrude. They'll take it out on my daughter if I don't do something about it. I done lost everybody else in my life to this curse I got, I'm not losing my daughter. 'Sides, I'm too old to go trying to hide from these bloodhounds. Do I look like James Bond?" He spit again. "I'll figure something out. Always do."

"What will you tell her about what happened here?"

He turned back one last time. "I'll tell her the truth for a change. It's what she wanted all along, for Junior to know, but she still loves Herbie despite everything. She never felt it was right to tell him herself. This way, everyone got what they wanted. Everyone 'cept me. That cursed secret was my meal ticket. Now I gotta deal with my shit."

"We all do eventually. Don't they have Gamblers Anonymous?"

"I'm not a joiner." He shook my hand and headed into the terminal. "If you're ever in Decatur, look me up. I dig your style, Boise."

CHAPTER 35

I spent the next couple days on lockdown in my room, drinking and eating and watching bad soap operas since the cable television was on the fritz again. Somehow those people's disturbed lives made me feel better about this ordeal.

I needed to venture forth and collect my investigation fees. Rent and bills would soon be due.

My phone had been silent except for Leber calling to get answers to questions for his report. I texted back my observations on our adventure, then stole back under the covers.

The Virgin Islands Archery Championship finals were coming up. There was little doubt that Isabelle LaGrange would easily qualify, so I decided to skip the early rounds. I needed to make a stop to see someone who'd been on my mind all week.

Yarelle Antsy might not like seeing me, but I couldn't get her off my mind.

I timed my arrival at the Bacon Distillery for noon, thinking she'd take a break for lunch. She was at her station, stopping the bottles, a small, pained expression on her face. At the top of the stairs, the lights in Gilroy's office were dark, waiting for the next occupant. For now, they mourned his death, too.

I'd rehearsed this encounter. As soon as she punched out, I made my way over.

"Hi."

"Boise. Oh gosh, Boise."

To my shock, she hugged me, like a friend, warm and close.

"I've been wanting to call you or come by or … " She shook her bent head. "I don't know what to say. I'm so sorry about my father."

What she really meant, and I could see it on her face and feel it in my chest like a deep cut, was "I don't know what to feel."

"Are you hungry?" was all I could think to ask.

Her demeanor brightened at my avoidance. We were both happy to avoid the subject of Gilroy Antsy. She chimed, "I am, a little. Actually, I wasn't, but now that you are here, I feel a pang for the first time all week. Is that weird?"

"Want to have lunch with me? My treat."

We ate together at a chicken fry joint a few blocks away in a lime green building. We avoided the subject of her dead father, which was a relief to me. The man wanted to give her a better financial life. He wanted security. He wanted his dream. And he killed for it.

"My next singing gig is in three weeks. I'm not sure I'm up to it."

"Why not?" I asked.

Her eyes cast down again, searching the empty plate for answers. He wondered then if she even knew the questions. "I guess because of what happened. I can see you're thinking about it. Isabelle says to go back to the tasks at hand, so I've been trying to rehearse and work. I've worked overtime all week. Then I go to Anna's to rehearse, then we go out drinking. But my voice. It feels like my vocal cords are going to snap. Like they're pulled to the thinnest point." She dropped her hands into her lap. "I don't know. It makes no sense."

"It makes sense. My voice cracks when I'm tired and depressed."

"You depressed? You always seem in control."

That was a laugh. "Thanks, but of course that's not true."

"So what? How do I get it back?"

"Your voice will come back when you've healed is my guess."

"I didn't even like him," she said, a tear running down her cheek. She quickly wiped it away with a napkin. "He's dead, but mostly I wasn't crazy about him as a friend. He had good dad qualities. He wanted all the right things for me, but it had to be his way. He was hard. A hard, driven man." She nodded, a picture in her mind to which only she could bear witness. "Sometimes, he ran over me."

Sounds from the kitchen and the street carried us out the door into the tropical heat. A man behind the counter--he seemed to know Yarey--waved while punching something into the cash register.

The knot in my stomach grew as we got closer to separating. This was the time. We were alone and we'd just had some kind of psuedo-date I'd orchestrated by showing up unannounced at lunchtime.

"So, uh, Yarey, I know this might be a bad time and if you don't want to you don't have to, but, uh, would you want to go see the archery tournament on Saturday?"

"'Course, silly! Everyone's going to that."

"Everyone?"

"Yeah, to support Isabelle. You're gonna sit with us, right?"

"Right. Yes. I'll be there."

"Great."

We had arrived at the punch clock in the distillery.

CHAPTER 36

My bed was scattered with discarded masses of clothing. "Masses" might be a strong word since I only owned a little clothing, but what I owned was on the bed, all discarded as unworthy. Everything felt either overdressed, the one suit and shirt, or underdressed, namely the shorts, t-shirts, pretty much everything I owned.

A knock at the door.

"What?" I bellowed. I needed to make a decision soon so I'd get there in time to sit next to Yarey. The knocking sounded again. I started to open it, then thought better of it and used the peephole despite my impatience.

"Dana! Perfect timing. You can assist." I pulled her inside and slammed the door. I was wearing only boxers.

"Jeez on bread, Boise, must we constantly repeat the clothing optional entrance. You don't even appear sauced."

"One beer so far today," I said, pointing at the empty on the bedside table. "Needed the carbs to get going." Then I remembered she was supposed to be off island. "What are you doing back, mi son?"

"Newspaper doesn't want to pay another night in a hotel there, so I'm back here. What's all this?" she asked.

"I need help with what to wear."

Dana picked through the options, pulling out a brown t-shirt and jeans.

"I'm gonna be hot," I mumbled. "What about this white one?"

"You been to an outdoor event here lately? Dusty as hell at these things. White will be dirty in no time. You want to wear what a woman likes. She'll prefer seeing you in jeans. Women sacrifice comfort in the name of fashion all the time, and she'll appreciate you doing it for her."

"Is that what you're doing?" I said indicating her ensemble of a halter top, cut-off jeans and her usual red cap.

"I'm not trying to impress a woman today. I'm just little ol' me."

"What about Annie?"

"She's off galavanting somewhere in Europe this week. So, what's new?"

***

The sun was high and clouds rolled around the heavens, welcoming us to the competition. We had about an hour before it was "go time," so I suggested some food and a beer.

"Boise, you just don't stop, do you?"

"Look at me, Dana? Do I look healthy?"

She looked me up and down then spun me around. "Fair enough, you've lost weight. What are you doing?"

"Working. Lots of working. I'm eating less."

"Good on ya. Where do you want to sit?"

"What about there?"

"Wrong answer. See that table over there? That's the judges' table. Who has the best view in the place?"

"Yeah, okay."

"Who?"

"Judges have a good view."

"Who's your queen?"

"You, Dana. You are my queen."

As I moved ahead of her, she smacked my butt. "Second row, we don't want to be too low."

"All right," I mumbled. Dana could be so bossy.

We spread out with seats between us on the hot metal bleachers. A few people milled about the field, checking this and that. A mourning dove alighted on one of the targets, cooed a couple of beats then flapped away. My eyes drooped. The end of all this madness had set in. Everything ached softly, especially my left foot and my trick knee. I wondered if that knee would ever heal properly or if it would ache forever. Probably permanent. The U.S. Army wouldn't pay for anything except rehab, which had improved things, but had left me with pain. The pain reminded me of Evelyn. It was why we met.

"Hi, Boise," said a soft voice from behind me.

I bolted upright, out of my reverie. "Hi, Yarey! I saved you a seat."

Out of the corner of my eye I saw Dana's smirk as she pretended not to notice my awkwardness.

"Dana," I said. She didn't look over. "Dana!" I said more loudly.

"Huh? Oh, Boise, did you call me?" She put her hand on her chest as if she was verklempt. "I am so entranced by this spectacle."

"Yes, it's quite a setup," Harold agreed, coming up from behind Yarey. "I'm Harold," he said, extending his hand. "This here's Yarey." Harold turned to me. "What's up, man? Why you wearing jeans in this heat?"

Everyone scooched around to make room. I managed to maneuver Yarey next to me while Harold plopped beside Dana.

"So what's your sign, Dana?"

"Did you just ask me a question from the seventies?" Dana shot back.

"Well, yeah, it's an 'in' line again, right Boise-boy?"

Harold seemed in a chipper mood. "Sure, Harry-pal, if you say so." I leaned close to Yarey. "Is he drunk?"

She held her thumb and index finger together and held them to her lips. I nodded. I asked Yarey to go get drinks with me. Harold had the full-court press going on Dana. Boy was he barking up the wrong tree, but Dana never let on. She enjoyed the male attention sometimes.

Once away, I asked Yarey about her coming with Harold. "He offered me a ride when he came by the distillery yesterday. I figured why not. No one else had offered a ride."

My face blushed. "Oh man, I, uh, don't own a car. Sorry, Yarey, I messed that up. I can get you home afterwards, how's that?"

"Yeah, okay," she giggled. "It's kinda fun to watch you squirm. Not driving is hot."

"It is?"

She rolled her eyes. "No, I'm kidding. Why don't you have a car?"

"Tired of driving," I said emphatically. "Living in L.A. can cure anyone of ever wanting to drive again."

"So how do you get around?"

"I manage."

"You mean with your little friend?"

"Dana? She's just a friend. But she does give me a lot of rides."

"I'll bet. You know, Harold has a point. Why'd you wear

jeans?"

"This seemed like a more formal occasion," I said.

She laughed and punched me lightly on the shoulder. Physical contact, a good sign. We got beers and snacks for everyone. Harold snatched a bag of Cool Ranch Doritos out of my hand. Before I even sat down, he was munching away while spitting crumbs and explaining archery to Dana in a self-righteous tone.

"He loves to talk archery," I said.

Yarey nodded.

It was already eleven-fifteen. "When's this gonna start?" I asked Harold.

He ignored me, still working hard on Dana, who looked like she was growing weary of the archery diatribe.

Three people walked out and took seats at the judges' table. Dana excused herself to use the bathroom. Without his target present, Harold's attention returned to Yarey and me. He leaned across Yarey's lap and stage whispered, "Dude, this is gonna be interesting right here."

"What?" I asked.

"That judge in the middle. Man oh man, what a shit-show."

I looked at Yarey, who seemed as lost as I was. "Harold, what are you talking about?"

"Aw, nothing. You'll see."

"Hey, how's Junior?"

"How do you think?"

"Why didn't you ever tell the kid about his parents?" I asked. "You knew."

Harold's gaze remained fixed on the field, but he was no longer in the present. His mind somewhere else. A dark place. Yarey winced at my blunt question. As Harold's non-response stretched out, she became more uncomfortable until she blurted, "Harold, you were telling Dana about the archery. Anything we should be looking for?" He didn't respond, so Yarey pressed. "Harold, what's that?" She pointed at a block with a number on it.

"Hey man, you ever had a family secret? Something you knew would blow the whole mess out the water like a torpedo?" Before I could answer, he spat, "Probably not, huh? So easy for dudes like you, with simple lives to point their simple fingers at us. Look at those rich, assholes, going around thinking they can do whatever they want." He paused, recognizing that his voice was rising and a woman behind us had begun to take notice. "Mind your own business, lady," he snapped at her.

"Easy, Harold, she didn't do anything," I said.

"Man, you aren't my dad. You aren't some knight in shining armor come out to rescue Junior, either. You want the money just like all the rest. They all want what we have. Well, now they got it. We ain't got shit, and I'm sure it makes everyone happy. Mom saw to that, didn't she?"

"You mean the reparations?"

"What the hell else would I mean? Man, it's like this, we don't have our inheritance, least not what we expected, and she kept us out of the business, even her precious Junior. And instead of doing it while she was around, she chickened out and did it after she died. Nice, huh? Easy to make decisions for everyone when you aren't around to face the music."

"You don't think what she did was right?"

"Shit man, it's her money. She can do whatever the hell she wants with it. I know that. But where's the love? Huh? While she was busy with that fucking reporter Adirondack Kendal."

"Here's another for you, Harold. Where were you when Francine was offed?"

This threw him, but he recovered quickly. "Herbie. Some brother that guy is. Family. My family. You want to know where I go, Boise? Man, don't you think I get tired of all the secrets, too? You know I didn't kill my mother. You know that. My sibs and I were just covering each others' backs."

"How could you be certain that they didn't do it?"

"Man, you just know. Like you know that you're hungry."

"So, where were you?" I pressed.

"I'm in a group. An anonymous group. We meet. No one talks, no one knows outside the group. I have a medical condition. That's all I'm willing to say. We've got too many secrets, and I'm more concerned with how my nephew is gonna live with his."

I wanted to tell him that I had family secrets too. But that was the point, wasn't it? My family secret could remain ignored as long as I wanted to let it fester in the corner. You didn't want to expose those you cared about to that level of scrutiny. Sometimes, as in Junior's case, it was so fundamental to who he was, his very genetic makeup, there was nowhere to run. How could he ever have a deep relationship with someone and keep something so fundamental about himself hidden? On the other hand, how could he reveal such a horrible truth and expect anyone to stick around? If you sat with that dilemma long enough, it could drive you mad. He would have no choice but to continue the lie. That's what I would do. I'd tell everyone my mother had abandoned me. That I'd never known her. On one level, a metaphoric level, that was true, but that didn't absolve him from living with the secret all his days. It would take a special partner to overlook Junior's lineage.

"Man, the short answer is, that kid is not good. He doesn't know what to do and none of us have an answer either 'cause there's no answer to something like that. Is there?"

He wasn't waiting for an answer. Yarey looked lost, but afraid to ask what was happening.

"And you," Harold pointed a finger at Yarey's nose, "you stay out of it. This is none of your concern. Now, let's just watch these archers. They deserve our undivided attention."

The competition had already begun, with various competitors coming and going from different categories and age groups. The final competition would be those at the senior level competing to go on as a representative of the U.S. Virgin Islands in international competition. Isabelle had qualified for this final round as expected, posting the best score average, having the most x's at seven, and posting the highest overall score in her category.

The crowd had begun to really pay attention in the last half-hour as the juniors and cadets finished their rounds.

Harold seemed to have calmed down. He leaned over after one girl who was fifteen-years-old finished her round and said, "Man, she's got the goods. I'd like to work on her stance and sightlines, but otherwise, she's got Olympian written on her back."

I was still reeling from our earlier conversation, but Dana had come back carrying more junk food. It took my mind off Junior's woes.

I still couldn't get over that, despite all that had happened the last couple weeks, Isabelle was here and performing at such a high level.

"How does she do it?" I asked Harold as we watched another competitor finish her round, moving us closer to Isabelle's turn.

"She's a different sort. She has this special focus. For all her physical gifts, it was her mind and emotional fortitude that wowed me when I first worked with her."

We continued like this, discussing the various competitors as they came and went. Harold found fault with everyone's technique, stance, or attitude on some level. He really knew his stuff. For some reason, at about one o'clock, they gave the judges a break for fifteen minutes.

"It's like the seventh inning stretch," Harold said, lifting his arms and yawning.

"We gonna sing take me out to the ballgame?" Dana asked.

"Ha, ha," Harold mouthed.

Everyone took turns going to the bathroom, first the women, then Harold and I. The bathroom sometimes produced my clearest moments of thought. For whatever reason the gentle echoing of the porcelain and the running water from the sink outside my stall, brought contemplation. In my lucid state, thoughts of Jermaine LaGrange swirled. The man had rage in spades. He had killed at least two people, that much was certain. But something was wrong in his motivations. He had made dire mistakes. Even assuming the man was justified, his rage was poorly directed. Like eating when what you really wanted was a hug from daddy. His was a crime of substitution, of misplaced justice. Who did he truly feel wronged by, and why hadn't he taken it out on them?

As I washed my hands I came back to the same thought I often had about motive: people much preferred to redirect their emotional energy anywhere but where it really belonged. Confronting your true emotional source was beyond daunting, it was only for those of a rarely brave nature. Murderers sometimes exhibited such bravery, but mostly, just like the rest of us, they substituted someone else for the person they never could or never would deal with directly. Usually someone from childhood. In Jermaine's case, I had no doubt his childhood had been a hot mess. For all I knew, his father, uncle, or mother were dead, so killing them was not an option, although even if it was, it was very unlikely he'd actually do that.

I finished washing my hands and did a quick flossing to questioning looks from the other patrons. Harold was outside the bathroom, waiting.

"I thought you'd fallen in."

"Sorry. I just got to thinking about Jermaine."

"Man, can we stay off all that depressing shit for an afternoon?"

"All right. We'll stay off that for the afternoon."

As we walked back, he stopped me. "You have a way of making me feel like I want to know what you know, so spill. What about this asshole you want to ask?"

"I feel like your grandmother and Kendal got screwed, because they did nothing to the actual killer. Sure, Gilroy put him up to it."

Harold held up a hand. "Let me stop you there. Gilroy killed 'em, not fucking Jermaine. Gilroy wanted all this to happen. Jermaine was like, I dunno."

"A substitute?"

"Yeah, that's it, a substitute. Gilroy's a fucking coward. If you're going to do something, at least have the guts to do it yourself."

I was about to mention that Gilroy did not intend to kill Francine, but thought better of it.

"It also got me thinking about who Jermaine really wanted dead. Who he felt wronged by. Didn't you tell me some story before about a judge?"

"Yeah, that's what I noticed today, too."

My skin broke out in a cold sweat. "What did you notice?"

"The judges, for today's match. The one sitting in the middle of that table, she's the same one who d-qed Isabelle's uncle all those years ago. That's why I was..."

I didn't even hear anything else he said. I could hear the crowd outside cheer as Isabelle LaGrange was announced.

As I raced back to the arena, Harold yelled, "Boise! Wait up"

CHAPTER 37

Bursting out of the hallway, I shoved through the milling people who guzzled beer, munched on fried food, and chatted about all of the mundane things people chat about. I heard a snatch of conversation as I rushed by a couple swaying to their own song.

"Hey baby, what's your smoke signal?" the man intoned. "You like arrows?"

Then I realized something, as everything shifted into slow motion, while I dodged and weaved through the crowd and Harold struggled to keep pace: my knee felt incredible, like some kind of lightning surged through it. Ever since the basic training accident had ended my military career, I had a slight limp, but every time my heart moaned to walk normally, I tried to be grateful for it could have, probably should have, been a lot worse. I should never have walked again. Now, here I was over a decade later, running with the practiced ease of my nineteen year old self. Perhaps I was the mother who suddenly has the strength to lift the car off her child. However, I wasn't going to save my child, I was going to save someone I didn't even know.

As I pounded up the bleacher steps I suddenly knew why I'd accepted the gun from Leber without a fight. Why all my protestations about guns were hollow. Why the pepper spray wasn't enough. Why the Taser wouldn't do, either. It was for this very moment. I would need to pull out the weapon before anyone else knew why and I could be executed for that. I wished there were time to do something more logical. Something less deadly, both for myself and for Isabelle. Surely she was misguided or she was the product of some elaborate brain-washing scheme triggered by the queen of hearts. Deep down, I knew that wasn't the case. Isabelle had made the choice to leave Harold and join Jermaine. Yes, she'd been young and impressionable, but she was now a worldly woman who could discern right from wrong. She'd had years to correct her error. She had chosen wrong and now stayed the course.

I burst out of the stairwell in time to see Isabelle move into position. It seemed so obvious now. Her training to shoot multiple arrows so quickly. That was not training for competition, it was training for an assassin. Jermaine LaGrange had turned his daughter into an assassin. That's what he'd meant when he'd said, "She was unbeatable at all of it."

She had already shot arrows at the target, all in the golden ring. She was exhibiting that legendary focus Harold spoke about. If my guess was right, her next shot would follow a pivot to her right, just as they'd practiced at the range over and over as I watched. Her target sat in the middle seat at the judges' table. Her target was Jermaine's tormentor. The female judge who had dared to stand up to him all those years ago and disqualify him from competition.

There were people between me and Isabelle.

"Move! Move!" I yelled, but most of the patrons were focused on the competition.

One fat man shoved me back as I tried to pass. "You ain't blockin' my view."

Then I pulled out Leber's gun. He stepped back, raising his hands, spilling his cup of beer over his shoulder onto someone's back. The victim of the spill turned and shoved the fat man. A commotion erupted as everyone joined the fray. Isabelle was nocking her arrow, ready for the final shot. She raised her elbow, just like Harold had taught her, just like he'd shown me. Her form really was perfect, even to my untrained eye. She had red facepaint on, a line in each direction. She had feathers in her hair, like extensions. She looked every bit the warrior her uncle had formed her into. She breathed calmly, exhaling as she pivoted on her right leg and planted her left, a slight bend in her knees. Perfect balance. The arrow centered on its target, right above the paper that said the name of the judge. I slid to a stop, also planting in a shooter's stance, my gun held firm. I squeezed the trigger, felt the recoil and saw my target jerk at the last possible second, the arrow flying upward and over the judge's head, glanced off a metal railing and landed harmlessly on a patch of grass.

Before I could see anything else, I was gang-tackled from behind and held down by three people. Harold charged up beside the woman and the two men holding me. The woman had already wrested the gun from my weary hand. I did not resist.

Harold yelled, "It's okay, it's okay. He's a private detective. Man, he's cool!"

They did not listen. They held me fast until Leber arrived. Leber must have heard my description over the radio because he was first on the scene.

"How'd you get here so fast?" I asked.

"I was here. Thought I should see this guy's daughter shoot." Then, as he put me into the front seat in handcuffs, he said, "I had a feeling about you and that gun."

"Is she dead?" I asked, feeling sick to my stomach.

"Nope. Where were you aiming?"

"Center mass, where else?"

"You a bad shot. You hit her thigh. She'll live."

I breathed a thick sigh of relief.

CHAPTER 38

A week later I wore a pirate outfit for a party at Dana's place. Pickering had paid me, but refused to give me my so-called bonus, claiming I'd technically failed to meet the criteria of one week. I took what he offered and paid my rent at both The Manner and my office.

Harold Bacon, true to his surfer nature, was casual about the whole thing, including paying me the remainder of my fee. I had amassed many hours on the case, exceeding his initial retainer.

I repeatedly tried to contact Junior. After leaving a dozen voicemails, my last call was met with the "I'm sorry, but this number is no longer in service" greeting. The Bacons refused me entrance through their main gate. Hillary had needed me at the end, but any illusions of us being long-term friends was madness. Then, I got a call from her late one night. I was dozing off on the used couch I'd gotten for my office while contemplating which straw fedor on my hat rack I'd wear the next day.

"Boise? This Boise?"

"Yes, it's Boise. Who's this?"

"Hill Bacon. You remember me?" She laughed knowing I would not forget her. She slurred the next sentence. "You ruined our family, you little bastard."

"Hillary, are you hitting the bottle?"

"No. How dare you! I'm, I'm tired. I take medication. It makes me drowsy."

What Hillary didn't know was that I was also a bit plastered on nine Guinnesses and a shot of vodka the bartender had poured as the last "I'm-cutting-you-off" shot. My stomach wailed like a cat in heat, which was why I hadn't lost consciousness yet, but had chosen to crash at my office which was a lot closer than The Manner. On the other hand, I held my liquor better than Aunt Hillary.

"Hillary, since I've got you on the line, what's the deal with Junior? I tried to come see him, but your bulldogs wouldn't let me on the property."

"Junior. You mean my son that I never got to raise, who I don't even know."

She paused. I imagined her taking a drink, probably champagne or white wine. Auburn lips against her pale skin. She was attractive in a broken and battered way, like a chipped and used piece of expensive china. I waited, willing her silently to tell me about Junior and maybe feel some guilt about not paying me.

"Taking a pill…with water. Helps me sleep. I don't sleep much anymore."

"Uh-huh." I wandered over to my desk and looked down into the wastebasket. I swore under my breath.

"What did you say?"

"Nothing, Hillary. That wasn't for you."

"You are a cheeky bastard, aren't you? Junior's gone. So's his

290

father. Herbie never could take it when things got hard. As long as he got to play the dutiful father and I resigned myself to playing the withering aunt, all was well. Once I told the truth, well, you can guess how that turned out. Like father, like son."

"What about their inheritances?"

"I'm sure they'll turn up in time to collect that, but the lawyers say it's going to be some time. This whole thing is a mess, and I plan to contest."

"Hillary. Please don't do that."

"Why-ever not?"

"Because the reparation package that Francine set up might be her only legacy. It would be something others could aspire to. There's not a lot of that in the world right now. She died for it."

She bellowed laughter into the phone. "So what, how's that my problem? I need to live, Boise. I need to live. Some selfish old lady has some dream of what, confessing at the end and making up for all the bad shit she did?"

"You'll have enough to live."

"You mind contributing?"

"What's that mean?"

"Well, big shot, if I can give up millions, you can give up what we owe you. Junior did send one text to me. Just one. He said we should pay you what we owe you. You believe that? He vanishes like the Loch Ness Monster and that's all he says to his mother. As if this was all my fault. I always get the blame."

She had a point. I should put my money where my mouth was. It was a couple thousand dollars. Was it worth fighting over? I stared at the green paper in the wastebasket, and was furious about something else. Why couldn't this goddamned building get a decent cleaning crew? Why was a sheet of paper I'd thrown in my wastebasket still there after a goddamn month? I had to call them and tell them what was what.

"Sure, Hill, keep it. Give it to the people who were wronged. Just remember, I supported and continue to support Francine and

Kendal's cause. I just proved it."

She laughed again. A spiteful laugh full of pepper and grease. "Here's hoping I never see you again, Detective."

The line disconnected. Even when it was derisive, I got a jolt out of being called, "Detective."

I dialed my building management company to complain about my wastebasket. By the time the nighttime voicemail finished talking about leasing opportunities and listing a special number to call about after-hours emergencies, my anger had wilted. I hung up, fished the green paper out of the wastebasket and dropped it back on top of the desk.

I muttered to myself, "If not now, when?"

***

That had been three days ago. I arrived at Dana's party to shouts of laughter and blaring music. Dana stood in the back, serving drinks while she watched Annie dance in the middle of her living room, her arms around one of the men who worked at the paper.

"What'll it be, Boise?" Dana asked, reaching behind her into a cooler and pulling out a Guinness. I put my hand on top of hers before she opened the can.

"Annie's back, I see."

"Yup," Dana said with a smile of contentment only a profound and long-lasting human relationship can bring.

"You got any selzer?"

She laughed as if I'd just told her the best joke of the year, then the grin fell off her face like the glue had melted. I pulled out the green paper without unfolding it.

"Why you pirate!"

"Arrrrr."

I shoved the paper back into my pocket.

Then she asked, "How many days?"

"Two."

"Good for you, Boise. I'm proud … "

"Don't get excited. I'm not much of a joiner. Nice party."

I didn't feel like spilling my guts right now to Dana, so I took my selzer and wandered away, saying polite hellos and laughing with whoever I ran into. I was only looking for one person. She wasn't there, so I flopped on the couch between a vampire who smelled like stale menthols and a devil-nurse whose mascara had started to run. I scooped party peanuts from a bowl and munched. I'd nearly finished the selzer. Nervous energy. God, I wanted a drink.

Leber appeared followed by some guy I didn't recognize. Neither of them wore a costume.

"You too good for a costume?" I asked, then shook Leber's hand. The guy with him said something I couldn't hear, then excused himself. Leber eyed my nearly empty cup.

"What you drinking?" he asked.

"Gin and tonic," I replied.

"What kind of gin?"

"Tanqueray," I said after a slight pause. He probably saw I had no lime and knew I was full of shit. Detectives.

"Uh-huh."

"Did you talk to Dana?" I asked.

"'Course, she's the hostess, isn't she?"

"Leber, I'm tired of seeing so much of you. You did me right, saving my life and all, but I need a break, what say another week before we chat."

"One thing, Boise. That whole Sherlock move on the boat." I stared at him blankly. "You don't remember? When were we out viewing Francine's crime scene. The nick in the side of the Bacon's boat, *High Hopes*. You thought it was from Francine's shoe."

"Leber, you never seemed like the 'I told you so' type."

"I'm not, but you must admit, it was a big error. Gilroy did it on *Distilled in Paradise*. There was a nick from her shoe on his boat too, but also a little drag along the outer hull as she went in."

"*Distilled in Paradise*. That's the name of Gilroy's boat?" I asked. He nodded. "I never got a good look at the name. So, you're giving me a backhanded compliment? Like Boise got the evidence right, but the location wrong?"

"No man, I'm giving you a compliment-compliment. Because of you, I was on the lookout for that evidence on Gilroy's ride. Barnes was impressed when I figured it out."

"You tell him you got the idea from me?"

He laughed. "You kidding? Hells, no. I'm taking full police custody of that deduction."

That's when I spotted Irene, seething sex. She had something, even if years of booze had used up some of her glow, she still had a way of putting a charge into me. She had her tattooed arms draped over the shoulders of a guy wearing a Ronald Reagan mask who was probably twice her age, if I knew Irene's taste.

I swatted at something tickling my ear. It tickled me again, and I jerked around. Someone in a bear costume was running her furry bear finger gently over my ear.

"Hey, man, what gives?"

"Your ear smells like honey, I was about to bite it," said the voice of Yarey Gilroy from inside the bear costume.

A giant smile spread across my face. "Just the person I was looking for. You want to get out of here?"

The Yarey Gilroy bear took my pirate hand, and we sauntered out of the party into the warm night.

I needed to go somewhere. I told her so. As we drove up into the hills, the moon-drenched hills seemed to writh as trees motioned in the wind.

At the gate, the guard examined us. Yarey knew him. "Going up to the house, Fritz. How are the kids?"

He said they were fine and buzzed us through. We circled to

the end of the private road. We settled down at the end of the driveway leading to the Bacon house.

The moon made the white walls glow, but I saw none of that sophistication. I didn't see the manicured hedges, the immaculate driveway, or the straight lines of architecture. I saw what she saw: the ravages of drought and the scars of war.

ACKNOWLEDGEMENTS

Dozens of people helped me complete this novel and bring it to publication. My wife, Ms. Marvelous, you are the light in my days, the stars in my night. Your belief and inspiration are the only things that kept me going when dark waves of self-doubt crushed me. Thank you for standing next to me when I handed pages to my writing hero and for always telling me what you thought, good or bad. You are my muse. Speaking of writing heroes, Michael Connelly, a writer I discovered solely on a book title, has inspired me with his story-telling. Ian Fleming's *Moonraker* inspired the dedication. To Sally Shore, who convinced me Boise Montague was interesting enough to carry a novel (now two). Ronnie Ashmore, a cop / writer, who kindly read my story and confirmed it wasn't ridiculous from a law enforcement perspective. My publisher, Acorn, and the amazing women who run it with a passion I am in awe of, Holly & Jessica. My diligent and encouraging editors, Michael Mohr and Laura Taylor, who tirelessly poured over the pages until they were perfect. Elena Felix, a great friend who discussed writing with me 4-5 days per week. She gave great advice about persistence, the only thing in this world that ever accomplished anything. To my kids, Ben and Miriam. You both inspire me with your gifts, caring and encouragement every day. To all my early-version readers who took the time to help me craft what I hope is a compelling story you suffered through the crappy self-indulgent research an development stages, especially Shane Valentine & R.D. Kard Any faults with the story and research are entirely my own.

ABOUT THE AUTHOR

Photo © 2018 Miriam Sachs

Gene Desrochers lives and works in Los Angeles with his wife, kids, and cats. He is originally from St. Thomas. *Sweet Paradise* is second novel. He has a Juris Doctorate from Tulane Law ol. If you ask he will regale you with his Caribbean accent and rowess.

9 781952 112386